A Fate of Onyx & Ivory

THE OBSIDIAN BLADE SERIES
BOOK ONE

O'JUNEA BROWN

This is a work of fiction. This story, names, places, characters, and incidents are the product of the author's imagination or are used fictitiously, and any resemblance to actual persons, living or dead, business establishments, events, or locals is entirely incidental.

Editing provided by Janna Harner

Cover design created by Lexi Esme

Dad, please don't read any of the smut scenes.
Mom, read them twice!

For the girls that got knocked down nine times and stood up the tenth time without any help.

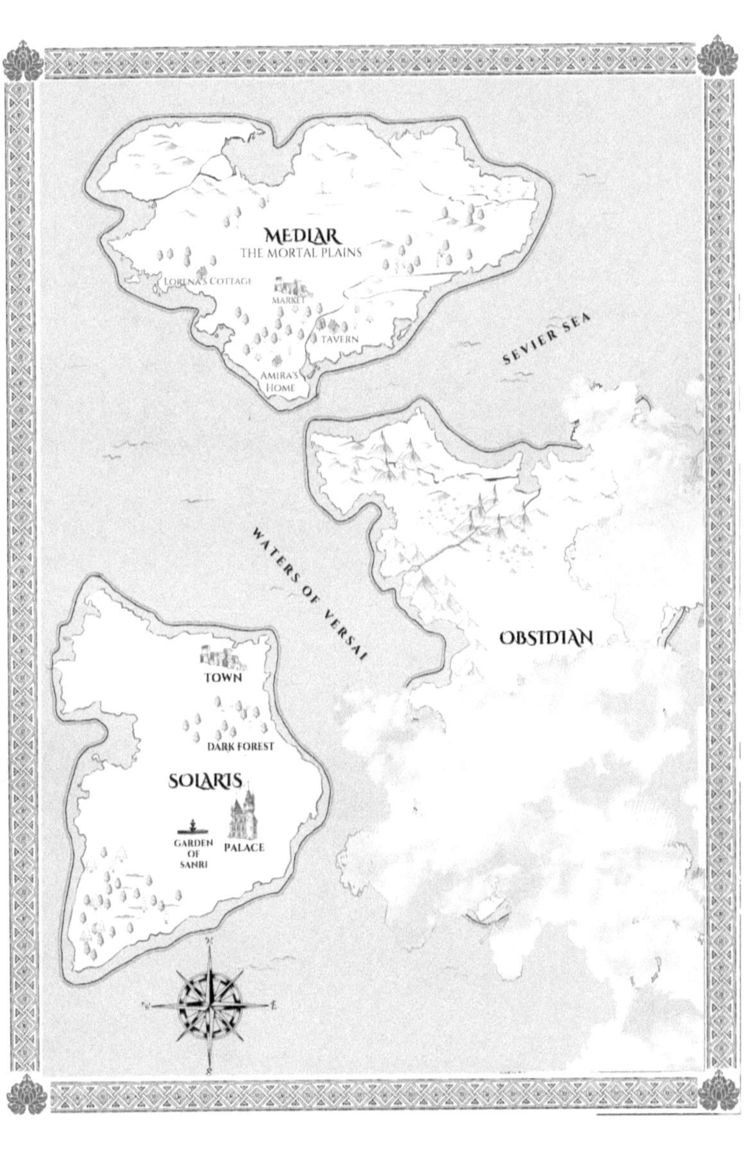

MEDLAR
THE MORTAL PLAINS
LORENA'S COTTAGE
MARKET
TAVERN
AMIRA'S HOME
SEVIER SEA
WATERS OF VERSAI
OBSIDIAN
TOWN
DARK FOREST
SOLARIS
GARDEN OF SANRI
PALACE
N
S
E
W

Author's Note

A Fate of Onyx & Ivory is categorized as dark Romantasy, but I want to clarify what that means for this book.

Is this book sunshine and rainbows throughout? No.

Is this book insanely demented and unhinged? No.

I decided to label it as "dark" because it includes more "dark elements" than a typical fantasy novel.

But I have heard through the grapevine that each book does get a bit darker. (What do I know though?)

Regardless, the content warnings can be found at the following link: https://ojuneabrown.carrd.co/#contentwarnings

Happy reading!

Playlist

"Confidently Lost"- Sabrina Claudio
"Running with the Wolves"- AURORA
"Toxic"- Kehlani
"Wrong"- ZAYN & Kehlani
"Witchcraft"- Frank Sinatra
"What Was I Made For?"- Billie Eilish
"Before I Ever Met You"- BANKS
"Beggin For Thread"- BANKS
"Lotus Flower Bomb"- Wale, Miguel
"You Don't Own Me"- SAYGRACE & G-Eazy
"Waiting Game"- BANKS
"Love Out of Lust"- Lykke Li
"Lovesick"- BANKS
"Only Love Can Hurt Like This"- Paloma Faith
"Another World"- Ruelle, UNSECRET
"Nothing Is As It Seems"- Hidden Citizens & Ruelle
"Bad Guy"- Billie Eilish
"Mind Games"- BANKS
"I Put A Spell On You"- Annie Lennox
"Judas"- BANKS

"Lies In The Dark"- Tove Lo

"Be wary of the one that brings death to those that are not at their end."

Chapter One

The sun barely breached the crowns of the surrounding trees as I swung open the door of the local tavern. Three pairs of eyes met mine before trailing from my face down to the supple curves of my hips. Each male remained leaning against the wall while sipping their ale as they continued their visual assault. Not a single one of them looked like they had bathed in the last month, maybe two. My nose scrunched at the thought of any of them naked and bathing. The male furthest to the right sucked his teeth loudly, severing me from my unpleasant thoughts. He ran his tongue across his bottom lip while offering me a wink and a nod of his head.

Great. Just what I needed before a cup of coffee had even graced my lips.

"Where is he?" I asked. Their eyes slowly returned to my face, a smile curving their lips.

I didn't have time for any of their bullshit today. Any day of the week, really, but *especially* not today with my mind consumed by thoughts of bringing home enough money to keep food on the table for the next week and midnight hunts in secret.

"Where. The fuck. Is he?" I asked again. Patience is already non-existent in my blood, but now it's not even a miniscule thought.

One of the other men ogling me from the moment I had walked in pushed away from the wall he was leaning on. Chugging the remainder of his ale, a devilish grin swept across his face as he wiped the liquid from his mustache. Handing the empty mug to the male next to him, he narrowed his eyes and strode in my direction. I stiffened while brushing a hand over my thigh to retrieve my knife, followed by a hushed curse. *Where the fuck is my knife?* I didn't even need to ask that question again because I knew I had left it at home. *I'm going to personally kick Alix's' ass for making me rush out of the house.*

The male that was still busy licking his bottom lip while surveying me, ignored his friend that was now drunkenly staggering over to me. His stench flared out around him, confirming my theory about them bathing to be correct.

"Alix, I know you're in here. Let's g—"

The staggering male grabbed the crook of my arm, pulling me into his soft, round torso, his blue eyes sunken in from a long night of drinking and heavens knows what else.

"How about you forget whoever it is you're looking for and come to the back with me?" he suggested with a quick wink of an eye.

The smell of mead on his breath damn near sent me toppling backwards.

"Let go of my sister you stupid fuck," a familiar voice came from a doorway in the back. Though I never broke my gaze from the male towering over me, I knew my brother was ready to bash his face in. The thought alone pulled the corners of my lips upward.

"I'm going to give you five seconds to get your fucking hands off of me," I said in the most sarcastically sweet voice I could muster this early in the morning. The men occupying the space around me laughed as the words left my lips. Another male grabbed my other arm, "You got a mouth on you, you know that? I think those pretty lips of yours need to be put to work."

Alix was damn near running toward me at that point, but the devilish smile I inherited from my mother was already evenly spread across my face.

Times up.

My knee sprang up between the first male's legs as I threw my head into the other man's nose. Both men dropped to their knees in seconds, receiving a fist to the face from my brother shortly after as a parting gift before we grinned at each other in celebration of the groaning men on the ground before us. I nodded my head in the direction of an empty table, hoping my brother would oblige. Alix knew the scolding he was about to receive but accepted my invitation by leading the way to the corner of the tavern where the empty table awaited us. Thankfully, no one felt the urge to avenge the two fallen men as we claimed our seats.

Before jumping into a lecture, I observed my baby brother for the first time in a long time. His bright eyes were sunken in from lack of sleep, sections of his hair were going in different directions, and just an overall exhausted appearance consumed him.

"Alix... this is getting out of hand. I know you think our current position is because of you but—"

"Don't, Amira. Don't fucking baby me. I'm sick of you always trying to protect me. Always trying to cover for me. Just let me come clean and tell mom and dad that I'm the one that truly fucked us over after we lost our land."

I reached across the table to grab my baby brother's hand while looking at his big green eyes I fell in love with the moment he came into this world.

"I will *never* stop protecting you. I took that oath the moment you wrapped your little finger around mine all those years ago," I said as Alix acted like he was distracted with something behind me. "You were only trying to help us get back on our feet. But you must know when to walk away, Alix. I'm trying my best to get back what you've lost by coming here, but I can't do that if you keep returning. I can't keep going out in the middle of the night to hunt additional game to cover your mistakes every time."

Alix slipped his hand from mine as he fiddled with a piece of paper on the table. After a few passing moments, his big round eyes finally connected with mine again. "You're right. I can't even argue it anymore." I sighed with relief at his realization and clasped his hand in mine again. "Thank you. We will get through this, I promise."

"Take me hunting with you! To help. Let me help, Amira." Hope flashed in his eyes after his request. Almost a silent plea for me to accept his offer.

"Alix, you're not—"

"Before you say no, let me grab us some drinks! Think about it, I'll be right back."

Before I could argue with him, his hand was snatched out of mine, and he was on his way to grab drinks for us. I placed my head in both my hands, contemplating letting my baby brother tag-along for at least one nightly hunting trip. At twenty years of age, you would think he was mature enough to handle it, but in the back of my mind I knew the real answer. He was so concerned with correcting his mistakes that he couldn't focus on making mature decisions.

Lost in thought, a hand settled on my shoulder with a firm squeeze. Not taking any chances, I grabbed the hand and twisted it, pushing their elbow upwards while exiting my seat. I hoped to hear a crack.

"Fuck, Amira! It's me! Look at me, it's me!" The poor soul yelled as everyone in the tavern placed eyes on us. I looked down to see a familiar, handsome face. His big brown eyes locked on mine as a lock of hair fell onto his forehead. A wince of pain plastered to his face as I realized I was still pressing upward on his arm. He leaned into the table while kneeling on one knee.

"Shit...I'm sorry, Knox. I just never know who has it out for us with my brother..." I paused, catching myself before I revealed anything too personal. Knox didn't need to know about Alix's gambling debts, and he sure as hell didn't need to know anything more about me or my family. He already tried to cross that bridge. I winced, remembering him begging me to meet his mother—just one of his constant efforts to make us official instead of just an easy fuck when one of us needed to get off.

I leaned down, helping him to his feet. He massaged his elbow gently, grimacing with the motion. "What's up?" I asked. Pulling out a chair as a peace offering.

I knew where this conversation was going before I even asked. Knox was a convenient option every time I drank too much wine when I wandered into town. A consistent, convenient option if I was being honest with myself. And there were a few others sprinkled in here and there when he was not around. Unfortunately, he didn't understand that was all he was—a convenience.

"What are you doing tonight?" He asked as he slid a hand around my waist. Without a thought, I removed his hand as I stepped away from his embrace. Placing my hands on my hips, I narrowed my eyes as I looked at him with annoyance. Of all people, he knew I didn't do public displays of affection. Nothing made me more sick than egotistical males needing to claim a woman as their property in front of others.

"I'm busy, Knox. And you know this isn't— " He held up a hand before I could protest. Paired with his charming wide smile, I almost felt bad for attempting to scold him. His brown skin glowing in the sunlight that's creeping through the doors of the tavern reminded me of just how handsome he was. For a moment I almost scolded myself for not giving him a fair chance at being in a relationship.

Snap out of it, Amira. You're just thinking about his skills in bed.

"I know, I know. But I'd be lying if I said I didn't want more. Just looking at those lips makes me weak. Give me a chance? One date. One *official* date. No sex. I won't even touch you or hold your hand if you don't want me to. But I *need* that chance." His begging almost turned my heart from cold to lukewarm as he bit his full lip. The sincerity in his words replayed in my head.

I stared into his brown eyes as he brought his hand up to brush his thumb across my lower lip. My brain was telling me to say no, but my heart was pulling me towards his. As I was about to answer, a crash came from the back of the tavern as we both whipped our heads in the same direction and back to each other.

Alix.

Sprinting toward the back room, we found chairs thrown to the side, playing cards scattered across the floor, and an entire round table flipped over. Scanning the room, Knox pulled me closer to him as both of our gazes landed on Alix in a corner surrounded by six men.

"Amira, listen to me. I know he's your brother but let me handle it. We can't take on all of them," he whispered in my ear as my eyes connected with Alix. Those big green eyes were filled with worry.

"Fuck. That," I gritted out through clenched teeth. I could hear Knox sigh because he already knew he had lost the argument. I placed two fingers between my lips and let out a loud, long whistle. "Get the fuck away from him. If you have a problem with him, you have a problem with me." The six men turned to survey the female voice that called them out. Their faces turned to stone as they looked me over. Moments later, each of them let out similar bellowing laughs. I tilted my head as they made their efforts to intimidate me.

"You heard the lady," Knox chided with a serious tone that I had never heard from him before. Crossing his arms over his chest, I noted him surveying the room for additional opponents or weapons as he subtly inched closer to me.

The biggest male grabbed Alix by his collar, "First, I'm going to drag your sister to the back and show her a good time. Then

I'm going to come back and watch my men break every single bone in your body before we send you back to your pathetic waste of a family."

"Two inches," I called out.

"What did you say?" The male questioned.

"Two. Inches."

"What the fuck are you talking about?"

Alix consistently twisted in the male's grasp in an attempt to escape, his eyes briefly landing on mine in a plea for me to leave while he fought alone. He knew damn well we would never abandon each other.

"I'm referencing what's in your pants. Someone of your size picking on my brother must be lacking somewhere else if you need to boost your ego so badly."

The male's face turned so red I thought he was going to combust as his friends burst into laughter. "Here the fuck we go," Knox muttered from beside me as he stepped away, putting a small distance between us and took his stance.

"As if we haven't been here before," I replied with a side glance and smile that was immediately returned. *I really should give him that date.*

Another male punched Alix in the face before jumping on top of him as the others stalked toward Knox and me. I was not sure if the men expected me to cheer on my brother and Knox instead of fighting, but they walked right up to me without a fighting stance. *Their mistake.*

My fist connected with one of their noses. The crunch was instant music to my ears as searing pain spread across my knuckles.

"You little fucking bitch," the second male said as he swung his fist at the side of my face. I ducked down to avoid his attempt, bringing my leg out to sweep his. As his body came crashing down to the floor, I jumped on top of him, straddling his body as I pinned his arms to the floor. I rained punch after punch on his hideous face. The darkness consumed me as heat flooded through my veins.

Amira.

Blood covered my knuckles as the male made a last attempt to grab me with his free hand.

Amira.

Another fist connected with his mouth as his lip split open, showing the blood collecting in his mouth as his head dropped back.

"Amira, that's enough! You'll kill him."

The darkness faded away as I snapped back to reality. Knox was pulling me off the male while I surveyed the rest of the room. All six of the men were laid out on the floor surrounding us. I glanced up at Knox who had a small cut above his lip. "I'm okay," he said with a smirk.

Alix.

I jerked my head to search for my brother as his familiar voice filled the room. My focus landed on him leaning against the bar in the back of the room, a small swell beginning to form under his left eye. "Right here sis."

I grabbed his face in my hands as his right eye had already begun to swell. He caught both of my hands in his as he brought them down from his face. "I know how to hold my own. Learned from the best... remember?"

A smile spread across my face before it quickly disappeared as my brain remembered to reprimand Alix for his behavior. My chastising began loudly while Knox tried to cover his laugh with a cough. I briefly paused my lecture to give him a glare, which ceased his laughing as he tucked his hands in his pockets and stared at the ceiling.

I started dragging Alix out the front of the tavern by his ear as Knox called from behind us in the doorway, "Think about my offer, Amira!"

Chapter Two

"For fucks sake, Amira. I told you I'd be home before breakfast. There was no need to come looking for me in the first place," Alix spat as we walked back home to the sound of birds chirping endlessly.

"And I told you that you better have your ass back home before sunrise," I hissed back as I pointed my index finger toward the sun. Alix rubbed his hands over his face before apologizing.

"I didn't even make anything. I didn't lose anything either... broke even. But..." he trailed off knowing my response wasn't going to be what he wanted to hear.

"This ends now. You're going to get hurt...or worse." Images of his body strung up in the town square, or pieces of him left in the woods for me to find flashed through my mind.

"Promise me that you're done with this stupid shit," I demanded as I stopped walking to look at him. My baby brother clenched his jaw as he rolled his eyes.

"Fine. I promise."

I stopped walking to look at him. I studied his face as if it was the first time seeing him in a long time. Stress was threatening to overtake his youth. The light that typically shone from my brother was slowly being sucked out of him due to his attempt of digging our family out of poverty, only to carry us in slightly deeper.

"Listen to me. The debt that you owe from gambling at the tavern is almost paid. Once I go to the market today and trade in the additional game I caught last night, you'll be debt free. I promise you that we will get through this. And I promised you that this would be our secret to keep. Have I ever broken a promise to you?" Alix sighed and threw his head back to the sky before answering, "No."

I huffed before playfully punching him in the arm, "And I never will."

We were silent for the remainder of our walk home.

We arrived with minutes to spare before I had to depart for the market if I wanted to get there before everyone else looking to make a sale. I waited to see if Alix would tell me to wait for him to accompany me, but I watched as he stalked to his room and flopped onto the bed.

I'm used to his empty promises of helping more, but it's grown more irritating with each passing day. At twenty years old, I was hoping the maturity needed from him would have kicked in by now, especially after I saved his ass today.

Filled with annoyance, I shrug into my coat and catch a quick glimpse of my mother. She doesn't blink an eye when I put my hand on the door to walk out without Alix anywhere in sight like he had promised in front of her at dinner the night before. I stalled for another five seconds just to see if she would make the effort to drag him from his room. Alix is the baby of the family, granting him special treatment from both of my parents. Without surprise, she sipped her morning coffee and continued to rock in her chair in front of the fire, offering a smile of pity.

The only one that would have accompanied me to the market was my father who was already giving a helping hand by chopping up the wood to keep the fire going for the next few days. I gave up on my mother opening her mouth and decided to leave. Before I closed the door, I glanced at my sister just to see if she would acknowledge my presence and possibly come in place of our brother. Tessa observed me with her usual uncaring stare. I'm used to her acting like she's the princess of the family even though she's three years older than me. She does everything in her power to make it known that she's too good to get her hands dirty.

Coming to terms with the fact that I wouldn't be receiving any help from my siblings, I shut the door.

Maybe this time I'll get kidnapped on the way there or get mauled by a bear and won't have to return home. "Wishful thinking," I muttered to myself. "That would make life too easy."

After saying goodbye to my father, I snuck around back and clipped the additional small animals I caught last night to my belt and heaved the deer carcass onto my back in one throw. I walked toward the familiar path.

Twice.

That's how many times I'm required to go into town this week and successfully trade my father's game at the market, plus the additional game to pay my brother's debt. Today just so happens to be that second day. In the past, I was a mere tag-along at my father's side for these ventures. But a few weeks ago, he had finally found me responsible enough to handle the task of collecting enough coin to put food on the table without his guidance. So far, I had yet to screw up the pedestal I'd been placed upon.

I cringed at the thought of having to go into town again. Everyone knew my family and not for good reason. We straddled the edge of poverty, although we'd done our best to portray otherwise. The stares that we received each time we went into town made my skin crawl. *The fucking looks of pity in their eyes.* Even if our poverty had yet to be declared, they knew. They all knew. Yet none of them had offered any of us a job regardless of how many times we had inquired. Gods knows what the reasons were for not allowing us to work for them.

Money wasn't a problem before, but ever since the King of Medlar had been replaced things have steadily gone downhill. The piece of shit took it upon himself to claim multiple parts of land that he deemed *unworthy* for the lower class, resulting in our loss of land along with the animals that once roamed it. Seizing that land severed our connection to the income necessary to live a comfortable life.

Now things were... different. *Stressful.*

And with a new king came a new army that patrolled Medlar on a frequent basis. Each time I left our home, I spotted men from his army searching places and interrogating our people. It was never like this prior to the new king replacing the old one. King Emyr was kind and helpful during his time as our ruler. He governed justly until his heart gave out on him unexpectedly, causing grief throughout all of Medlar. Before we had time to process the loss of our beloved king, the counsel had appointed King Malik to the throne of Medlar without a vote or request from the people that lived within it.

I bristled at the events that had taken place over the past six months.

If it weren't for my father being as good as he is at hunting, my sister and I would have sold ourselves just to put food on the table each week. I let that possibility come to the front of my thoughts for a moment and almost made myself sick. We may no longer have our wealth, but I'm aware of the many wealthy men in town that would have killed to have my hand in marriage--the superficial men solely obsessed with looks and nothing more that is. I resembled my mother, known for her glistening golden-brown skin and loose luscious curls that framed her heart-shaped face.

I'm sure they would love to show me off as a shiny trophy in terms of marriage, but I'd rather bathe in piss for the rest of my life instead of being their shiny toy for everyone to admire.

Nevertheless, helping my father came with its perks. The additional muscle and endurance were handy when my mother sent me to the town tavern to fetch her only son and bring him back home. Yet she never asks why he's always there. The task rarely ends without us having to fight our way out due to an inebriated bet he placed on a random card game that he didn't have the funds for to begin with—his typical good-willed attempt to dig us out of poverty that had yet to be successful.

Unfortunately, muscle doesn't stop the weather from making it feel like I'm going to catch frostbite before I reach my destination. The twenty-minute walk to town wouldn't be so bad if this awful wind would stop. It's the dead of winter and my boots are already ripping at the seams, allowing for the cold to nip at my feet. I try not to waste money whenever I can, so I donned the same boots I was gifted from my parents years ago. I realized a year after I received them that they were already too small, right along with my coat. Unlike my sister, I would rather put food on the table than spend money on upgrading my wardrobe.

After what felt like an eternity to get to the market, I searched for the man that frequently cut my father a deal and threw in extra when he could. To my dismay, the area where his tent usually resided was vacant.

Shuffling forward to search the area for additional merchants to work with, a solid frame smacked into me as I turned the corner. Thankfully, two large hands grabbed my arms, preventing me from tumbling backwards.

"Amira?"

Fuck. What is with my luck today?

"Hey…" I tried my hardest to remember his name, but all I could remember was the way he climbed on top of me weeks ago and drove me into pure bliss before I found myself sneaking out in the middle of the night. "How are you?"

The raise of his eyebrow and arms across his broad chest let me know he wasn't going to put up with whatever bullshit excuse I was about to sell him. "Not even going to acknowledge what you did huh?" He asked as he stared at me waiting for a response. I shifted on my feet as the weight of the carcass was taking its toll on me. His blue eyes burned a hole through my skull as he awaited an answer.

"Listen, uh..."

"Oliver. For fucks sake, my *name* is, Oliver."

"Right. Oliver. Listen, it was a one-time thing. Don't get me wrong, it was great. But relationships aren't my thing. And currently I'm freezing with a dead animal on my shoulders. So let's move on from this?"

He stiffened at my statement before finally standing tall and spitting at my feet. Shaking his head of blonde hair, he stalked past me with a look of disgust. As he blended into the bustling movement surrounding us, I let out a breath.

That went better than I thought it would.

After passing dozens of tents either selling items or looking to trade for items other than what I could offer, I came across an older merchant that took interest in my belt of smaller rodents. The small bag of coin was just to pay off Alix's debt. Knowing that I could relieve him of the stress he had been carrying for months made my heart squeeze. Unfortunately, he showed no interested in the deer carcass, nor did any other merchants.

With a lack of available options, I reluctantly pinpointed the woman that consistently gave my father a hard time when it came to selling or trading. And by the look on her face, I knew I was about to have the same fate if I attempted to work with her. After this morning's freezing journey, I was in no mood to put up with anyone's bullshit.

As I sauntered over to her table, I realized that I had never really given her a close look when I came with my father. I was so focused on learning the negotiating tactics that he used, I omitted everything else from our adventures in order to memorize his methods. Now that I was by myself and had to focus, I noticed how awful she looked up close. She was a short, scraggly old woman with black hair accompanied by a few streaks of grey that reached her lower back. Outside of her piercing blue eyes she didn't have much else going for her looks wise, and the scowl on her face informed me that she was equally displeased to see me.

"What worthless piece of game do you have for me this time child? Hopefully something better than your tiresome father provided three weeks ago," she hissed with irritation overflowing in her voice. As I was about to answer her, another woman appeared at the tent and was greeted with a warm smile. I shifted the weight of the deer on my back, watching their friendly exchange as the woman perused a few small trinkets. The vendor smiled before turning back to me. Her face resumed an etched scowl.

What the fuck had we ever done to get on her bad side? My father is anything but mean, so I know he couldn't have done anything to warrant her behavior toward us. And this was my first time interacting with her.

"Excuse me, I was here first. And I'd like to—"

A vicious glare came from the merchant's ice-blue eyes that caused me to stop mid-sentence. The tips of my fingers felt cold as anger consumed me.

I peered into those blue eyes of hers and dropped the carcass on her table, not caring what goods were laid across it for her to sell. She scolded me, hinting that she'd be offering less coins for the carcass – if any at all - solely because of my actions.

I glanced around to confirm that there were no other buyers at the market. After confirming that she was the only option to bring home money to my family, it registered that she now had the upper hand. I forcefully shoved my pride to the side and apologized. With a glare that could slice a colt to the bone, she gave a snort, "Not interested."

My blood ran cold. She was my only option to provide money needed to get my family through the week with a full stomach and other essentials. Grinding my teeth together, I squeezed my eyes shut before taking a deep breath.

"Please."

A sly smirk played across the old hag's face as she surveyed the carcass and waved off the other customer. Running her tongue across her teeth before the corner of her mouth lifted into another smile she spoke, "Fifteen coins."

"Fifteen!" I blurted out. Anyone that was within hearing range now placed their focus in our direction. The hag allowed her merciless smile to slowly spread across her small face. "Maybe you should have considered your actions before your impulsive, little outburst".

I surveyed the carcass knowing very well it was worth considerably more than her offer, maybe even double what she had proposed. It dawned on me how disappointed my father would be if I returned with such a small amount. Anxiety crept its' way in, threatening to take over. I could feel the typical beads of sweat forming on each of my palms along with my breathing beginning to shorten.

"Listen, I'm sorry about how I acted when I got here," I said quickly moving closer to the table. "But I'm exhausted, hungry, freezing, and I'm just frustrated. Can we both just move on from this?" I asked through a forced smile while fighting the urge to cringe at the begging that was tumbling from my lips. If there was one thing I hated more than begging, it was being vulnerable.

Her smile faltered and a distant look flashed within her blue eyes before focusing back on me.

"I tell you what," she leaned on the table, "I'll give you forty coins. Actually, make it forty-five, if we have an agreement that you'll come back tomorrow and work for me." I studied her with skepticism. After how rude I was to her, she wanted me to return and *work for her*?

"If you bite your lip any harder it'll burst child," she quipped while eyeing me in annoyance. I surveyed the deer one last time, pretending to weigh the options that I had been given. I looked back into her grizzled face. Something shone in her eyes, something that had me wanting to reach again for the knife that I now knew had been left at home. I tensed. Her demeanor changing in an instant gave me an uneasy feeling. But with our current financial state, I didn't have another choice.

"It's a deal," I said and flashed her a broad smile while extending my hand for her. She grimaced at the sight of my hand but shook it to complete the deal. A dead look in her eyes was paired with the same sly smirk from before, causing me to slowly bring my hand back to my side as I studied her.

I retrieved my father's pouch from my pocket, handing it to her for payment and thanking her. I turned to leave, wearing a wide grin on my face thinking about my family's reaction once they found out the amount I'd brought home.

"Took you long enough," Tessa barked at me with a scowl on her face as I burst through the door. Without a word, I threw the pouch on the thick, wooden table. "Maybe you can help count those since you barely help out around here." Her jaw almost hit the table along with Alix and my parents when they saw how much silver spilled from the tan bag.

"What did you do to earn this?" My brother asked slowly, shock seeping onto his youthful face. I let him know the merchant offered me the coins in exchange for me returning to the market tomorrow to work for her.

My father jumped up so quickly from his chair that I was sure he would knock over the table.

"Who did you make this arrangement with?" He cried out. I glanced around the table as my siblings and mother looked unnerved. I chewed on my bottom lip before I gathered enough words to form a coherent sentence.

"The lady that always buys from us when Carlisle is away."

"Heavens above…" He let out a long breath. "You made a deal with the short lady, with the long dark hair? The blue-eyed old scraggly lady?"

"Yes, that's her," I replied as unease began to settle in my stomach.

"What the hell were you thinking, Amira?" He shouted back at me. "Were you even thinking?"

My face held a blank expression of confusion. He had never spoken to me like this before and my brain was searching for a reason for such an outburst. I followed the precise instructions that were given to me. I went to the market, made a deal (*more than we could have asked for),* and came home. Subtly, I looked over at my mother whose hands were trembling so badly that she had to set her cup down.

"Does somebody want to tell me what the hell is going on here?" My brother asked with confusion replacing the shock that was on his face moments before.

When my father spoke, his eyes were wide with concern. "You just made a deal with one of the last suspected witches in town."

My body went rigid after what my father had said registered in my head. Could I run back to the market and retract our agreement? Surely she would agree to reverse it if I asked her. After a few moments of silence, I snapped back to reality knowing that deep in my heart, *deep in my soul…* I couldn't fix the mistake that was already made.

My heartbeat thumped an unsteady rhythm as the weight of my realization became too heavy to bear.

Chapter Three

We may have our moments of bickering and banter, but we spend our meals together as a family every evening. And though we don't have much, we enjoy what we have with each other regardless of the day's petty annoyances and disappointments. We all had a love-hate relationship floating between us. Yet, family was the backbone to my strength and determination, the reason I willed myself to get out of bed each morning. The turn of events within the last year attempted to throw us into a hole of poverty that we couldn't dig ourselves out of, but we still sat at the dinner table and loved each other in the ways that we knew.

Naturally, my sister was trying to mask her worry about the bargain I made earlier in the day and was doing her best to distract me from it as we gathered for dinner.

"This soup could use a little more seasoning, but it'll do," she said while bringing a spoonful of the soup I made to her mouth. Tessa had a dry sense of humor mixed with an aggressive personality, which was part of the reason we didn't always get along. It also didn't help that she refused to show any type of emotion.

"Why don't you go pick up a few more seasonings tomorrow at the market?" I replied, sipping the last bit of my soup from the bowl. "Oh, that's right," I placed my bowl down and looked at her across the table. "Helping out isn't your strong suit."

I should've known better than to start an argument with her when I knew she was only teasing me. But I was already on edge thinking about my stupid agreement from earlier.

"You think you're better than me because you can walk to a market a few days a week?" She quarreled. Tessa cocked her head to the side as she rested her elbows on the table, clasping her hands under her chin.

"I know how to do a lot more than that, but the answer you're looking for is *yes*. Among other reasons."

"And what would those reasons be besides laying on your back when you sneak out at night to go into town?" Tessa countered, crossing her arms across her chest while leaning back in her chair. Alix tensed at Tessa's words as my parents never flinched at the information provided.

Before I could process my actions, I had already leaped across the table and grabbed my sister's hair as she swung her fist into the side of my face. To my dismay, our father pulled us apart before I could get a proper hit in.

"Enough! I have one son. Not three. Act like the women that your mother and I raised you to be," he instructed before narrowing his eyes at Tessa. "Apologize to your sister. Amira is right. You need to start helping more around here. You and Alix both. No more exceptions."

Tessa narrowed her eyes at me before that devilish smirk that always brandished her face before a smart remark appeared. "Sorry, Amira. We all know it was a false accusation of you being on your back since you're still a virgin and all," she jeered while swallowing the last bit of her soup. Despite what my sister thought, I was not a virgin. Far from it actually. But I refused to share those details with someone whose face I wanted to smash against every solid surface in our compact home. *Daily.*

My fingers curled into themselves once more, ready to land on my sister's jaw whenever my mother shouted, "So help me, if the two of you say one more—"

Her words were cut short by a rap at the door. Alix and my father slowly stood from their seats as the noise repeated itself—the second strike being louder than the first. The door flew open, revealing nothing but the chilled night air.

"Well, that was quite odd don't you think?" My brother asked while staring at the empty doorway.

"Eh, the wind is picking up outside. Could have been that or an animal seeking shelter," my father reasoned as our mother clenched her necklace as if it would protect her.

"Or it could be *them*," my sister said with a sinister smile.

"Give it a break with your bullshit, Tessa. *They're* not real," I spat back at her.

Her head tilted to the side as her smile grew wider, "Sounds to me like you're scared that they are."

I glowered at her before my mother told her to be quiet.

As children, my mother would tell us old wives' tales about the *immortals*, beings that lived to be hundreds or thousands of years old. She would tell us of the dark ones that would come in the night to take us from our families if we didn't listen to our parents, making sure to clutch her necklace when it got to the most bone-chilling parts. She rubbed her thumb over the dark glass pendant that held swirls of purple and blue, emphasizing the ghoulish details. Her stories were so detailed that my siblings and I would pile on top of each other in one bed with the covers pulled over our heads to protect ourselves. Alix was so little that Tessa and I put him between us to protect him. Once we got older, we caught on that her stories were inconsistent and made up just to get us to follow the rules.

"Well, if they are real, hopefully they take you instead of us so we can finally get some peace and quiet around here," Alix quipped, causing my parents and I to laugh. Tessa scowled at him but let a laugh slip through her full lips.

My father closed the door, putting all three locks in place before announcing that he'd be turning himself in for bed. My mother followed behind him as we forced her to turn in early while we tidied up for the night. Kissing the top of our heads, she halted before leaving the three of us for the night. "Your bickering has to stop," she said, looking pointedly between me and Tessa. Alix seemed to disappear as she focused her attention solely on us. "You're bound by blood. Act like it," she snapped with a caring glare at Tessa and me. "You're sisters whether you like it or not. Through thick..."

Tessa and I rolled our eyes before our mother tilted her head with a menacing glare, reaching for her shoe as a threat if we didn't finish the saying she had taught us at a young age.

"*And thin*," we gritted out through forced smiles.

Content with our forced answer, our mother left us to clean up after dinner. Though Alix insisted on helping, we forcefully declined his assistance due to it always leading to an even bigger mess than when we started. The water fight that broke out last week resulted in two broken dishes and multiple bruises on each of us. The memory tugging the corner of my lips up into a smile as I replayed our laughter in my head.

"Let me help dry those so we can get to bed," Tessa broke me out of my memory with her mellow voice. I handed her the drying rag as we worked in efficient silence. "I'd be lying if I said I don't enjoy our banter," she said while curling her lips in to suppress a smile.

"Fuck you," I countered while bumping my hip into hers.

"Hey, watch where you throw that thing," she retaliated, causing us to laugh with true sincerity.

Finishing the dishes, I bid my sister goodnight and began

pushing in the fragile wooden dining chairs before heading to bed. The notion that Tessa had something on her mind was floating through the air as she cleared her throat from behind me, causing me to straighten.

"I'm sorry for the virgin comment at dinner and ratting you out for sneaking to town in the middle of the night. That was a low blow...even for us. We don't spill our secrets, and for that, I'm sorry," she rattled off at lightning speed.

"It's okay. No harm done," I replied in truth. Our parents didn't even blink when she let it be known that I snuck out on occasion, meaning they most likely already knew. What neither they, nor Tessa, knew was that fifty percent of the time it was to hunt in order to pay off Alix's debt.

"Was my statement true?" Tessa blurted out. I was already walking away from our conversation when I paused at her question. "About me saying that you're a virgin. Was it true?"

I turned around to face my sister before I slowly shook my head no, watching a flash of shock cross over her face before disappearing.

"Why do you ask? Actually...why do you care?"

"Because you never talk about any...men. And I was starting to wonder if—"

"If I liked women?" I finished her sentence before she could begin rambling. She nodded her head in agreement to my question as she unapologetically stared at me. "No. I prefer the male *appendage* just as much as you do," I quipped as she grimaced at the word "appendage," making me smirk.

"Then why do you never speak of marriage? Or children?"

"Because I refuse to sit around hoping and waiting for a knight in shining armor to come save me. If that's what you want to do, then do it. But don't try to force your hopes and dreams onto me. I don't need children or a husband to make me happy. To have a life worth living," I spat back at Tessa while trying to figure out why her question had caused such a rage and anxiety.

"Is it though?" She asked in a calm and collected voice.

"Is what?" I gritted out.

"Is this life one you find worth living? Do you truly think this is all you have to offer in this lifetime? Or are you lying to yourself about what you feel deep inside there?" She pointed at my heart with her final question.

"Goodnight, Tessa."

Unfortunately, when my head finally hit the firm pillow on my bed, I couldn't fall asleep. My mind raced with the worst thoughts possible about my deal with that evil bitch. Was she going to bind me to some spell to make me her eternal slave? What if she turned me against my own family? I wanted to cry myself to sleep, but that emotion was long gone. I hadn't cried since I was an adolescent. When you're required to grow up fast and learn how to help provide for your family that's what happens to your emotions. You become numb to all of them and everything else *very* quickly.

Suddenly, the plethora of questions that Tessa threw at me snaked their way into my mind. It burned me to the core that she could read me better than anyone I knew. Only Tessa knew that I had always felt out of place, that I had constantly felt like the black sheep of the family—the black sheep of Medlar for that matter.

Maybe that's why we bickered so much. I confided in her so much when we were younger that she knew all my secrets, all of my true feelings about anything and everything.

My anxiety swirled as heat consumed me before squeezing my eyes shut and rolling onto my side.

I peered out my window at the stars above me. Since childhood, I'd always found myself intrigued with the stars and everything surrounding them. The bright lights illuminating the dark sky reached out to soothe my mind. They couldn't talk back, but they're who I'd always talked to during the good and the bad. Tonight, I pleaded with them to help guide me. To make me feel that I had not done something terribly wrong, something that I couldn't make right. A slight calmness blanketed my conscience as I shut my eyes.

Or was it the darkness I always called to instead of the light?

Chapter Four

When morning broke, my mother was standing in the doorway of my bedroom. She hadn't greeted me or woke me up in the morning since adolescence. I usually woke up on my own, got dressed, had my breakfast, and walked out the door to help my father without a word from anyone. This morning, she stood there as if it was the last time she would ever see me.

"Good morning," I mumbled. "Is there something wrong?" I asked as my mother clenched her jaw with watery eyes.

"How could you do this to us? Have I not taught you to use your head?"

Moving from my bed, I planted my feet on the floor. Her posture straightened as I slowly strode toward her. "What are you talking about?"

"What if her intentions aren't pure once you get there, Amira? If you don't come back... I don't know how we can survive without your help. Your father has taught you everything he knows. Your siblings haven't had a chance to—"

"And what if her being a witch is another one of your myths

like the immortals you filled our heads with when we were children?"

My mother opened and snapped her mouth shut.

I don't know who I woke up as this morning, but I walked over to my mother and peered into her hazel eyes, "I am not the oldest one in the family nor the male. Why are you not relying on Alix or Tessa to help like you rely on me? Why are you consistently putting all of our troubles and problems on me? I'm the one that stepped up when it should have been all of us."

She narrowed her eyes as her mouth formed a thin line, refusing to admit the amount of responsibility that had been placed on my shoulders.

"It would be nice if you gave me space to breathe every once in a while, or a simple thank you would suffice." I studied my mother's face a bit longer. "From the moment I was born you've expected more from me than Tessa or Alix. Why is that? Can they not have just as much responsibility as me? Or am I just not good enough?" The words were flowing from my mouth effortlessly. Everything I had kept inside of me for years was spilling out without a second thought. "Would it hurt you to give a damn about the weight that's constantly being set on my shoulders? I have no purpose in this world outside of breaking myself to care for all of you."

I felt the burning sensation before the realization set in. I knew that it was coming, but it was still a wave of shock. *A slap across the face.*

After I collected myself, I looked back into those hazel eyes I loved as a child. "At least there was some sort of contact between us before I left." She covered her mouth as she turned to leave. With sadness pooling in the pit of my stomach, I closed the door and got dressed for the day that lay ahead.

I stalked out of my room and into the area where my family had gathered. All eyes were glued on me. My father had no problem portraying the hurt he had in his round eyes. I glanced at my mother who showed no emotion from our encounter moments before. Quickly wrapping myself in my coat for warmth, I made my way out the door with a nod to everyone before loudly closing it behind me. Part of me thought one of them would run out the door to accompany me to my death sentence, and the other part of me knew that was wishful thinking. Frankly, I would have settled for a simple "goodbye" from any of them.

My chest tightened at the silent confession.

A couple yards from home I heard a rustling from behind and turned to face what was chasing me. Tessa's face came into view as she jogged after me while still buttoning her thick coat.

"Slow the fuck down, will you? Heavens knows the last time I made an effort to run."

A stared back at her, baffled at what her reasoning could be for chasing after me. "Did I forget something?" I questioned while searching her hands for an item I must have left behind. She huffed. "No. Father demanded I walk you to the market to meet the merchant."

"That's not necessary. I can handle myself. You're a burden more than anything."

Tessa glowered before passing me to walk ahead. "You forget that before you became father's favorite, it was I that taught you how to defend yourself."

She did have a point. Tessa dated a man for a year or so that was a guard at the walls of Medlar. As long as we've lived here, we've never been told why a guard wall was needed to surround our village. And despite them being together, he left Tessa in the dark when it came to the reasoning for the wall, enforcing that the subject was not up for discussion numerous times.

Nevertheless, he taught her fighting techniques that were required to be a guard. She in turn taught me at a young age, causing us to challenge each other on a weekly basis. This would result in her drawing a circle in the dirt and the two of us practicing the techniques while Alix cheered from the sidelines.

Despite her telling the truth, I refused to give her the satisfaction of being right. Declining to reply to her statement, I continued walking to the market next to her in silence.

When we arrived, the old hag was standing inside her tent. Her eyes were always blue, but today they looked ice blue. Cold. Unfeeling.

"I'm here to work," I said while fidgeting with a crystal on her table.

That familiar cruel smirk spread back across her face as she looked to my left, eyeing Tessa up and down. "My darling child, I never told you that the work would be here. I only requested that you return to work for me."

Panic rushed through my body causing me to stand straight up, Tessa joining my stance.

Anger was close on the heels of the panic I felt rising. Anger at this lying witch for withholding her true intentions. Anger at my family for thrusting me into this situation in the first place, but mostly anger at myself. I didn't realize what I had agreed to yesterday in the heat of the moment.

"I told my family that I was coming to the market to work. They'll expect me to return home today."

"You are of age, are you not?"

"Twenty-four," I replied through gritted teeth. I peeked at Tessa from the corner of my eye and saw the look she would get before pouncing.

"Then I am correct in saying that you are of age, and you've made a bargain for a job that you're old enough to consent to. Therefore, you'll be doing the job that you agreed upon. Otherwise, I will have to declare that you've stolen my coin and are backing out of the bargain. Are you aware of the consequences of that in my realm?"

Her statement caused me to stiffen as the bustling around the market drowned out whatever word venom Tessa was spewing next to me. *What does she mean by realm?* I swallowed the unease climbing up my throat and fought to gain back the control I was losing.

"Your realm? What the fuck are you talking about?" I shot back. She returned her cold stare to my face, but I noted a sparkle in her eyes for the very first time. Not one time in my twenty-four years of life had I ever let someone swindle me, and here I was. I looked like an incompetent idiot and the sun hadn't even fully risen yet. *What a wonderful start to the day.*

"Okay then. Where would you like for me to do the work?"

"You can't be serious," Tessa barked as she stared at me in disbelief. "I'm not letting you leave here with her. She doesn't look like you can trust her as far as you can throw her," Tessa snorted, "Which doesn't look like it'd be very far."

"It'll be at my cottage. Short distance from here on foot. Feel free to find it yourself, or you can wait for me and we will walk together," the old hag informed me while still ignoring Tessa and tidying up her table without casting a glance at either of us.

"Can I go home and let my parents know the change of plans?"

"Send the pleasant one to inform them," she said while sneering at Tessa.

I didn't want to cause a scene, as she did make a point that I took her coin after I had already agreed to the deal, so I settled. Tessa told me not to leave the market and that she'd be back with our father to sort everything out. I waited for her return as others came and went throughout the day.

My sister, nor my father ever showed.

The heat of panic crept its way back in as I realized I wouldn't have a choice but to leave without their return as the merchant began to pack away items from her table.

"My sister hasn't come back yet, could we wait just a bit longer?"

She didn't utter a single word in response to my question as I waited. After loading up her belongings, she glanced at me with raised brows, a subtle cue to start walking behind her. With one last search for familiar faces in the outskirts of the market, I accepted that they weren't coming. I cautiously trailed behind her.

The walk through the forest to her home was anything but pleasant. Unease coursed through my veins as shafts of sunlight filtered through the trees above. There wasn't a single bird among the canopy, leaving only silence to linger between us. When we arrived at the small cottage in the middle of the forest it didn't match the witch's lair that I had formed in my mind. *Did my father lie to me? Is she an actual witch or did my parents just not care for her and created this myth?*

The cottage itself was small and welcoming as we approached. As we got closer, I noted the walls of dark weathered stone were covered in patches of moss and vines that intwined with one another. She pushed open the dark wooden door which loudly groaned in protest. She carelessly walked through, a stark contrast to my wariness. I was only halfway through when she released the door, declining to hold it open for me. I stumbled under its weight, shoving the swinging door back open. I followed behind and surprise swallowed me whole at the view before me. The home was immaculate, yet very dark. Not an ounce of color was present in the entire cottage, which didn't bother me in the least. While most would be terrified of the ambiance before me, I had always gravitated to the dark, finding comfort rather than grief. A quick grin played across my face as I was reminded of the huge contrast between me and my sister and mother who both loved to parade around in anything brightly colored.

At least they enjoyed the finer things before our poverty struck.

Contrary to what I believed a witch's layer would look like, the inside was warm and inviting despite the darkness that the stone walls provided. The hardwood floor creaked as I strode across in awe at the home. Each piece of furniture was clearly crafted from the surrounding woods of the forest. Had she carved them herself? The firewood crackled in the compact fireplace that she lit as I walked up to an old wooden desk that had no less than fifty crystals laying upon it. Each one of them gleamed despite there not being an ounce of sunlight coming through the two small windows. Intrigued by their beauty, I outstretched my hand to touch one.

"I wouldn't do that."

Her whispered command startled me so badly that I involuntarily snatched my hand back, smacking it on the corner of the desk in the process. "Fuck," I cried out. "Why not?" I glared at her while rubbing my searing knuckles.

"Questions can either get you further in life or get you further into trouble. I'd stay clear of the latter while you're here."

I had mustered up the courage to ask another question about the crystals when a huge black cat jumped from the top of a skinny black bookshelf. I reached out to pet the four-legged animal, causing him to retreat. Bending down on one knee, I attempted again to put my hand out toward him, but quickly brought it back in as my heart skipped a beat. *Not a pupil in sight.* His eyes were only a swirling mist of green.

"What's his name?"

"Thackery. He doesn't like to be pet."

I briefly narrowed my eyes at her statement. If he didn't like to be pet, why didn't he flinch at my gesture?

"What kind of cat is it? His eyes..." The cat went to take a step towards me, but it stopped instantly. A single black paw remained extended in midair as his gaze remained on me, as if it were fighting against an invisible tether.

"You need to be more concerned with your work girl. Not with the cat, nor the crystals."

"What exactly *is* my work here?"

Her smile was brighter and wider on her small face than before.

"Come."

Unease settled in my stomach again, the same wave of heat from my anxiety reminding me of its constant presence. At some point I must have let her subtle threats get to me.

Or maybe it's just the dread of working for her.

The agitation coursing throughout my body seemed to alter the shape of the cottage as we walked, stretching the size of the rooms we passed. They seemed impossibly large. I rubbed my eyes and looked again. The hallway appeared to be an endless trail with multiple windows casting streams of sunlight upon the walls and hardwood floors below. How could such a small cottage contain such a long hallway? With an abrupt stop, the old hag opened the door to our left. The light from the windows in the hallway seemed to slice through the pitch darkness, revealing a large room with floor-to-ceiling black bookcases.

"Dust every book on the shelves," she ordered.

I squinted in the darkness, relying on the light behind me to reveal the room within. As if the room understood my acknowledgement, sconces lit among each wall providing additional light. The hairs on my arms stood as I swallowed, processing how they were lit on their own. I gaped at her in surprise as I walked further into the room. The room was massive with wall-to-wall bookcases and additional carts filled with books and trinkets.

Surely, I must have been imagining this. How could a small, country cottage house a room large enough to fit in the king's palace? I pivoted to ask her what the point of this task was and to demand an explanation for the room's size, but she had vanished. The door closed behind her with a subtle thud.

As I observed the bookshelves, I noticed the thick layers of cobwebs, dust, and dirt. A glance upward revealed three large black chandeliers that provided no additional light, and a ceiling littered with thick cobwebs. A shudder traveled through me as I thought about how many spiders probably lived comfortably within these walls.

Running my fingers across the books lining the first case, I stopped in my tracks as I noticed the titles on their spines. Not a single book was in my language, nor were they in any language that I recognized. I placed an index finger atop one to remove it from the shelf as a flicker of light caught my attention. A solid black crystal was shimmering in the low light of the sconces. My lips parted at its beauty, its sleek appearance asking to be in the palm of my hand. I swallowed as my body drifted toward the stone; hand outstretched to touch it. To hold it. *To keep it.* She has hundreds here anyway; she wouldn't notice one missing. *And how much could I sell this for at the market?*

Just as I had made the decision to pick it up, the door opened with a loud thud. I jerked my hand back, turning quickly towards the sound. A pile of dust rags was thrown unceremoniously onto a black end table. The old hag then shut the door without even showing her face. I began to grind my teeth as I walked over to where they laid and peeled off my top layer.

"Thanks for offering to take my coat," I murmured to myself as I hung it upon the hook next to the door, grabbed a rag, and got to work.

Chapter Five

After what seemed like endless hours of work, the old hag walked back in with her usual grim expression. "Your work for today is done."

I placed the dirty rags under the end table and followed her out of the room. Contrary to the initial walk to the library, the house now seemed to shrink the more we walked toward our exit. Once we reached the front of the cottage, she unlatched the door, making a gesture for me to leave.

"You're not going to walk me back?" I questioned as she opened the door wider for me to leave.

She flashed me a look of disgust. "It's getting late, and I have things to do. Did you not pay attention to your surroundings on your way here, child? How will you ever find where you're going in life if you're not paying attention to the simple things?"

I opened my mouth to deliver a wicked remark, but within the blink of an eye I was already standing outside with the closed door. Confused, I looked at the window to my right and saw the black cat staring back at me. I forced myself to look away, setting my sight on the forest ahead. Though I told myself there was no need to panic because I've traveled by myself before to the market, back home, and around the village, there was a voice in the back of my head telling me that I should turn around and beg for her guidance. I swiveled back to the door and knocked. Silence answered as the wind blew through the few curls that had fallen from my bun and now fell loosely around my face.

Did I really think she would answer?

Above, daylight was fading into the distance as the sun began to set. *It's only a brief walk to the market and I can make it there before sunset.* If I can make it to the market before then, I'll have no problem making it back home. I pushed down the fear attempting to take control and shuffled my feet toward the trees ahead.

After some time, blaring alarm set in. The brief walk I experienced earlier had come and gone. Reality set in that I had no idea where I was. I fought to suppress the rising panic and lost the battle within seconds. My breathing turned shallow, convincing me that my lungs were going to collapse from the heaviness in my chest. My face simmered with the heat of anxiety promising to devour me. "Get a grip Amira," I said out loud with clenched eyelids.

I opened my eyes to find myself on all fours in the middle of the forest. The trees before me doubled as the panic consumed me. I reached my fingers to my lip as blood trickled down from the force of my bite—a bad habit that formed during childhood.

This anxiety is going to ruin me.

Gathering myself, I gained my footing before moving forward. Moments later, every hair on my body rose at the sound that traveled between the trees. I turned in circles waiting for it to present itself once more. Catching my breath, I continued to walk when the most vicious growl I had ever heard repeated itself. I whipped my head around to find three large wolves staring at me several yards away from behind the trees.

This is how I die. How could I be so stupid to leave home without some type of protection again? Two stupid mistakes in one twenty-four-hour period had placed me in this situation, lost in the woods of my childhood watching as three wolves salivated over their next meal—an absolute idiot who couldn't even remember to strap on her knife.

Slowly, the wolves prowled toward me in unison. Terror swallowed me whole as my eyes fixated on the three figures in front of me. In my years of hunting with my father, I had never seen a black wolf, let alone three.

RUN.

My body and mind were begging me to run instead of admiring the jet-black coat of the wolves. But something pulled me toward the one in the center. Its' huge eyes never wavering from my gaze.

RUN.

I took an involuntary step forward as beads of sweat trickled down my back.

RUN.

The force that was pulling me toward the pack snapped. My breath released from my lungs, burning with a blazing fire. I turned in the opposite direction and sprinted as fast as my body allowed. The three animals were immediately behind me, but not moving as fast as wolves should.

They were taunting me.

My legs wanted to give out, and a few moments later they did just that. My body forcefully told me it was done and allowed for my knees to buckle under my weight. Involuntarily, I crashed to the ground as the wind was knocked out of me. The wolves prowled only a few yards away. The mere sight of them so close caused me to clench my eyes and accept my fate. I'd rather die than give up a fight, but I knew when to accept a loss.

With my eyes clenched and sweat dripping down every inch

of my body, I heard a loud thud and the sound of paws sliding against dirt. My eyes sprang open to see huge white wings obstructing my view of the three black figures that continued to advance on me. The male figure glanced back at me with a face that was more handsome than Remy, the God of beauty himself. His long ivory hair gleamed in the sunset. Along with his blue eyes that were now staring into my soul. My heart pounded as my surroundings became a blur. The sounds of the forest and wolves were now silent against the thundering beat of my heart as I drank in the sight of the male before me.

Moments later, he turned his vision back towards the wolves where they had halted at his arrival. Without hesitation, he began walking towards them as they stood their ground. There was a silent stand-off until the pack began to run in the opposite direction as if they had forgotten about their dinner that they were chasing moments before.

Did they just make a silent truce?

I stumbled to my feet to ask him who or what he was, but his striking features left me frozen in place. His eyes narrowed as I gawked at him, acting as if I had never been in the presence of a man before. "S-Sorry," I mumbled as I slowly stalked forward. *What am I doing? Just because he saved me doesn't mean he won't hurt me.*

I was barely a foot away from him when he tilted his head to the side, his eyes softening. *Those intense blue eyes that I couldn't rip my gaze from.* My breath hitched as he slowly reached out a hand toward my face, stopping inches away from my cheek. His eyes flared as if he realized the heat between us was about to burn us alive. Before I could open my mouth to protest him depriving me of his touch, he shot into the sky with one flap of his vast white wings. The instant cold that floated across every inch of my body at the loss of his presence didn't go unnoticed as I reached my fingertips into the space where he was mere seconds before.

While I was happy to have my life spared, my mind wandered back to paranoia. Saved or not, I didn't know how to get home.

And what the fuck just happened?

In front of me, a glimmering line of stardust was floating far into the distance. I reached out to grab it and stared in awe as my hand went straight through. The dust wound through the trees, a thread of light through the otherwise impenetrable forest. With no other alternative, I followed its' path. *Perfect... my hope was now placed in the hands of a non-existent rope.* After a while, I looked ahead and noticed the market was within eyesight. I felt a rush of relief. The moment that I realized where I was, the rope vanished. A lone figure stood pacing at the edge of the market, movements both frantic and familiar.

Running full speed toward the market, I locked eyes with my father. I couldn't slow down quick enough, resulting in me colliding with him so hard that he stumbled backwards.

"Where have you been?" He shouted while clutching my shoulders so tight I was sure I'd have bruises by morning. "I've come back here three times since Tessa delivered the message and you weren't here." His hands were trembling against my shoulders. Though I'm sure Tessa relayed the interaction, I let him know how I had been fooled into thinking the work would be at the market and that I wasn't allowed to return home to tell him about the reality of the bargain.

"You went to her *home*? Are you out of your mind, Amira?"

"What was I supposed to do? We made a deal, and she threatened me with the consequences that would come with backing out of an agreement in her realm. I waited hours and you nor Tessa came for me." The color drained from my father's face.

"Her realm? What do you mean by her realm?" He questioned me.

Rage crept its rearing head into my father's eyes. As badly as I wanted to reply, an answer couldn't be provided because I didn't have one. When I inquired about her world she never answered, and I hadn't pushed. Tears welled as I eyed my father, frustration building a teetering tower within. He placed his coat on top of mine and began to lead us home. The adrenaline coursing through my veins had made me unaware of the chill from the night air until now.

Chapter Six

When we reached the front door, my mother opened it, throwing her arms around me in an embrace I hadn't felt since I was a young girl. Grabbing my face, she examined me, apologizing for our quarrel that morning. I stared at her blankly, our heated argument feeling like it had been weeks ago, not that same morning. While she embraced me again, I noticed Tessa staring at me from her place at the table. Making eye contact, she stood from her seat before speaking.

"Amira, I— "

I held up my hand before she could utter whatever bullshit excuse she had conjured for not keeping her word and returning to the market.

"You left me. You abandoned your sister to figure it out for herself. You—"

"I did *not* abandon you. I ran as fast as I could back here, but I..." She looked off into the distance. "I got turned around halfway home. I can't wrap my head around it because I can walk that path there and back with my eyes closed. But it took me hours to get home. I can't explain it...," she looked away from me again without finishing her argument. "I'm sorry."

I didn't have it in me to fight, nor the energy to question her bullshit excuse. And I *definitely* had nothing left in me to explain the man – or whatever he was – that I had encountered in the forest. The more I thought about it while eating the bread and broth my mother prepared for me, the more I wondered if what I saw was real. Was it possible to hallucinate when adrenaline and panic consumed you?

I found myself sitting in the wooden rocking chair in front of our home staring at the big round moon that hovered above when the door creaked open from beside me.

"Can I join you?" Tessa asked as she stood next to the additional chair inches away from mine.

"If you must," I replied while still staring at the full moon above.

"Amira, I wanted to tell you— "

"Let me stop you there," I said while holding my hand up to her. "I don't want to hear whatever excuse you're going to feed me about abandoning me. I do whatever I can to make sure we don't lose what little we have left. And you decided—" Before I could finish my statement, my sister stepped in front of my view, cutting me off.

"Heavens above, Amira. For one second can you please close your fucking mouth and listen to me?" She seethed while narrowing her eyes and towering over me as I remained seated. I leaned back in my chair, waiting for her to continue. "Thank you," she said as she let out a tiresome breath and reclaimed the seat next to me. She began slowly rocking before speaking. "I did not abandon you today. I don't know how to explain it, and as badly as I want to, I can't understand it but I got...lost." My gaze snapped to her at the last word she spoke. How could she get lost on a trail we have been able to follow with our eyes closed since we were children?

Tessa stopped rocking and brought her dark green eyes to focus on mine. "Regardless of today, and regardless of our consistent bickering, you're my sister. I would never leave you, let alone abandon you. And I would hope that deep down you know that to be true."

My heart squeezed at her words as I nodded my head in understanding. Because I did understand. We would give our lives for each other, no questions asked. Same for Alix.

"I just want you to know that the reason I give you such a hard time is because you don't know your worth. You don't know what's out there in the world for you because you're so focused on taking care of us. And I love you for that. But spending all of your time and focus on us takes away from the time you spend trying to figure out who you truly are," Tessa explained while looking straight ahead. When she reluctantly looked at me again, tears lined her eyes. The visual made me jerk forward. I had never seen my sister cry before.

"Tessa are you... do you know something that I should? You're scaring me," I said while struggling to process her emotions and mine.

Tessa leaned over in her seat and grabbed my hand. "What I'm trying to say is, I will always come for you. I will always find you. And I will *always* protect you." My stomach dropped at her words. My sister had declined showing emotion ever since I'd known her. I tightened my grip on her hand, squeezing gently. The door opened once more, and she swiftly let go.

"Surprised you two aren't gouging each other's eyes out. Are you sick or something?" Alix quipped before my mother followed out the door behind him. Tessa gave up her seat for our mother before I had the chance, settling next to Alix on the stone ground.

"Are you okay, Amira?" Our mother asked while rubbing my hand resting on the arm of the chair. "I know you had a long day.

I think we've all had a long day worrying about you if I'm being honest," she admitted while turning up one side of her mouth. "Your brother won't admit it, but he wouldn't stop pacing. And your sister was such a frantic mess when she returned that I thought she'd need a doctor. I've never seen her so hysterical." My head whipped to Tessa as she glared at our mother. "Oh, save your evil glare for someone else. I taught you that look and I'll be damned if my own daughter intimidates me with it." Tessa's glare turned into a deep smirk at our mother's words.

I studied the face of the woman that raised me. Her slap to the face before I left was the first time she had ever laid a hand on me. Neither she nor our father had ever laid a hand on us. I suddenly wanted to ask her why in that very moment she chose to raise her hand to me, but as if hearing my thoughts, she released my hand and cleared her throat to speak. "I wanted to talk to the three of you," she said while clutching the arms of her chair.

"Tessa did it!" Alix spat without any context.

"Did what?" My mother inquired with a look of confusion as she glanced between all of us.

"I don't know. I thought we were in trouble, so I figured I'd just blame her and get it over with," he replied while scratching the top of his head. Without follow up, my mother whipped her shoe off and aimed it perfectly at Alix's shoulder, causing a yowl to escape as we laughed. Once our laughter began to fade, we focused back upon our mother to allow for her to speak.

"I know that with having siblings comes bantering and quarrels. But what I will not settle for is not having your brother's and sister's backs. If you want to argue and pummel each other that's fine. But as soon as it's over, I expect you to hug and make up directly after. This life..." her voice broke at her words. "This life is too short to not appreciate the ones that the heavens gave us to love." Her eyes roamed each of our faces as we remained quiet. "You love each other, care for each other, provide for each other, and you *fight* for each other. Understand?"

"Yes," the three of us answered in unison as a broad smile floated across her slender face. Her hazel eyes brightened in the moonlight as she stood to leave. Alix called for her as she was halfway out of her seat.

"Mom?"

"Hmm?"

"Could you tell us one of your stories?"

A look of shock and amusement passed over her as she sat back down, surveying Tessa and me. We nodded our heads in agreement while playfully rolling our eyes.

"If you insist," she said as she began to rock back and forth. "Here we go..." Tessa quipped and flinched, preparing for a shoe to fly her way. But our mother simply laughed and continued her tale.

"The tale of the slave and the savior," she said before licking her lips. "There once was a woman that served day and night to survive after her family was slayed in the night, working her fingers to the bone for a family she barely even knew. Yet, she had no place to live without them as she no longer had a family of her own. They paid her no mind, except leaving her the scraps to eat after their late-night meals, and a thin bed to lay at night." My stomach felt uneasy at her words. "A guest arrived one fine evening to join the family for their meal. His smell encapsulated her senses and threw her into a sea of lust. Upon time for him to leave, the woman quietly followed him outside to catch one last glimpse of his handsome face as they rarely allowed guests into their home. His tanned skin and bright brown eyes shining in the evening moonlight were all she needed to see one last time to burn the memory into her mind." My siblings and I had involuntarily leaned forward at the emotion that her words carried into the night. "As she reached the front steps, he stepped from the shadows grabbing her by the wrist before he offered her a lifetime of freedom if she took his hand. Shocked, she yelled at him to let her go, and so he did. But his eyes, his demeanor called to her.

"What are you?" She asked the handsome male before her. *"Only a shadow of your fate my love,"* he replied in a soothing voice. As his dark wings stretched from behind him, he reached out his hand once more. Without hesitation, she placed her hand in his as he whisked them away to a world of love, immortality, and solemnity where she wished to live out the rest of her mortal days in happiness."

Our mouths hung open while we watched a single tear fall from our mother's eye as she smiled and gazed at the moon. In my twenty-four years of life, she had never told a tale of immortals that provided a happy ending.

Without additional words, she stood and placed a kiss atop each of our heads before returning inside. My siblings chatted quietly, their presence a comfort I had forgotten over the last few years, their conversation already moving to light, trivial topics and gentle jabs. My eyes followed our mother's retreating form, the ending of her story leaving something jagged in the air behind her, like a hangnail caught on a loose thread.

If the slave's happiness was a *wish*, not a "happily ever after," how *did* she spend those final days alongside her dark-winged savior?

I returned my gaze to the moon.

Perhaps the story of the Slave and the Savior didn't have a happy ending after all.

At long last, I finally crawled into bed with a full stomach. My mind graciously shut out everything from this dreadful day except the angelic face that I witnessed in my time of despair. *Will I ever see that face again?* That was the only question that still floated through my mind as my head hit the pillow that night. The image of his pale, porcelain-like skin was seared into my mind. I pressed the palms of my hands into my eyes, hoping to erase the unknown male's stunning features that had left me breathless and saved my ass from the possibility of death.

I thanked the stars above that I had fulfilled the bargain and made it out of the forest alive and in one piece. My survival meant a return to poverty and bone-breaking work as I cared for those I loved. Surprisingly, I smiled at the thought, nestling deeper into the worn mattress.

I'd do it all over again—the deal, fleeing the wolves in the woods, all of the fear and anxiety. I'd gladly bear that burden again if it meant coming home to their smiles, banter, and humor. They were what made life worth living.

When I successfully calmed my mind enough to drift off to sleep, I did see that face again. In my dreams.

And it was just as stunning as it was in my time of distress.

Chapter Seven

I awoke the next morning startled by a loud knock. I threw on my garments and ran out of my room to find my family sitting at the wooden table with horrified eyes.

"Is no one going to answer that?" I asked. They stared as the pounding grew louder.

My father reluctantly stood from the table and opened the door to find *her* standing there. The room remained silent, save for my mother's gasp. Not a single word left his mouth as they stood eye to eye. "Time to work," the old hag projected at me from over my father's shoulder.

"My work was completed yesterday," I disputed with fists clenched at my sides.

"Ah, but who said it was complete child?"

"Like hell it isn't," my father spat, baring his teeth.

She looked him up and down.

"Let me clarify," she said, her lips curling upward as her eyes gleamed in delight. "Your daughter did not state when the end of our arrangement would be, nor did I. Therefore, her work is not done."

"No daughter of mine takes orders from a filthy..." his words trailing off as he studied the frail older woman in the doorway. And for a moment I was sure my father had taken his last breath.

"A filthy *what*?" A devilish smile played across her slender face. "Don't be scared to call me as you see fit. Or are you afraid to speak the words?"

The hairs on my arms were standing so high there was no chance they couldn't be seen from afar. My father walked over to the table and grabbed the pouch with the silver coins still inside, holding it in her direction. "We don't want the money. Take it back and leave us be."

As much as my heart hoped that she would take the pouch and leave, I knew that wouldn't be the case. Her ice-cold gaze remained where I stood as I turned to gather what I would need to leave.

Throwing essentials for the day into my bag, I could hear my father cursing as I focused on the day's work ahead.

Items and courage in hand, I walked around my father standing in the doorway and into the unwelcoming morning chill as snowflakes danced in the air. The old hag was already several yards away waiting for me with her arms crossed and a sneer on her face. I could hear my father's heavy feet pick up pace against the thick snow on the ground behind me. Fearful of his intent, I shut my eyes for a moment to prepare myself.

Denouncing any ounce of pride he had left, he begged her to take him instead to complete our agreement. With my heart sinking further than the core of the earth, I assured him that I'd be okay. Sorrow filled his big brown eyes while he looked at me as if he would never see me again. I extended my arm to embrace him, but the old hag grabbed my wrist turning me to walk. I took one last glance back at my father to see my mother and siblings standing in the doorway. Tears rolled down my mother's face as she held on tightly to the dark piece of jewelry hanging from her neck. Pressing my teeth into my bottom lip, I forced myself to look away. We've had our differences, but I can't bear to see my mother cry. Especially when it's due to my stupid decisions.

Light footsteps treaded through the snow behind me as the old hag wandered ahead. Tessa had pushed through my mother and Alix, sprinting toward me as she glared at the wench that was determined to drag me to hell. She stopped inches from me before grabbing my hand. "I know we rarely see eye to eye, but as I said last night, I did not abandon you. And never will," she said through staggered breaths. I studied the beauty of my sister's face for the first time in years. "Father didn't send you after me this time..." I said while looking away from her big green eyes.

"And he didn't last time either," she said firmly.

My head whipped back to her gorgeous face as the words left her mouth. *She followed me to the market of her own free will.* A lump swelled in my throat. She brought her other hand to mine, pressing a necklace into my palm. The necklace was an exact replica of my mother's necklace which she now clutched in her own palm, hovering in the doorway as she watched our exchange.

"I will always come for you. We're sisters. Through thick..."

"And thin," I finished up our childhood quote as the old hag grabbed my wrist again, yanking me from Tessa's hold. I subtly shook my head as Tessa clenched her fists, silently begging her to remain calm. Fearful that the hag would see me put it on, I shoved the piece of jewelry into my coat pocket as I began walking forcefully backward, the grip on my arm surprisingly strong and insistent.

I willed my eyes to focus back on my father's face. He knelt on both knees, hands buried in the snow, and I knew deep down that would be the last time I saw those loving brown eyes.

Chapter Eight

The walk back to her cottage seemed longer this time around. I kept telling myself it was only in my head, but I knew that wasn't the case. My gut had never been wrong, and I wouldn't let today be the day I second guessed it. The scenery I surveyed the day before wasn't the same as today's. The trees seemed to be spaced much closer together and were more withered than the ones I noted yesterday. The flowers that bloomed on the forest floor weren't even of the same family along this pathway.

Fuck.

To make matters worse, the closer we got to the cottage the colder the weather turned. Naturally, she hadn't uttered a word to me since we left. And during this time, it dawned on me that I had never asked her name.

"What's your name?"

Hesitantly, she answered, "Lorena."

"Okay, Lorena. Is there anything that you want to know about me?"

Just as I had assumed, no reply. Relief swarmed me as the cottage came into view.

"What are my *duties* today?" I asked in a mocking tone.

"Same as yesterday."

"Fine by me," I muttered while reminding myself that I was already halfway through dusting all the books when I finished yesterday, even dusting the shelves themselves out of good faith. *Definitely not doing that shit again today.*

That left me with only the last half to finish. I could have my task finished before sundown and then I'd be on my way home. A spark of hope crept into my mind that maybe she just wanted me to finish the books and that would complete our bargain.

Lorena pushed through the front door—once again failing to hold it open for me—and found her place on the stool in front of her workstation. Silently, she began threading the needle that she would be using to sew.

"What are you working on?" I figured the possibility that making light conversation would help with the tension forming between us.

"The books aren't going to dust themselves."

"You never even asked my name. Are you just using me strictly for work, or do you even care to know anything about me?"

"We both know the answer to that."

"Amira. My name is, Amira."

Slowly, she looked up from her thread to meet my stare. "If it wasn't for your beauty, you would be worthless. Get to work."

My eyes flared as I was tempted to connect my fist with her face. With an exasperated breath, I gathered my self-control and made my way to the back room. As soon as I opened the door and stepped inside, dread washed over me. A room three times bigger than the one from yesterday waited before me. I spun back to the door to ask her what the hell was going on, but there he was. The black cat once again sitting in the doorway. "Are you at least going to tell me what the hell is going on since she won't?" I hissed at him. He stared at me as if he could see straight through to my core. With every ounce of courage in me, I reached out my hand once again to pet him and to my surprise he didn't move. Slowly, I pet his round head and scratched behind his ears. Within mere seconds of me petting him, I heard swift footsteps coming down the hall as he darted up a nearby bookcase.

"Are you here to play with animals girl, or are you here to do your work?"

"Funny you ask that because I have a question as well."

"Your question is irrelevant."

She slammed the door shut behind her with a grunt.

Rage had finally overflowed as I hit my breaking point. I clasped the door handle, only to find it was scalding hot. I snatched my hand away, muttering a group of vile words that would make my mother faint. Against my own will, I grabbed the extra rags on the end table from yesterday and began dusting.

"Count your fucking days," I hissed at the closed door.

I was aware that a huge chunk of time had passed because daylight was fading through the small window in the room, but it felt like I had barely put a dent in dusting off the remaining books. When I reached the seventh bookcase, there was a shelf filled with the most beautiful crystals I had ever seen. Exact replicas of the crystals from yesterday. *"Don't touch my crystals,"* I mimicked Lorena to myself with my hands on my hips while twisting my mouth.

Although they were all beautiful to the naked eye, there was a specific one that I was drawn to. The same shimmering onyx stone from yesterday glistened in the minimal light. *Can energy radiate from an inanimate object?* I shook off the feeling and convinced myself it was only because I hadn't had anything to eat or drink since this morning and was becoming delirious.

Coincidentally, I noticed a glass of water and loaf of bread on the end table next to the rags. *When the fuck did that get there?* I went to take a break to indulge in the small meal, but noticed at the top of the bookcase the black cat was staring at me again. His head bobbed back and forth, from me to the food in my hand. Something in his expression told me not to trust the small meal that was provided to me, so I put it down and turned my attention back to the crystals.

Reaching out my hand to grab the blue crystal, I heard a loud purr. This time when I looked at Thackery, his eyes were narrowed.

"Alright then," I said to him, "You tell me which one to grab."

I reached my hand towards the violet crystal. No reply.

I attempted the clear crystal. No reply.

I stretched my hand towards the green crystal. No reply.

Irritated, I extended my hand towards the shimmering black crystal that called to me, and a faint purr surfaced within the room.

"You know this place better than me I guess," I whispered to the four-legged companion.

Picking up the black crystal I jerked back as if a jolt of lightning went straight through my body, followed by a flash of white light. When I opened my eyes and stood up straight it was as if I was in someone else's mind, as though I had been transported into another person's perception of me and I began to see myself through their eyes. I was pleading for my life with tears streaming down my face. I looked down to see chains around my waist, wrists, and feet. I was in a room surrounded by blank walls and chained in the middle of the floor. With panic rising, the vision began to get cloudy as if someone was trying to pull me away.

"Why are you doing this to me?" I could see myself asking whoever was standing in front of me.

A subtle husky laugh consumed the room.

"Find someone else to detain. Her soul is not up for negotiation."

I knew it was a male's voice, but who? They began walking

toward me as I could see the light leaving from my own eyes through the vision. One last cry for mercy, and I was gone. I stood over my own dead body. As I stared at myself lying on the floor, I could feel a warmth within my hands. Before I could relish in the comfort that was consuming my body, another jolt of lightning rippled through me, and I was back in the present state. Sweat encapsulated my entire body. I glanced to the top of the bookcase and the black cat's eyes were wide with warning.

Terror consumed me as bile rose in my throat at the vision of my own dead body replaying in my mind. If this vision was real, was Lorena involved? Was she detaining me for herself? My thoughts tumbled over each other as I racked my brain with questions. Why did she care so much about these books that clearly hadn't been touched in *years*. Her words played in my head as I drifted back to reality. *If it wasn't for your beauty, you would be worthless.*

Realization struck. *She never made this bargain just to work for her.* She wanted what she couldn't have. And what she could no longer have was my youth. Vexation washed over me, and rage once again filled every inch of me. As if someone else was in the room, I heard a voice urging me to run. Dropping the crystal back to the shelf, I snatched my coat from the hook and bolted directly for the door, swinging it open with the cat on my heels. *Thank the stars the simmering handle was now cool.* I was halfway to freedom when Lorena stepped around the corner. The sight of her alone made me clutch my coat tighter.

"Going somewhere so soon?" She crooned.

The devilish grin she now wore sent a shiver down my spine, as if melting ice dripped down my back.

"Why do you truly have me here? Why are you having me work? You don't care about those books. I can tell that room hasn't been used in years."

"From the look in your eyes, child, it seems that you already received your answer through the crystals I told you not to touch." She said as she brought both hands to her side and splayed them wide.

"I don't know what you're talking about," I spat. I swallowed as a giant lump of dread settled in my stomach.

"Lying won't get you very far, Amira. You see, with the way that magic works, when you have a vision through someone else's eyes they have the vision at the same exact time. And although what you saw was quite true, I have no intentions of killing you. Preserving your youth is a long and slow process. And unfortunately for you, that is the route that I'll have to take."

I stiffened. *MAGIC.* Fuck... my father was right.

"Your beauty. It's so...unique," she drawled. "The things I would do to have it all over again." Her eyes flashed with vice.

I felt my legs shaking beneath me, threatening to buck under my weight. I fought to steady myself. My entire life I'd been a fighter and I refused to die here without a battle.

"Move." I commanded. My words laced with conviction and my head held high.

"Proceed as you wish, child," she said while taking a small step to the side.

I took one step toward her, and a jolt of pain I'd never experienced paralyzed me in seconds. My legs finally gave way, and I screamed in pain as I slammed into the wooden floor. I could barely raise my head to look at her when I saw Thackery swipe at a lit candle ahead.

One second. That was all it would take, and that's all I would be granted. That was all I needed, and he knew it. Because Lorena's focus was taken off me, her hold had been broken when her focus was displaced. With everything that I had left, I pushed myself off the floor in one leap and bolted toward the door. She had magic on her side, but she didn't have my youth. I willed my legs to run as fast as I could, and this time I knew exactly where to go because I knew my way home. I was confident I could make it home if I kept running. When I was no longer in an open field and had made it into the forest, I knew that I was safe to run straight home. The only issue was that twenty feet to my right, she was there, running at my speed through the trees.

"How the fu—"

The same wave of pain and paralysis seized me before I could act.

"Silly girl. Did your parents never teach you that your mortality is nothing compared to magic?" She studied me with a click of her tongue, "Or do they prefer to keep the truth a secret?"

My thoughts halted at her question in the midst of panic and pain. *What truth?*

With the raise of her hand, a thousand more jolts of pain traveled through me. I knew that she had shattered every bone in my right arm from the intensity this time around. Another scream found itself trapped inside my throat.

"Or did you decide not to listen to them and did as you pleased?" she asked while moving toward me. The same shattering pain went down my left leg. Another scream tried to leave my mouth, but it wouldn't open.

"You unraveled exactly what I needed from you, and you still willed yourself to run. Are you not willing to help your elders, child?" A cold laugh escaped her. "Killing you slowly preserves the beauty, but I would be lying if I said that I didn't enjoy it as well. I had planned to do it humanely over time through food and drink, but you just had to be a nuisance and ruin my plans," she hissed while planting her foot on my already shattered leg. "I'm in a good mood today so I'll let you decide. What limb would you like to lose next?" A deep smile spread across her pale face.

Sweat began rolling down my brows. I wanted nothing more than to stand on my feet and fight like hell, but there was nothing that I could do to compete with her magic. Another wave of pain coursed through my body from head to toe, leaving me lying face down in the snow. My body went limp as the acceptance of defeat neared.

"Oh, you can't be giving up this easily can you girl? At least make it fun for me," Lorena spat as she kicked me over to my back. Opening my eyes revealed her standing over me with round eyes and a wide-toothed smile on her face. She raised her hand, conjuring a ball of light in her palm.

"You should be thanking me, Amira. At least you won't have to go back to that pathetic thing you call a family. A life of poverty at that," she stated. "In some ways you could say that I'm saving you."

I squeezed my eyes shut and threw out my unharmed arm to accept my fate and brace for the pain soon to come. I'll die before I begged this bitch for my life. "For what it's worth girl," her eerie voice flowed through the air. "That bitch of a sister never made it back to you because her mind was so easily manipulated by my magic." My eyes popped open at her words. "It was so easy to place a hex upon the trail she needed to follow back home that I didn't even need to lift a finger." My lips peeled back at her words, at her malicious smile plastered upon her ugly face. *Tessa.* I had blamed her for not bringing our father back to the market, but Lorena had prevented her from finding her way home in time. My eyes squeezed shut again as a ripple of pain traveled from the tips of my toes to my lips. I willed every fiber within to keep my scream from leaving me, not wanting to give her the satisfaction of reveling in the sound of my pain.

But time stopped. Everything stopped. The hum of the wind, bristling of the trees, and Lorena's horrendous voice ceased.

I opened my eyes to see her frozen directly above me and the screams that were being held captive finally left my mouth. My brain said to run, but my body was still too broken. The wave of pain that crashed over me brought stars to my eyes. I feared I was going to black out in my only window of opportunity. That's when I noticed the figure standing directly behind her.

The immaculate face from my dreams was here again with those deep-set sky-blue eyes. I watched as he slowly brought his lips to her ear. "If you come for her again, I'll kill you. If you even so much as think about her, I'll kill you. Let this be the last warning since you didn't heed the first." And within the blink of an eye, he wrenched her right arm until it fell from her body to the ground beneath her. Though she was frozen, I could see the pain in her eyes. I watched as her arm disintegrated into the ground and a wave of heat washed over me. A warning that I was about to faint.

As he shoved Lorena to the ground, his eyes fixated on mine before kneeling next to me. He reached out a hand to brush the stray hairs from my face, causing my head to jerk back from his touch. *A touch filled with fire.*

His eyes narrowed at my reaction and before I could protest him touching me, he slid both arms underneath my limp body as he prepared to lift me into his arms. Panic flared as my vision began to blur. He gently rose to his feet with my body pressed against his. A slight tilt of my head caused our eyes to connect as the brief moment of softness I witnessed before flashed across his face and poured into my soul. His eyes narrowed, and a mask of indifference quickly replaced the brief vulnerability. With one flap of his beautiful white wings, we ascended into the sky and my surroundings became a colorless blur.

Chapter Nine

My eyes remained closed, but I could tell I was no longer in the forest, nor my home. My body ached something terrible, which forced me to stay still. Was I dead? Was this all a dream? It had to be a dream, although being dead was a huge possibility as well. And if I am dead... how long will I have to wait to transfer to the afterlife? The events that I just witnessed didn't exist in the real world—a man with wings, a witch, magic. I'd heard tales about creatures with wings, but I chalked those up to myths from stories passed through time. *I really should've stopped listening to my mother's stories.*

I felt a wave of cold rush through my right arm, the shocking sensation forcing my eyes open. A woman with an angelic, tan face, long white hair pulled back into a ponytail, and light teal eyes stood directly over me. Though she may have been the most beautiful female I had ever seen, I had also never screamed so loud in my life. She jumped back quicker than any human could have.

"I'm so sorry if I hurt you. I was only trying to help. You were so limp when he brought you here and I didn't want you to wake up in the same state as before," she quickly exclaimed.

I blinked way more times than necessary to collect myself. "Oh...who brought me here? Where am I?"

"You're in Solaris. Raine brought you here. He didn't quite explain everything that happened, but he said you were in so much pain that you had blacked out." A grimace began to form on her oval-shaped face. "If you're okay with it, I would be happy to keep helping you." I've never been one to trust strangers so quickly, but the warmth and smile that formed on her face made me feel comfort.

"I'd appreciate that very much. I'm still in quite a bit of pain," I stammered while scanning the room. The aesthetic was nothing short of breathtaking. Given my family's current predicament, I'd never seen a room so spacious and bright. To look down from my bed and see marble white floors with hints of gold flecks shined to perfection and a wall full of windows with a balcony was not something I was used to every day.

My hand flew to my chest instinctively, seeking the familiarity of home. *I never put the fucking necklace on after Tessa handed it to me.* Dread engulfed me as my fingers met bare skin. Eyes wide, I opened my mouth to express my concern for the vacancy.

"You must be looking for this," the gorgeous female said as she reached into her pocket. She revealed the silver chain with its obsidian stone glimmering of purple and blue hues at the end. Relief flooded every bone in my body as she extended the piece of jewelry to me. "It fell from your garments when you were brought in. Figured you might want something that's so pretty back in your possession." A genuine smile spreading to her high cheek bones as she dropped it into the palm of my hand.

The tall female stepped closer as I closed my hand around the gift my sister had hurriedly given to me. Hovering her hands above the limbs that Lorena shattered, she studied them intently before speaking. "You might feel a cold sensation, but it shouldn't hurt. If I can finish everything right now you should be good to move around in just a couple of hours."

"What are you?" I blurted out before I could stop myself, which caused her to wince. "I'm so sorry. I didn't mean it like that. I've just never experienced anything like this. To say I'm confused is an understatement."

A sincere smile spread across her face at my apology.

"Oh! That would make sense why you've looked bewildered since you've awakened," she said with a chuckle. I wrung my hands together nervously, questioning exactly how bad I looked after what happened.

"I'm assuming that you're from the mortal realm?" she continued. I nodded my head in agreement as I provided a sheepish smile. Did they dislike humans here?

"To answer your question, I'm Fae. In short, we were born into magic and immortality. Some of us possess different magic than others, while some don't possess any magic at all. My main source of power is healing, so you're in a bit of luck today." She winked and once again that comforting smile was back on her face.

"May I?" she asked while hovering her hands over my body next to the bed. I gave a nod of approval, along with a genuine smile sweeping across my face.

As she warned moments before, a cold sensation rippled over the limb where her hands hovered. And just like she promised, not an ounce of pain arose. A sensation that felt like everything was fusing back together slithered its' way beneath my skin. Before I could process everything that was happening, she announced that she was done.

"You should be able to sit up in bed, but I would advise against attempting to stand until the morning. I'm not quite sure how well my magic works on mortals."

"If I can't stand, how will I care for myself?" Panic began clawing itself back to the surface. "If I don't fully heal by morning, how will I get back home?"

She didn't seem too shocked with my questions until I

mentioned the word *home*. The genuine smile she offered fell from her face as she nodded to portray her understanding of my concerns.

"I am going home...aren't I?" My voice projected in a higher pitch than I'd intended.

"Well, as far as caring for yourself goes, we have servants for that so no need to worry. But, when it comes to you going back home...you'll need to talk to, Raine." Panic had successfully clawed its way out.

"I want to speak with him right now," I exclaimed.

"Of course. As you wish. Give me a few moments to retrieve him," she said as she exited the room with a nod.

I thanked her before she left and wondered how I got into this position within the last few days. Not only did I have no idea where I was, I didn't even know who had brought me here on a personal level. Just when I had begun to spiral down a black hole of thoughts that scared me so badly I thought I would be sick. A knock on the door brought me back to reality.

"Hello!" I called, smacking my palm to my forehead. *Why would I say hello?*

"May I come in?"

His husky voice alone was enough to have every hair on my body stand up.

"Yes," I replied while pulling the sheets all the way up to my collar bone.

He opened the door, took one step inside, and closed it behind him without moving any further. Being in his presence was like looking at a god. *How could anyone be this attractive?* His rectangular face accompanied by that strong jawline was unheard of back home. The hooded icy-blue eyes was the final stroke to the masterpiece.

The silence was so heavy I felt like I couldn't breathe.

"Well, first I want to say thank you for saving me," I said hesitantly. "My memory is a little fuzzy, but I know that I wouldn't be here right now if it weren't for you.

He crossed his arms across his chest and leaned against the door with a thud. Strands of his snow-white hair fell to the sides of his face, causing him to run a hand through the thick locks. I swallowed at the visual, wondering what it would be like to run my hand through the same strands. He cleared his throat, meaning I was gazing at him like a fucking idiot. Heat flared its way up my neck in embarrassment.

"Don't mention it," he said with a blank expression.

His face was so unreadable I didn't know how to follow through with the rest of the conversation.

"I'd like to know when I'll be going home. I'd really like to get back to my family. I don't want them to worry about where I am."

"Noted." He answered with the raise of a single brow and subtle nod.

"Does that mean that you'll be taking me home? The kind girl with the gorgeous eyes let me know that I shouldn't attempt to stand until morning. Which I completely understand, but would you be able to take me home once I'm healed? Or let me know how to get back home?"

"That girl is my sister, Raya. And no, you won't be going back home tomorrow," he answered in a cold voice.

"Oh, do I need to stay here a bit longer to heal before I go back?"

"Healed or not, you won't be going back home anytime soon. I suggest you make yourself comfortable, Amira. Snap your fingers twice if you need assistance. Otherwise, we will check on you in the morning." His face held the same cold stare that he entered the room with, along with the tone to match it. If Tessa were here, it would be a standoff on who could portray the least amount of emotions.

Heat flared within as his off-putting demeanor sunk its teeth into the atmosphere. Nice Amira was now hiding in the shadows.

"Look, I understand you're supposed to be the one in charge here. And I understand that you saved my ass back there. But that doesn't give you a right to hold me hostage in a foreign place. If you think—"

Raine held up a single hand to stop me from speaking, causing my eyebrows to shoot upwards. "Your rambling has become quite irritating," he declared before brushing off the front of his tunic. "I'd rather keep this short and sweet."

"I'm sure that's your standard in bed as well," I whispered to myself, causing Raine to narrow his eyes. *Shit. How could he hear that from all the way over there?* I stiffened as he took a few steps closer.

"Despite what you may think Amira, I'm not holding you hostage here just for the sake of it. It's to keep you safe. Lorena is a very powerful witch, but fortunately for you, she's not powerful enough to break the wards of Solaris. As long as you're here she can't harm you. And trust me, after what happened back there, she's searching high and low for both of us." Raine took in a deep breath and released it before retreating backwards. "But by all means, if you'd like to be a careless damsel in distress once again, I can drop you back off where I found you. Just say the words."

Damsel in distress? Ice flooded through my veins at the sound of those words leaving his mouth. I couldn't release a single word from my mouth once again as I opened and closed it.

"Thought so," he spat as he turned his back and exited the room.

After a few seconds passed, allowing me time to process our interaction, I was able to form words again.

"What a prick," I mumbled to myself. I crossed my arms over my chest while glaring at the closed door. My usual witty remarks had escaped me in the moment, but luckily that had been short-lived. A knock on the door sounded. I sat up straight ready to tell him how I really felt about his cold attitude.

"Thank the heavens your back because I want to know who the fuck you think—"

"I think you're looking for someone else," a sweet voice answered from a crack in the door before I could finish my rant.

I swallowed my embarrassment before answering, "I'm so sorry! Please come in!"

Two older women shuffled in with polite smiles and a tray in each hand. A smile pulled at my lips as I noticed each movement they made was in unison. I quickly surveyed them, noting their features easily portrayed that they were siblings with their pale skin, long grey hair, small frames, and matching dark brown eyes. The more I studied them, the more youthful they seemed despite their aged features. Both females carried monotonous traits, yet their smiles and confidence could brighten any room they stepped in.

"We just wanted to bring you a warm meal in case you awoke from your slumber. Sorry to disturb you," one of the women rattled off. Before I could thank them and introduce myself, she hurried the other woman out of the room and followed behind her while softly closing the door.

I stared at the door perplexed by their actions. Moments later laughter exploded from within before I reached over to down the glass of water, falling back onto the plush mountain of pillows behind me.

Chapter Ten

Being confined to this bed until healed caused hundreds of thoughts to flood my mind about how I ended up here and how I was going to get home. Outside of those two worrisome issues, another question that I kept revisiting was how can that girl be his sister? She's so kind and he's nothing short of an asshole.

I desperately wished to snap my fingers to bring Raya back to my room for comfort, but I was terrified of getting *him* instead. I could tell nightfall had come through the wall of windows to my right, and I didn't want to bother anyone while being a guest. But of course, I really needed to use the bathroom as well. I put my right hand in the air and snapped twice. Within a few moments I heard two subtle knocks.

Raya popped her head around the door, "Did you need something?"

I released a deep breath that I was holding once I saw her face instead of Raine's. "This is kind of embarrassing, but I really need to use the bathroom and I know that you told me I couldn't stand up on my own until the morning," I rushed out in a single breath. "I didn't want to hamper the healing process any further."

"Oh! Not a problem at all! Here, let me help." She beamed while gracefully striding toward the wall of windows to pull the curtains together.

Raya helped me rise to the side of the bed, and to my surprise she lifted me into her arms in one swift motion. I blinked multiple times in confusion before fixing my stupor. She looked at my surprised face and chuckled, "Yeah... being Fae has some perks, strength being one of them."

While she walked me over to the bathroom, I couldn't help but observe I was in a completely different outfit than what I had come here in. Raya must have noticed that I was studying the new wardrobe, letting me know that the servants who brought me my meal had changed me. A flood of relief washed over me knowing that it was two female servants who swapped out my clothing. Maybe that's why they ran out of the room in a hurry earlier.

She sat me down to use the bathroom and told me to call for her in the other room once I was relieved. Sure enough, she came right back to get me and asked if I needed anything else for the night. I let her know I was comfortable, and she laid me back into the bed. I felt as if she were my own sister as she carefully pulled the covers up to my chest with that same warm smile from earlier. The thought caused my heart to slightly squeeze as I reflected on my strained relationship with Tessa.

After I thanked her, she sighed while smoothing her night-gown. "I know that he can be a bit of an ass sometimes, but he does mean well. He just hasn't known how to show emotions ever since we were kids."

"Oh... I understand. I did ask him when I could go home and he told me that it wasn't happening." The brightness in her face vanished and she smoothed her dark blue nightgown again.

"I can't really change his answer because that's his call to make as High King of Solaris. But I could try talking to him for you."

High King?

"I would greatly appreciate that."

"Of course! You know, I feel quite rude for not asking previously but, what is your name?"

"Amira. I'm sorry, I should have introduced myself."

"Well, you did kind of lose consciousness, so I think we can let it pass this time," she said while trying to hide her laugh. "I'm Raya, by the way."

"Your brother let me know your name, and it's very nice to meet you."

She headed towards the door and turned back around. "You can snap twice in the morning when you wake up, and I'll make sure that I'm the one to pop in and help you. Get some rest. You'll need it." With a flick of her wrist, she closed the door behind her.

When Raya left it felt as though the room knew that I was overly tired once again. The lights dimmed down and the fireplace turned on. My eyelids were so heavy I couldn't fight the exhaustion consuming me even if tried. And to my delight, I drifted into one of the deepest slumbers I'd had in years.

Chapter Eleven

It wasn't long before my eyes reluctantly fluttered back open. A cold breeze swept overhead, causing me to shoot up from under my warm bedcovers. Oddly enough, I still felt like the room understood my emotions because in my moment of panic the balls of light along the walls brightened. I looked in every corner of the room and saw nothing except expensive-looking furniture. I clasped my hands together to stop them from shaking, pulling them to my chest as I began to lay back down. My head was about to hit the pillow when I saw movement out the corner of my eye. With my neck almost snapping in half from the quick movement, I looked out onto the balcony. I couldn't tell if my mind was playing tricks on me, but I was almost certain that the black cat from Lorena's cottage was out there. I had the strongest desire to jump out of bed and run through those glass doors to see if my eyes were deceiving me, but I remembered Raya's orders on the healing process. I calmed my nerves and decided to lay back down. I'd been through a lot today. Clearly that amount of trauma could cause anyone to be delirious. Slowly, the lights dimmed until fully submerging the room in darkness again, sending me back into a sound sleep.

The sun shone through the double glass doors, waking me from a deep sleep. Sitting up in bed, I remembered the odd feeling that I had felt in the middle of the night. Did I really see that black cat from the cottage, or was I going crazy? I closed my eyes, took two deep breaths, and snapped my fingers twice. In a moment's time, three faint knocks on the door were heard. "Come in!" I yelled with a smile, waiting for Raya's bright face to show. While her tanned face did peak around the door, she was anything but bright. Her facial expression was a portrait of concern. It was then that I noticed another set of feet standing right behind her as she opened the door wider.

"Are you dressed, Amira?" She inquired through wide eyes that she kept shifting to the side as a warning that someone was behind her.

"Yes. Come in," I replied while trying to hide the worry in my tone. She opened the door further to step inside, and that's when I noticed Raine right on her heels. My stomach sunk into the soles of my feet as soon as we laid eyes on each other. Raya could sense the air was getting thicker with every passing second and decided to thin it out.

"How do you feel this morning?" she asked with a strained smile.

"I feel much better. Do you think I could finally stand on my own?"

"I believe so," she beamed, "Let's give it a try."

Gliding over to me, she slowly pulled the covers back, providing me time to adjust my nightgown over myself. Raya helped bring my legs to the edge of the bed, taking both of my hands in hers with hopeful eyes. I willed both legs to ease to the floor and firmly pressed my heels down, standing up to eye level with her. We both looked at each other and beamed with excitement. "You did it! Let's take some baby steps," she said while walking backwards and willing me to follow her. "Perfect! Try to walk back to the bed by yourself." My hands were slowly released from hers. I turned around and effortlessly walked back to the bed. As she clapped with excitement, I ran back over and threw my arms around her. Thankfully, the impulse embrace was reciprocated.

"Thank you so much," I nearly screamed into her face. "Now I can return home sooner rather than later!" I exclaimed with a smile on my face. The pit of my stomach plummeted, noticing that her smile faltered when mine lifted. She peered over at her brother and back at me.

"Why don't you go grab her some breakfast, Raya." Raine issued a command to his sister, rather than a suggestion. His bright, icy blue eyes remained fixed on me. It was in that moment that I realized I was in a nightgown and wanted to cover myself. I was convinced that Raya could read my mind because she walked into the bathroom and came back out with an oversized satin robe that she wrapped around my body, tying the thin ropes together.

"Any foods you don't like?" she asked while forcing a smile.

"Not that I can think of," I replied with a smile of my own. I had never been allowed the privilege of being picky with my food.

Advising that she would be back soon, Raya purposefully left the door cracked behind her. Not long after, Raine closed the door all the way with the heel of his boot. Walking to the opposite side of the room, he sat in an all-white velvet chair trimmed in gold and crossed an ankle over his knee.

"As you can tell from yesterday, I've never been one to beat around the bush, so I'm going to get straight to the point." His blank expression was still present as he smoothed a wrinkle in his slacks. "Though you're fully healed, you're still not going home any time soon. I know that this will sound strange to you, but you can't jump to different realms in such a short time."

My heartbeat slowed while trying to process his words.

"Different realms?"

"As you've noticed, you're no longer in Medlar, Amira. When I rescued you, I beamed us back to where it was safest."

"And that would be Solaris?" I asked through my own blank stare.

"Correct."

"What the hell makes it so safe here?"

"Well, that's no way for a lady to speak," he said, a corner of his mouth turning upwards. "It's part of a world other than your own. You'll find that many things are different within this realm, along with a lot more…" His head tilted to the side. "*Magic.*"

"Why wouldn't you just take me home instead of here?"

"As I informed you once already, I knew that Lorena would follow us. And I have no desire to fight someone of that caliber in such a weak realm. While I'd win, Medlar would suffer. To keep you safe, I brought you here as she has no access to Solaris."

My mind was trying to process how I could be in a different world other than where my family exists. I swallowed the unease attempting to swallow me whole and continued with my questions. "What happens if I return right away? I'd rather take my chances being *boomed* or whatever you said."

Raine's jaw ticked as he studied me for a moment. "It's called *beaming.* And traveling through multiple realms in such a short period of time can have an effect on the mind that at times can be irreversible for humans."

"But Fae can travel as often as they like? Whenever they like?"

Raine flashed his teeth before following up with a chuckle, "You're catching on." I seethed at his arrogance and clenched my teeth together so hard that I feared they'd crack at any moment. Remembering I was on his grounds, I unclenched my fists and teeth to continue interrogating this asshole.

"So, how long are we talking?"

"Since it was your first time, I would suggest waiting a couple of weeks." He quickly glanced over my face. "Two or three…three to be safe."

"*Weeks?*" I realized I was shouting but I didn't care. "You expect my family to not go looking for me for *weeks*?" I was so irate that I began laughing out loud. "What if Lorena goes after them because she thinks that I went home?"

"I have that issue handled."

"*Handled?*" I choked out, my voice hoarse from hysteria.

"Lower your tone when speaking to the High King."

"I don't even know what the fuck a High King is, therefore, I will speak in whatever fuckin' tone I feel is appropriate at the time. And in this specific time, I find that my tone is *very* appropriate for me," I spat back at him. That same sly smile swept across his face at the same time he swept across the floor, bringing him mere inches away from me.

"Would you like to test that theory again?" he asked with a sinister stare and a raised brow. He's challenging me. He may be used to weak women where he's from, but I'm not from here. He can kiss my ass if he thinks I'm going to back down from an egotistical prick like himself. "Are you that weak that you can't last a few weeks without your family? Tell me, do you rely on them that heavily to survive, damsel?"

Heat flared from the inside out as my fists clenched. I'd rather be pummeled to death than have a random man degrade me. I stepped closer while tilting my head upwards to meet his glare. One additional centimeter and our noses would touch. "With all due respect High King... go fuck yourself," I said with a full spread, sinister smile sweeping across my face.

If looks could kill, I would be a pile of ash under Raine's boot. The male in front of me was seething at my suggestion, and I was relishing at the thought of getting under his skin. Just as his lips peeled back and his breathing increased, Raya opened the door with a tray in hand.

"Breakfast for three," she chimed while shifting her eyes back and forth between the two of us.

Chapter Twelve

Raine didn't bother to eat breakfast with Raya and me. As soon as she came through the door with our food, he angrily stalked right past her to leave, slamming the door behind him. It took everything in me not to swing the door back open and either demand more answers from him or somehow force him to take me back home. I had to remind myself that I was human and didn't possess a single ounce of magic in my *mortal* body. Unfortunately, with that realization, I didn't see myself being able to force anything out of Raine at the moment.

"You've barely touched your food," Raya acknowledged, her concerned teal eyes shifting to my full plate.

"I'm sorry. Everything is delicious. I just can't stop thinking about my family and how they're probably worried sick about me right now." When that last sentence left my mouth, my stomach turned into knots because deep in my soul I worried that my siblings wouldn't step up to help my parents. An even deeper knot formed as an uneasy feeling washed over me with the thought of possibly never getting the chance to mend our relationships.

"I understand. There are days when I miss my family too."

My eyes shot up to meet hers. "What do you mean? You have Raine." After my statement threw me into my own thoughts, my eyes grew wide. "Where are your parents?"

"I don't know."

"As in you have no idea where they are?"

"Years ago, I woke in the middle of the night to find my mother's crown on my bed. When I went to take it back to her in the morning she was gone, and so was my father."

"And no one has been able to find them?"

"Raine and I did our best to find them, along with the army of Solaris. We found nothing, not even a trace."

I'm not sure how long we sat there in silence as Raya stared off into the distance of my balcony. I let her know that I was sorry to hear about her parents, but she gave no reply. While we were both lost in thought I finished my meal and began to collect our dishes to put them back on the tray. As I reached for Raya's cup, her slender hand grabbed my wrist, startling me as she yanked on it to bring my face inches away from her own.

"No matter what you're told during your time here, nothing is what it seems. NOTHING, Amira," Raya blurted out to me as if her voice was going to crack. And for a moment her eyes were slightly darker.

"What do you me—" I went to ask her to elaborate, but my bedroom door flew open.

Raine walked into the room without announcement. "I hope you enjoyed breakfast," he said while sheathing a dagger to the belt resting at his hip. I looked back to Raya who was now smiling as if her quick outburst never happened. "It was delicious," I said while evolving a fake, minute smile of my own. "Thank you."

"Good, because you're going to need it for where we're going today."

"You've lost your mind if you think I'm going anywhere with—"

"We're going to the Garden of Sanri," Raine cut me off without considering my refusal.

"Garden of what?"

"You'll find out soon enough."

"Will Raya be coming with us?"

Raine answered before his sister could open her mouth. "I'm afraid Raya has quite a few things to do today to prepare for Spring Solstice." Curiosity got the best of me before I could demand that she accompany us.

"What's Solstice?" I questioned while looking between the two of them. Raya jumped out of her seat.

"I'll explain the holiday and its festivities to you when you get back later today." Her smile was so wide I thought it'd split her face in two. "Let me run you a bath and grab you some clothes for your journey."

~

An hour later, Raya was guiding me down the hallway to the front door of the palace. I don't know which one I was in more awe of: the palace itself or the two female servants not allowing me to bathe myself and get ready for the day before I left my room. Everything in sight was white marble with gold accents. When we reached the peak of the stairs, Raine was waiting for me at the bottom. His blue eyes shone brightly against his grey pants and white tunic. The only accessory he embellished was that same dagger from earlier resting on his hip.

His eyes swept from my feet to the top of my head. "I could give you a tour of the palace when we get back if you would like?" He offered with a rare smile before clearing his throat and adopting that same blank expression. I examined him through glaring eyes.

What happened to the asshole from earlier?

"As much as I would like that, don't think that I've forgotten about our conversation earlier," I said while gripping the railing so hard my knuckles began turning white. With a shrug of his shoulder, he held his hand out while waiting for me to descend the stairs. Making my way to the bottom, I walked past his hand making sure to bump it with my shoulder. When I glanced back, I saw Raya standing inside the double doors holding in a laugh by biting her tongue out the side of her mouth. Raine shot her a glare that even made me cringe. She waved goodbye to me and went on her way, turning back towards the hallway.

Outside, two white horses were waiting for us. Raine stood next to one and gestured for me to get on. While I took a leap of faith to mount the horse, I felt both of his hands grab my waist. Butterflies filled my stomach and made their way up my throat. I desperately tried to get settled atop my horse without making eye-contact with him but couldn't avoid seeing him smirking out of the corner of my eye. Two authentic smiles from him had been produced within a few hours. *What the fuck has him so giddy?*

"I'm assuming that you know how to ride a horse?" he asked dryly.

"Guess we'll find out. If I can't, it looks like I won't be going," I answered just as dryly while shrugging my shoulders.

"It entertains me to hear you think that I won't put you on the back of my horse and feel you bounce behind me the entire way to the garden," he countered with a menacing stare.

I felt the heat rise from the pit of my stomach all the way up to my cheeks.

"Shall we just jump straight to you getting on my horse, Amira?" His voice was filled with such solidity that I wanted to curl into a ball. But I wouldn't provide him with the satisfaction of that sight.

"I know how to ride a horse," I said through gritted teeth, never dropping his gaze.

"Shame."

Effortlessly mounting his horse, he looked straight ahead as we moved out toward the gates.

I've never been a shy person, quite outgoing on the contrary. But being around Raine made me want to run and hide in a corner somewhere. I almost begged him to let Raya come with us so that I wouldn't be so on edge. And it was in that moment that I realized I would be by myself with Raine in a place that I knew nothing about.

Chapter Thirteen

I realized that Raine and I hadn't uttered a single word to each other on our way to the garden just as we came up to a large golden gate that slowly opened for us. I waited for him to go forward before I willed my horse to do so. As we entered, my lungs filled with the purest form of air encapsulating us, and I gasped at the air's sweetness. My horse slowed its pace at the sound. Raine must have noted that I was startled too as he turned around for the first time since we left the palace grounds. Stationing his mare, he offered a hand for assistance. I thought it wise to take his offer this time around because I wasn't trying to land face first off my horse and lengthen my stay in Solaris with another injury.

"Welcome to the Garden of Sanri, Amira." Raine threw his arms out wide, accompanied by a smile equally as wide across his face. The morning sun beamed down on his pale face, and I studied his features carefully. I don't know if I had ever seen a smile so beautiful. *This is the most confusing man I've ever met.*

"It's lovely," I exclaimed with a smile of my own.

"Walk with me?" he asked as he offered the crook of his arm to me. I'd be lying if I said my stomach didn't take a leap to my chest.

I was staring at the most beautiful man that I'd ever set eyes on, and yet I was worried about if I could even trust him. Regardless of the million questions swimming around in my head, I hooked my arm in his and looked straight ahead. While walking, he told me about the history of the Garden of Sanri and what makes it so special. The fruit and vegetables that grew there replenished themselves without aid. What wasn't eaten fell to the earth and grew again over time. The water was the purest water known to man (along with the air) and if a person bathed in it, their skin glowed for weeks with a shine that resembled the warmth of the sun.

Raine walked up to a peach tree and plucked one from the lowest branch. "Taste it," he instructed. I scrunched my nose as I pushed his hand away from my face.

"No thanks."

His shoulders sagged as he loosed an exasperated breath. "How long?" he asked after staring at me while the silence encapsulated us.

"How long what?" I asked while crossing my arms across my chest.

"How long are you going to put up this charade that you hate me? One moment you're okay being in my presence and the next you despise me." A genuine laugh escaped me before I could stop it.

"You think that's a charade? You have been nothing short of an asshole since you've brought me here! You won't even let me go home to my fuckin' family!" My words were flowing from my mouth like a river.

"Language, Amira." My eyes flared at his response.

"Oh, fuck your standards!" I seethed at his reprimand as he took a few steps closer, his voice barely a whisper as he bared his teeth.

"How about you stop acting so weak and helpless without your family to coddle you. I'm not trying to be an *asshole* toward you. I'm trying to protect you. To protect my people. My realm, from Lorena and whatever destructive plans she's come up with to get to you." My eyes darted back and forth across his face at his words.

"I don't need your fucking protection, Raine." A subtle shudder ran through his shoulders as his name left my lips. A tiny smirk played on my lips at his reaction. I popped my hip out while waiting for his response.

"Fine. If you want to take the risk of beaming back to your realm then I'll do it. If you're too weak to spend a few weeks without your family to lean on for stability, then I can't help you. But I have a strong feeling you *can* survive without them for that small amount of time." My arms dropped from my chest at his judgement.

"I know that I can survive without them, but can they survive without me?" I replied while practically screaming in his face at this point. The shock, the realization that formed across his face calmed me while his tense demeanor mellowed at my words.

"You take care of them, don't you?" He asked while searching my face.

"As much as I can," I answered solemnly, hugging myself while rubbing my arms. Raine wet his lips and looked away before returning his focus back to me.

"Finding you on the ground in that forest showed me how you can be hurt. How brittle your human body was... and still is. I won't let it happen again, Amira. And I don't regret for one second bringing you back to my home instead of Medlar."

My surroundings were a blur as his words filled the air. Maybe he wasn't the asshole I so badly wanted him to be.

Forcing myself to breathe I stepped forward, reaching for his side. He didn't move but kept his focus on me. Warily, I took the peach from his hand and sunk my teeth in. It was like taking a bite out of a forbidden fruit. I'd tasted many peaches in my lifetime, but none came close to the deliciousness and purity that this one offered. I devoured the entire thing in less than a minute and didn't feel an ounce of shame afterwards. Surveying my delight, Raine instructed me to drop the pit right where I was standing. My gaze fell to the ground as I dropped the remains of the delectable fruit. The peach stone disintegrated into the ground within seconds, resulting in a flashback of Lorena's arm disintegrating in the snow after he had ripped it from her body.

Nervously, I looked back up at Raine who had wandered ahead of me to an apple tree. I

reached him as he plucked an apple from a branch I couldn't reach even if I jumped.

Slowly, he raised the apple to my lips. Taking a step forward, I hesitantly placed my mouth on the fruit while holding his stare. Tension sifted through the air. *Is it possible to fuck without touching each other?*

As my teeth sank into the sweetness, electricity flowed through my veins but without the pain. I stumbled backwards from the shock and Raine caught me by the waist. Time passed slowly in my mind while he made sure I was stable before stepping away from me with a smirk that quickly disappeared.

Just like my delicious peach, the apple core disintegrated into the ground in mere seconds.

"Shall we?" he said, offering his arm once more. And again, I found myself taking his offer, this time with less skepticism.

He walked us to the pond that held the water he had told me about, and my mouth popped open. I was staring into a pool of golden honey. Each ripple carried a lace of glimmer with it. Raine dipped one hand in and held it up in the sunlight, releasing a gleaming stream of water that was tinted gold.

"You can jump in if you want to. But I feel the need to remind you that you don't have any spare clothes with you," he stated with a hint of challenge in his blue eyes. As much as I loved a challenge, this was one I was willing to lose. "Why come all this way if you're not going to indulge in what this realm has to offer?" He questioned with a calm that made my spine straighten and shiver at the same time.

I looked back to the pond and dipped my hand in, holding it up to the sunlight. That same golden honey was now shining on my bare, golden-brown skin and making its way down my forearm. I dipped my hand back in, scooping up a palmful of water and took a sip. My head jolted back, and my eyes burned as if I were looking directly into the sun. My throat was so hot that I wanted to scream, but it wouldn't release. Within seconds another jolt came through my body, and I was looking at my life through someone else's eyes once again. I was sitting upon a throne with a long white dress bedazzled with gold jewels to match the jewelry placed upon my neck and wrists. A gold crown with diamonds and pearls sat atop my head to complete the ensemble. When I finally took my gaze off myself, I noticed that Raine was sitting on my right, holding my hand. My eyes snapped back up from our hands to see Raine looking at me seated next to him with eyes as white as the marble floors of the palace. When he went to stand, my body took one last jolt and I was back to the present in the garden, laying on the ground with my head in Raine's lap.

"What the fuck was that?" I could feel the sweat beading at my hairline as if I was trying to break a terrible fever.

"Once again, that's no way for a lady to talk," he reminded me while pushing a stray curl from my forehead. "Some Fae who drink from the waters of Sanri have visions and some don't."

"Then why didn't you stop me? I'm not even Fae, what if something worse happened?" I yelled at him with wide eyes.

"Because I figured if there was a possibility of you seeing the future it would be much easier than me having to explain it to you," he answered with that same calm that had sent a shiver down my spine earlier.

"Excuse me? And what exactly *is* that future that I'm supposed to see?" At this point I had jumped up and was seething while standing over him as he remained kneeling on the ground.

The last bit of self-control I was clinging to had decided to make its exit.

Raine calmly regained his footing as he stood, showcasing his dominance by towering over me. "That future includes you sitting by my side as queen of Solaris, Amira. And not only will that happen, but you will grant me the heir to my throne as well. In return you'll never have to lift a pretty little finger ever again in your lifetime." The blood drained from my face as my fingers began trembling. "If you'll have me that is."

"Like hell I will!" I screamed at him and turned to walk back to my horse. Raine grabbed my wrist and flung me to his chest.

"The fact that you think you can hide your attraction to me is admirable to say the least. Let's get back to the palace so that you can get cleaned up before dinner."

I gazed down at my clothes and noticed the amount of dirt on them due to my episode I had when I drank the water from the pond.

"Don't flatter yourself," I exclaimed and mounted my horse without his help. It wasn't graceful by any means. But I refused to let him put his hands on me again.

I prepared myself for a long, silent ride back to the palace, but I blinked and found myself at the front door. I gaped in confusion as Raine stepped to my side.

"Welcome to the land of magic my future queen," he said through a tilted smile, opening the door for me to walk in.

Why the fuck didn't we just do that in the first place?

Chapter Fourteen

I made my way back to my room, making sure to bring out my inner child by stomping my feet as loudly as possible and slamming the door shut behind me. I may not have been able to fight Raine, but at least he'd know my distaste for him.

My sister had enthusiastically talked about the day she would get married, but we didn't share that same desire, and I refused to be forced into a marriage with someone I had just met, let alone someone that I was terrified to be around. I sat in the same chair Raine sat in last night and caught his scent hidden in the fixture. Of course he would smell absolutely divine, a stark contrast to the rotten attitude that he carried around.

Just as I had calmed myself down, there was a knock at the door.

"I heard your wrath being taken out on the innocent door and thought you could use some company," Raya offered with a hint of humor.

"I just don't understand what I did to get on your brother's bad side." Walking over to my bed, I threw my arms out to the side and free fell on top of the cloud-like pillows.

"I don't think that you're anywhere near his bad side, Amira. He has that same attitude and demeanor with everyone that he first meets. I don't think he knows how to tell you how he really feels. Anytime he sees you his aura instantly changes."

"Well, he could've fooled me. He can tell me that he's basically forcing me to marry him, but he can't be nice to me?"

"*Forcing what?*" Raya asked with concern.

"Raine told me that I'm to be seated at his side as queen of Solaris."

"I'm sure he didn't mean that it was a requirement," Raya retorted.

"Well, he did say that it's my choice at the end of his speech. But he couldn't at least court me first? Or heavens forbid, scale back on being an asshole in the least?" I sat up suddenly, throwing my hands in the air out of frustration. "I've never been interested in marriage. And children are out of the question. So he can forget his request of me providing an heir as well." Raya threw her head back as laughter consumed her. Narrowing my eyes at her odd behavior, I asked her what was so funny.

"Sorry. I forget that you're not one of us sometimes," she said while wiping away tears of laughter. "Mortals and immortals cannot have children together. Even if you were able to bear his child, the change would be too much on your mortal body. Fae and other immortal females only carry for five months. Our offspring grow quicker than mortal offspring." Raya winced at the last half of her statement. "Basically, your body would not be able to handle the rapid growth of an immortal baby."

"Has there ever been a half mortal and half immortal Fae?" I asked as Raya completed the rest of her giggling spell.

"I've heard old wives' tales of the sort over the past centuries. Supposedly, decades ago one was born but no one knows whether it was within the mortal or immortal realm, nor how long it even survived in the world. And of course, no one has ever seen this child or knows any particulars of the story. Tale as old as time naturally," Raya pursed her lips accompanied by a shrug of her shoulder. "How about a tour of the palace? You seem stressed and you haven't even been here two full days yet."

"I think that would help to clear my head," I agreed and followed her into the hall.

We started outside of the palace, where I instantly regretted not taking the time to marvel in its beauty earlier. The exterior was complete with white stone and gold accents. Yards away I noticed the front gate of solid gold that opened to a white stone bridge that led to the front yard of the palace. And beyond the gates the trees had bloomed into the brightest colors that the naked eye could behold.

"How long have you lived here?" I asked Raya in awe of the beauty the palace held, even on the outside.

"My family and this palace have stood the tests of time that's for sure," she answered with a lighthearted laugh. "This year will be 350 years of us ruling Solaris, which makes this year's Solstice a very special one." Strong waves of pride rippled off of her as she finished her statement.

I whipped my head toward Raya. "I'm sorry, did you say 350 years?"

She looked at me with bewilderment.

"Yes. Were you not aware what immortal meant or..."

"I was aware. But it never quite registered in my mind that immortal could equal to hundreds of years," I had to look away from her out of embarrassment, "I'm sorry, everything is still so new to me." I could feel the rush of blood to my cheeks as silence filled the air between us. "You promised to inform me what exactly Solstice is before I left this morning," I reminded her in hopes of changing the subject.

"That's right! It completely slipped my mind that you're not aware of the festivities. Every year Solaris celebrates Solstice to welcome Spring. The festival is celebrated throughout all the land with high hopes for the upcoming year. Though it's a holiday of mysterious roots, it's mostly associated with rites of passage, music, food, and romantic gestures," she explained. I noted the strain in her voice when she stated *romantic gestures*. "Solstice is celebrated for three days, but the climax of the holiday is found within the final hours that holds the main event that everyone looks forward to."

"What happens in the final hours?" I questioned, curiosity getting the best of me.

"That is something that must be experienced, rather than explained, Amira," Raya answered with a happy tone. "Come, let me show you my favorite place on the outside of the palace."

Raya walked me to the back of the palace where the most beautiful flowers bloomed, accompanied by a white stone foun-tain. Every piece of grass reminded me of the jade stones I would see at the market with my father. There was not a brown patch in sight. A petite bench sat along the back of the white stone wall overlooking the immaculate stone fountain. I noted a few more benches carefully scattered throughout the garden, making sure that all the best spots for a view were marked. The rows of flowers had no problem getting their share of the attention as bumble bees bounced to each one. Nothing in eyesight should be ignored, but the lotus flowers floating leisurely in the glimmering water of the fountain dwarfed the beauty of the surrounding garden.

Noting my gaze on the lotus flowers, Raya gestured me over to the fountain and picked one up from where she sat at the stone edge. "Did you know that the lotus flower symbolizes purity, over-coming adversity, and rebirth? Regardless of what realm you visit, all of them believe that the lotus flower represents positivity in nature," she informed me while laying the flower back in the water. "These beauties will only grow within mud and as the lotus blooms, the blossoms unfold one by one. Of course, these survive within the fountain due to enchantments placed by my aunt when they first arrived here." Raya released a breath before continuing. "My mother used to tell me that like the lotus flower that is born out of mud, we too must honor the darkest parts of ourselves and the most painful of our life's experiences, because they're what allow us to birth our most beautiful selves."

I glanced at Raya and saw the tears in her eyes ready to overflow.

"You miss her," I said with sorrow lacing my words.

"Every moment of every day."

After a moment of silence, Raya quickly wiped her eyes and straightened her back. I was about to ask her what was wrong from the look of concern on her face, but I felt his presence before having to ask. Raine was sauntering down the back palace steps wearing white pants and a light grey tunic, leaving the top two buttons undone. It irked me how attractive I found him.

"Enjoying your tour of the palace, Amira?" Raine asked with a small smile, irritation lacing his words. I grew irritated as well trying to figure out what he could possibly be upset about now. My memory ran its course as I remembered his offer from earlier about touring the palace. The trivial part within me reveled knowing that his frustration came from my choice to have a tour of the palace grounds without him.

"Yes. Raya is the *perfect* guide."

"Is she now?" he inquired as he tossed a quick glance at his sister.

"And she finally gave me insight on Solstice. When is that by the way?"

"Spring Solstice is in eight weeks' time," he replied. "Shall I show you around the inside of the palace?"

I looked down to see his hand outstretched toward me in offering. I loved to devour every chance I got at shoving this prick's arrogance right back up his ass.

"I think Raya is doing a good enough job with showing me

around. Thank you though." I patted Raya's shoulder and focused back on the lotus flowers.

"Raya has responsibilities to tend to for Solstice. Come." The demanding tone in his words startled me, placing my attention back to him with his hand still held out for me to take.

I glanced at Raya who was now standing and dusting off her skirted two-piece turquoise outfit. She remarked that she does in fact have planning to tend to regarding Solstice but promised to catch up at dinner. She nodded her head to the two of us and made her way up the palace steps and through the glass doors. With an annoyed sigh that I made sure Raine could hear, I started walking towards the steps, ignoring his hand once again. Before I could make it two steps past him, he grabbed my arm, turning me around to face him. "You'll find that you will be begging for my hand soon enough, Amira. Might as well take it while it's offered." Chills rippled through my core while he stared into my eyes.

"I'll take my chances," I quipped, snatching my arm from his grip. Something told me that he willingly let me out of his grasp, but I decided to take the win in stride. With a chuckle, he passed me and started toward the palace.

Once stepping foot back inside, I realized I hadn't got the chance to appreciate its full beauty. But if the front was as beautiful as the back, I didn't know how I missed it when we left that morning. The reasoning for my lack of observation most likely being because I was fuming at the fact that I had to spend an entire morning alone with *him*. The white marble on the floor shone with swirling gold accent lines flowing through it, and the long hall was lined with art I had never seen.

Before I could inquire about the art pieces, Raine led me into a room lined with a wall of glass. It was one of the most breathtaking views that I knew I would ever see in my lifetime. Rows of sunflowers decorated the open plane outside of the glass windows. Scattered along the flowers were statues discolored and aging from the sunlight. All I wanted to do in that moment was lay in the middle of the sunflower field and bask in the sun.

The open wall distracted me so much that I didn't notice the remainder of the room was lined with bookshelves. My body shut down at the realization of what I was surrounded by. I was convinced the walls were closing in on me with flashbacks of being in the woods at Lorena's cottage dusting those awful books. Phantom spurts of pain shot through my limbs as I remembered hearing my bones break from her craft. I trembled, hearing her wicked laugh ring through my mind as I recalled it unwillingly. The vision of me chained to the middle of the floor flooded my mind, causing me to hyperventilate. Darkness had consumed most of my vision when I noticed Raine holding me by my shoulders while repeating my name. My anxiety had banked for a day or two, but it was coming back with vengeance in this moment. The tips of my fingers felt cold as I fought to tame the rising panic.

"Amira, please talk to me. *Amira*."

"I'm so sorry," I stammered as my eyes wandered around the room. "I remembered being locked in Lorena's library surrounded by bookshelves and then I remembered a vision I had from touching one of her crystals."

I winced at how stupid I sounded from my rushed explanation.

"Nothing can hurt you here, Amira. What was the vision?" His eyes narrowed in on my face.

"I saw myself chained to the floor. Before it was over, I found myself standing over my own dead body," I confessed while staring off into the distance of the sunflower field.

"Amira, listen to me. And listen to me carefully. There is no one in this realm or universe that can take you from me. I will tear anyone and anything apart that looks in your direction without asking you first. Do you understand me?"

I wanted to answer him, but I was in shock at his chosen words that I couldn't process my own thoughts quickly enough.

"Answer me, Amira. Do you understand me?"

What did he mean by taking me from him? I didn't belong to him. I didn't belong to anyone, But I damn sure didn't belong to this asshole.

I searched his eyes for answers to the questions that were swarming in my head. "T-take me from you?" I felt myself teeter again at the words that left my lips. Raine brushed my hair from my face, as he brought me an inch closer to his.

"I meant what I said at the garden, Amira. Whatever decision you decide to make is yours. But the heavens don't lie. They never have." I swallowed hard as my eyes narrowed at his statement.

"Lie about what, Raine?" We were so close that I could feel his cool breath on my face. His scent of cinnamon and musk consuming me as one hand left my shoulder to cup my face.

"The heavens don't lie about fated mates, Amira." I jerked myself from his grip, knowing that he willingly let me go. "I felt it the moment I saw you running from those wolves in the forest. I wanted to grab you then, to hold you and never let you leave my protection again. But I knew I couldn't take you from your realm without reason. Without breaking the treaty."

My lungs burned from me ceasing to inhale or exhale. The burning look in his eyes let me know the seriousness of his statement. His piercing blue eyes were staring so deep into my soul I was sure he could command me to crumble, and I would without question.

"I-I don't even know what a mate is," I stammered through incohesive thoughts.

"It means that I have waited for you every single day of my life for the past three-hundred and twenty years. Every Fae is fated to someone in this world but that doesn't always mean they will find them. But you're here and I'll be damned if I let you go without a fight." Raine's firm grip had somehow made its way to my waist as we talked. I pushed his chest where both my hands laid just as firm. His hold didn't falter.

"You have been nothing but an ass since the moment you brought me here. And now you expect me to accept some kind of *mating call*?"

Raine released a laugh so loud his chest vibrated.

"It is not a *mating call*, Amira. It is a bond that cannot be broken. When two mates find each other, the other would rather die than let them go. And I am sure that my world would burn if you declined to accept our fate."

I was so focused on his words that I didn't notice my body was now firmly pressed to his. There was no air between us, just like my lungs that were still burning from my refusal to breathe. My eyes wandered to his lips and back to those blue eyes that constantly found mine.

"I'm sorry for my behavior when you first arrived. The mating bond was taking a toll on me, and I wasn't prepared. That's still no excuse for how I treated you. But I will make it right," he promised while brushing a thumb over my bottom lip. "I know I just dropped a lot of unexpected information. This was not how I wanted to let you know my feelings for you. Let's go get washed up for dinner," he suggested while taking my hand and guiding me back upstairs to my room as I remained in a fog of disarray.

"I'll send Raya to get you when it's time for dinner. If you need anything prior, you know how to call for us. Otherwise, anything and everything here is yours to explore. You don't need one of us to leave your room, but it would be my pleasure to complete a tour of the palace whenever you wish," he said, letting me know his wishes as he turned to walk away. "That includes a tour of my bedroom if you're ever interested in that as well." He gave a small smile and continued walking down the hallway. Those same butterflies from earlier started to make their way from my stomach and up my throat. I quickly opened the door to my room and shut it as soon as I was inside. Sliding down the door while those butterflies settled back down in the pit of my stom- ach, I started replaying the day in my head. How could Raine go from being so cold the previous day, to being someone that vows to protect me the next?

And what the fuck is a mate?

Whatever it was, he must be lying. If mortals and immortals can't bear children, how can they be mates? Attempting to process my thoughts only furthered my curiosities. Curiosities that had no business existing.

Chapter Fifteen

At dinnertime it was hard to look at Raine without thinking about the events that would happen if I took him up on the offer of venturing into his bedroom. I moved my hand toward my chest to fidget with the only piece of home I had managed to bring with me. *Shit.* I must have forgotten to put the necklace on this morning after my heated discussion with the *High Asshole of Solaris.* I made it a point to admire the gorgeous, dining chamber surrounding us to avoid the sensual thoughts in my head that stemmed from his offer. Raya had expressed that it was her favorite room in the palace because of the beauty it held, but her description didn't do it justice. The long golden table with white accents could fit up to twenty people at a time if needed. I couldn't stop my fingertips from gliding across the smooth surface every other minute if I tried.

Unfortunately, Raine must have noticed that I was avoiding eye contact at all costs and decided to bring me back to the present moment. "Let me know if you need something smooth to rub after dinner since you can't bring the table with you," he said with a seductive look that would bring most women to their knees, me being one of those women if I weren't so headstrong on telling him to fuck off.

"Raine, give it a rest. She's human. Not Fae. She doesn't fawn over you like the rest of the idiot women in Solaris. She's not interested. Right, Amira?" Raya presumed with confidence beaming through those teal eyes on her heart-shaped face.

"Right." I answered with a look of disgust at Raine. It was a half honest, half lie of an answer but convincing, nonetheless.

Raine grunted at my reply and raised both palms to the ceiling. Mouthwatering food arose from the table in front of us, along with plates and silverware. Raya let a subtle laugh slip at the sight of my mouth wide open in bewilderment. "Wine?" Raya asked without a glass or bottle present.

"No thank you. I'm not really a drinker anymore," I politely declined. I saved myself the embarrassment of confessing how I used to drink myself silly at the local tavern back home, ready to fuck any attractive male willing to leave me the fuck alone and never talk to me again afterwards.

Raya raised her right palm to the ceiling and four glasses of wine appeared. "Well, one thing is for certain. You can't count to save your life," I said to Raya while laughing. She snapped her head to Raine and inquired why four glasses presented themselves instead of three.

"Because I don't need an invitation after all these years," a deep voice projected from the doorway. Startled, I turned around to see a tall, handsome male standing in a black and grey ensemble. Though he looked young, shades of grey ran through his dark shoulder length hair.

"Yet, you annoy me every time I hear your voice or smell you for that matter," Raya retorted. The random male walked behind her chair and kissed the top of her head. "Come on love. Don't be like that in front of your guest." Raya swatted at the man behind her. The unnamed guest walked over to me with his hand out. "You must be, Amira. You are just as gorgeous as Raine described.

I'm Eryx. Best friend of honor, soon to be brother-in-law to Raine," he said with a smile and wink toward Raya.

"*You're engaged?*" I yelped to Raya with my voice cracking as I shook the male's hand.

"Absolutely not. This asshole is delusional and has been ever since we've meet."

"She'll come around as soon as I convince her to lay in my bed," Eryx said with his eyes locked on his apparent future wife. Raya stood from the table out of anger, almost knocking over her chair. Her teeth had peeled back as she seethed at the male's comment.

"Enough of your idiocy, Eryx. Take a seat and shut up," Raine said with authority while remaining unamused. Eryx sat down but didn't wipe the Cheshire cat grin off his face before grabbing a glass and pouring the deep red liquid to the brim.

"Honestly Raine, what is the point of him being here? It's Amira's first dinner with us and you invite this idiot," Raya argues while crossing her arms.

"Because, even though sometimes you forget, I'm the High King of Solaris, and I can invite my best friend to dinner any time I want," Raine answered with dominance in his voice. When I looked at the hurt in Raya's eyes, I couldn't stop my mouth from opening if I tried.

"That doesn't mean you have to let him disrespect your sister," I said before I could stop the words from tumbling out of my mouth. Raya placed her hand on my thigh under the table in warning, but I wasn't the least bit worried about Eryx. I'd tussled with men back in Medlar without a single scratch to show it. He may be twice their size and have the added benefit of Fae strength, but I still had no intentions of backing down.

Unfortunately, it wasn't Eryx that she was warning me about.

"This is not your argument to partake in, Amira," Raine spat at me with glowing eyes. My breath hitched while looking at the white that took over the blue hue of his eyes.

"Relax, Raine. She doesn't under—," Raya spoke in an attempt to stop my belittlement.

"Then she will learn her place just like you will soon," Eryx spat back.

I clenched my jaw, shooting Eryx and Raine a glare regardless of how terrifying Raine looked. I could see my fingers beginning to tremble from my anger. Heat flushed over me, warning me that my panic was threatening to strike as I contemplated leaping across the table.

"Oh, she thinks she can fight you Raine," Eryx said with amusement in his voice. "Shall we move the table and chairs?"

"Shut up," Raya said through gritted teeth. "Eryx thinks he's special because he doesn't know how to get the fuck out of people's minds when he's not invited in."

"He can read minds?" I asked with embarrassment, remembering my thoughts about laying in Raine's bed at the beginning of dinner. I felt relief knowing he had missed those particular, sordid details.

"Oh, but I was in the hallway. Thanks for the visuals," Eryx said in my direction with a sinister smile. A look of horror swept across my face, causing Raine and Eryx to burst with laughter. I didn't have to touch my cheeks to know that my embarrassment was showing.

"Make him stop, or we're leaving," Raya demanded of her brother.

"Alright, Eryx. Enough games," Raine said while tilting his head with a smile in my direction. The blue of his eyes made a full return as he sipped from his glass.

"You're going to have to get used to this idiot for the next couple of weeks, Amira. I'm so sorry," Raya said, apologizing on behalf of the two assholes sitting across from us.

"A couple of weeks? I thought—"Eryx started saying but stopped when he received a vicious glare from Raine.

Raya could sense my panic from the questions forming in my

head and placed her hand back on my thigh in warning once again. I relaxed my shoulders and reached for a glass of wine against my better judgement. Taking a sip from my glass, I willed my eyes to look in Raine's direction. The ice blue eyes that had now resurfaced were locked on mine, causing my heart to skip a beat and cough due to choking on the wine. Raya patted my back and started placing food on my plate, noting that I must be famished from today.

Cutting into the roasted chicken caused the steam to rise up to my nose. I caught an odd, sensational smell. My twitching nose caught Eryx's attention.

"It's the smell of magic. You'll get used to it, but it tingles at first. Even though the food is made by the servants here, they still use the little amount of magic they possess to season the food. Which you'll soon find out is what makes it so delicious."

Skeptically, I took a bite of my food. As much as I despised my sister, she was an amazing cook, but I'd never tasted anything like this in my life. Everyone at the table chuckled, including Raya at the startlement displayed on my face at the delectable taste.

"Just wait until you taste the food at Spring Solstice," Raya said with that familiar smile on her face. "If you decide to stay that is."

After dinner, Raya accompanied me back to my room. We found ourselves sitting across from each other on my bed, but not speaking for a long time. The two of us were enjoying the silence and each other's company, but the air was getting thick awaiting my questions.

"Why do you let Raine talk to you like that?" I selfishly blurted out.

"As High King, he can talk to me however he wants. I can ask him to stop, but at the end of the day, I'm only his second-in-command of Solaris. Thankfully he doesn't speak to me like that in public. But it drives me mad when he does it in front of Eryx."

"Why does he even let Eryx speak to you the way that he does if you're second-in-command?"

"Because Eryx has been his best friend since childhood and like a brother to him. In Eryx's mind he's second-in-command, but due to the bloodline he can't change my rank in Solaris."

I glanced out to the open space of my balcony as I wondered what it would be like to have a rank of nobility. *To be someone worth something.*

"And what of you marrying him? Will you?" I questioned her.

"I would rather rip my eyelashes out one-by-one," she answered me in disgust. "He's been trying to get my hand in marriage since I can remember. Part of me is convinced that Raine keeps nudging him on in hopes that Eryx will get to marry into the family one day."

Raya produced a laugh that was slightly filled with unease as she fiddled with the intricate patterns of the quilt we sat on.

"Can Raine force you to marry, Eryx?" I asked warily. Raya slowly turned her head back to me.

"He can try." And for the first time, I saw her beautiful teal eyes turn to night.

Chapter Sixteen

I woke up feeling more anxious than I had when I went to bed. After Raya and I talked a little longer last night, I bathed and got into bed. My thoughts made it hard for me to fall asleep. I was conflicted on the fact that I missed my family, yet I was happy to be away from them. Happy not having to bear the burden of my father and keeping them alive. Happy not having to see my sister's annoying face every morning.

I rolled out of bed and listlessly sauntered into the large bathroom. After splashing water on my face to wake myself up, I froze while taking a hard look in the mirror. I barely recognized myself this morning, though I knew I was still the same girl. The girl with golden-brown skin, long dark curls, and light brown eyes with hints of green speckles was staring back at me. But I was convinced everything on the inside was changing. I released a long breath and dressed myself in the clothes the servants laid out for me the night before, accompanied by the obsidian stone that was set within my necklace. I was settled on getting cozy in the chair in the corner of my room and reading a book I plucked from one of the library shelves downstairs when loud voices echoed up to my room.

I rushed to the top of the stairs and listened to three different voices getting louder by the second. Raine, Raya, and Eryx were in the dining room having a heated discussion that I couldn't quite make out or understand so far away. I convinced myself to go back to my room because, after all, this wasn't my family. I had no business getting into their quarrels when I wouldn't be here much longer anyway. My hand was already pushing my door back open when Raine's voice got so loud with Raya's name that my door rattled. On impulse, I bolted down the stairs and into the dining room where the three of them looked at me in irritation. Raine's eyes were filled with white clouds again, but this time I noticed black lines that resembled veins trailing from his fingertips to his forearms. Noting where my eyes were fixed, he returned to his normal stature and walked back to his seat at the table as the black veins faded from view.

"Everything okay in here?" *Stupid question, Amira.*

"Does it look like everything is okay, *Pixie*?" Eryx spat in my direction causing me to flinch.

"This is exactly what I am talking about, Raine. He exudes evil and hatred everywhere he goes. She asked a simple question, so why the name calling?" Raya's hands were shaking while talking to her brother.

"What's a *Pixie*?" I asked as if that was the most important question with three angry Fae surrounding me. Naturally, they all ignored me as if I was a piece of lint on the floor.

"There will be no further discussion on the matter, Raya. I suggest you help make him feel at home sooner rather than later." Raine went back to sipping his wine as Raya looked at me with tears in her eyes, bolting past me out the door and up the marble stairs. Glancing at Eryx to see him casually rolling his eyes, I turned to follow Raya. It didn't take long before I found her sprawled out on the bed in her room.

"Want to talk about it?" I asked, placing my hand on her arm while she lay facing the large bay window.

"What's there to talk about? Eryx is moving into the palace and Raine declines to see why I find that to be a problem," she said through small gasps of air indicating that the tears she was contained in front of the others had finally found an escape route.

"I'm so sorry, Raya. If it helps, at least your room is right next to mine, and you can always come sleep there while I'm still here." My lousy attempt at comfort was barely working.

"And what happens when you're gone?" I winced at her question before she continued making valid points. "When I must be here with the two of them. *Alone.* My brother could care less about me. He shows it more and more every day." She was sobbing at this point. I sat on the bed to comfort her when another voice came from behind us.

"Please spare us the dramatics, Raya. You will not dictate how I rule Solaris or *my* palace." Raine was standing in the doorway with his usual blank facial expression that made my blood boil.

"I'm your second-in-command Raine. You wouldn't even hear me out on why I prefer that he doesn't live here," Raya sobbed to her brother.

"I know why you're concerned about him living here. You have my word that he won't touch you or make any advances during his stay here," he promised.

"You swear on our family crest?"

"I swear."

I'm not sure how convinced I was of Raine's promise, but Raya seemed more at ease after hearing it. Once her tears had ceased, she announced that she was going to take a warm bath. I hugged her tighter than usual before she left. I was in the process of closing my bedroom door when Raine slipped a foot in between the door and its frame.

"I'm sorry that's how you had to start your day," he apologized.

"It's okay. I've just never heard a voice make a room shake on its own before," I answered honestly.

A smile flashed across his face. "I can make other things shake too."

The butterflies must have awakened from their slumber because they began flying around in the pit of my stomach again as I started fiddling with the doorframe.

"Have dinner with me tonight," he requested. *Or was it a demand?* I wanted to decline his invitation, but his sky-blue eyes were staring into mine. "Just dinner. Out back in the garden. Nothing else." He added onto his invitation. I realized I was holding my breath and battling the butterflies in my stomach at the same time.

"Okay. Just dinner," I agreed. He nodded his head with a closed lip smile and walked away.

I laid down for a short rest before dinner and awoke to the servants knocking at my door. Drowsily, I let them in and kindly told them that their services weren't needed. They huffed a laugh. "The High King has requested that we prepare you for dinner. And we always fulfill his requests." I almost rolled my eyes but didn't want to offend them so I politely smiled and nodded in understanding.

Over the past few days, I had learned their names—Millie and Ellie. It was clear they were the "mothers" of this place, always making sure everyone was cared for appropriately while keeping themselves in shape to move with the hustle and bustle of the palace. *Always making sure I was cared for.* As if I was someone of importance.

I knew servants didn't possess as much magic as most Fae, but they still used a small amount while assisting me to get ready. Millie would always ask what color I was feeling for the occasion and with the wave of a hand an outfit of that color would be laying on the bed ready for me to slip into, even placing a charm on my necklace to help it match my outfit if needed.

But tonight, I wasn't asked what I wanted to wear. A gold and white sundress was laid out for me on the bed. After Ellie put my hair into a loose bun with two curls falling in front of my face, I slipped into the dress and noticed that it revealed more cleavage than I'd usually show. Millie acknowledged me trying to pull the dress up higher for coverage and gently smacked my hand away. She waved over the front of the dress with her hand and two to three more inches of my cleavage was covered. She winked at me and let me know that I could meet Raine in the garden for dinner now. They both slipped from the room, Millie quietly closing the door behind them.

I slowly made my way to the back of the palace. I was fully aware that I was dragging my feet down the hall, my stalling futile as my steps inevitably brought me to the hall leading to the garden. I was nervous, but mostly I felt like I was showing too much cleavage and there was nothing I could do about it. The form fitting dress just so happened to show off every inch of my ample curves that I worked hard to hide. Muttering to myself about the dress, I finally made it to the back stairs and saw Raine in the garden. He was sitting at a table that wasn't there before with a glass of wine in his hand. His eyes followed me as I began descending the stairs.

Even though he was over thirty feet away, his eyes were still mesmerizing. So mesmerizing that I missed a step and slid down four stone steps right onto my ass. Before I could wince in pain, Raine was at my side asking if I was okay. I knew I'd have a bruise on my bottom in the morning, but I insisted that I was fine. I protested, but still found myself in his arms as he carried me to the table, seating me in the chair opposite of his and carefully pushing it up to the table.

"You sure do know how to make an entrance, Amira." Hearing my name on his lips had my stomach doing flips I didn't know that it could do.

"Happy to keep you entertained, *High King*," I countered, putting emphasis on "High King" with an eyeroll. He gave me a small glare before regaining his composure.

"I hope you like what I've chosen for dinner tonight." And with the raise of a hand, multiple dishes of food graced the table in front of us. "I wasn't sure if you wanted wine, so I didn't request it," he added on.

"No thank you," I said while staring at the food being placed onto my plate by a male servant. I hadn't cut into anything yet, but the sweet smell of magic was already making its way to me.

We began eating our meal while having light side conversation. I didn't mind most of the silence because I was enjoying the delicious food and breathtaking scenery surrounding us. Each time I observed something new in the garden a small part of me was upset that I would be leaving Solaris so soon. When we finished our meal, everything vanished from the table except our drinks. Raine asked if I'd like to go sit on a bench to overlook the fountain, and not wanting to miss the opportunity to see something so beautiful under the moonlight, I agreed.

"You're probably confused on why I asked you to have dinner with me tonight," he said while staring out at the fountain.

"Well, it is quite random to be honest. Did I do or say something wrong again?" I asked with concern. He gave a sidelong glance at me and let out a breath, turning his attention back to the fountain.

"No. You've done nothing wrong at all. I actually asked you to have dinner with me so I could apologize."

I stared out at the fountain in silence as well, not knowing what to say.

"I lost my temper with you at dinner yesterday and I'm sorry. I shouldn't have let Eryx speak to you in that manner as well. I can assure you that behavior will no longer be tolerated from him nor myself," he exclaimed.

"And will it still be allowed for him to speak to Raya in such a manner?" I questioned with curiosity and a small amount of bitterness.

"I'll let him know that he is to speak to her as he would any other second-in-command. And to respect her as well." His gaze remained fixed on the fountain before us.

"I think she would appreciate that. As second-in-command and as your sister," I commented after a long moment of silence. He finally looked at me after I spoke.

"When we go back in, you'll notice that your room is next to mine now. I moved Eryx into your old room and provided you with a larger room." My stomach sank thinking about how Raya will have to sleep one room over from someone she loathes so deeply.

"You can relax about Raya's room being so close to his. I've put a charm on the entrance of her room so that he can't enter without her permission," he said, reading the concern on my face.

We sat on the bench embracing the night air and the complimentary light from the stars gleaming through the garden. It wasn't until I found myself half asleep on Raine's shoulder that we decided we should head inside for the night. He walked me to my new room next to his and on the way there I wanted to knock on Raya's door to ensure she was okay, but I resisted. Arriving at my door, we both stopped as we silently stared at each other.

"Thank you for joining me for dinner tonight. And for accepting my apology." His low voice was a soothing hum to my ears.

"Thank you for inviting me and providing a place to stay," I responded while soaking in the perfection that he was. Since I laid eyes on him, I've wanted to take those snow-white strands of hair between my fingers to see if they really were as soft as they looked. It took Raine clearing his throat to stop me fantasizing about my hands tangled in his long, thick hair.

Saying goodnight in unison, I turned to open my door but felt the urge to turn back around. Turning on my heel I was met with our faces being mere inches apart. We stared into each other's eyes for several seconds before I felt his lips on mine. I knew that a man of his caliber would be intoxicating, but that was an understatement. One of his arms wrapped around the small of my back and his other hand braced himself against the doorframe. After several minutes, he pulled his lips from mine, and I snapped back to reality. He stood me back upright, kissed my lips one last time, and bid me goodnight with a smile.

I waited for him to force us both inside of my bedroom (part of me praying to the stars he would), but he opened my door with one wave of magic and strolled into his room closing the door behind him. I stood in the doorway alone and confused about what had just transpired within the last few minutes of the night.

Chapter Seventeen

I woke up well rested the next morning due to finally sleeping through the night. After a restless hour spent wondering what happened the night before and what that kiss meant between us, I finally fell asleep under the warmth of my blankets, aided by the warm fire that the overly kind palace lit while I dozed. *Am I becoming friends with an entity?* I mused.

Getting out of bed, I realized that clothes were already laid out for me for the day. Millie and Ellie had begun to lay my clothes out for me the night before if I was out of the room later than usual.

The weather was warmer than Medlar the moment I arrived here, and it hadn't changed. Slipping into the white sundress that was chosen for me, I put my hair in a bun and made my way to the stairs for breakfast.

Both doors to the dining hall were closed and upon opening them I only found Raine at the long table. I'm sure he noted the look of confusion on my face because he offered a tilted smile and held his hand out offering the seat next to him. I offered my own small smile back and nervously made my way to the offered seat.

The servant pushed my chair in, presenting me with a cup of coffee.

"How did you sleep?" Raine asked while relaxing his back against his chair. My eyes were stuck on the opening of his light-blue tunic, revealing his chest, yet leaving just enough to the imagination. As a result of my delayed answer, he asked again.

"Great!" I accidentally yelled in his direction, letting my nerves get the best of me. Raine laughed and conjured the food to the table. Again, I got a small, sweet smell of magic, as well as the unimaginable magnificent smell of the biscuits, sausage, bacon, and eggs before me. The servers began placing food onto our plates and refilling our cups of coffee. I was doing my best to bite my tongue from asking him what the hell was up with last night when he beat me to the punch.

"About last night Amira, I would apologize but then I would be lying to you. And that's not something I'm willing to do." He was looking at me with such an intense stare that I wanted to curl into a ball in my bed with the covers pulled all the way to the headboard. Before I could stop myself, word vomit was leaving my mouth like I had a sickness that couldn't be cured.

"Then what was it? Why did you do it? From the moment I got here you've been nothing but rude and downright evil to me," I grimaced while averting my gaze. "Aside from last night."

Raine stiffened.

"Raya informed me of my behavior toward you and I had to agree with her. She has a knack for knowing when I'm attracted to someone and unfortunately, I go about it the wrong way." I eyed him wearily,

"So, this happens often is what you're telling me?" Raine did that same childish smile and took a sip from his cup.

"No. It does not happen often, Amira. So once again... do you accept my apology?" A few moments passed of us staring and assessing each other before I answered.

"I do...again. Don't make me regret it." A flash of white came over Raine's eyes before he smiled at me and took a bite of his food. "Just know that there won't be a third granted."

I couldn't help the next question that tumbled out of my mouth due to it running through my mind since it happened. I had refrained from mentioning it, afraid of him laughing in my face at the thought of me seated next to him on the throne.

"The vision that I had in the Garden of Sanri... what does it mean?"

His fork froze inches from his mouth as his gaze connected with mine.

"Well, what did you see?" Raine inquired while setting his fork down. Still fearful of his reaction, I explained how I saw myself next to him upon a throne in full detail. His features never changed, making him seem unfazed by what I had just explained to him. "My guess is that you saw that vision because the waters of Sanri portray the life you wish to live. They read your future based off your feelings and thoughts. Perhaps you see more for yourself in Solaris than you'd like to admit. A life filled with happiness and love. Possibly with someone to share those feelings with."

My mouth popped open at hearing Raine's hardened, gravelly voice speak to me about love and happiness. Is this something that he's even experienced in his lifetime? *Is this something that he even wants for himself?* And if so, why hasn't he found it after more than *three-hundred* years?

"I see," I answered, still in a stupor from his chosen words. "And do you think that will happen? That I'll find love while in Solaris?" I was shocked at my own question but kept a blank expression and my head held high while waiting for his reply.

"I already gave you that answer when I told you what I felt in the forest the first time I laid eyes on you, Amira," he answered with an expression as dark as the night sky. The rush of heat that raced throughout my body and settled in my core was too much to bear as I adjusted myself multiple times in my seat. My mouth turned dry as I replayed his words in my head without offering a reply of my own.

We finished our breakfast in silence and waited for the servants to clear the table. "Do you mind if I go back to the library today?" I asked before I changed my mind after remembering what happened the first time I visited the gorgeous chamber.

"Amira, I've told you before that you have free range of the palace. You have no need to ask if you can go somewhere," he answered with annoyance in his tone. I started twirling my fingers together.

"Right. But what if I don't remember how to get there?" He let out the loudest laugh I've heard from him since I arrived. He stood from the table and offered me his hand. Guiding me to the library, he opened the doors and my breath hitched. I had forgotten how breathtaking the view was but became quickly reminded of how badly I lost myself the last time I was here due to the resemblance of Lorena's rows of bookshelves in her library. Taking a few steps inside, I began to settle my breathing and run my hands along the random book spines that lined the never-ending shelves.

"Are you sure that you'll be okay in here by yourself?" Raine questioned, concern lacing his words.

"I'm not afraid anymore," I answered with confidence. I felt his hand on the small of my back and turned around to face him. His lips were as close to mine as possible without touching.

"You have no reason to be afraid of anything as long as you're with me." Before I could return an answer, our lips were together, and my legs were wrapped tightly around his waist. Carrying me over to the nearest desk, he gently laid me down with his hand cradling the back of my head. Instinct taking over, I began to raise the blue shirt that had brought out the sparkle in his eyes at breakfast. After raising the hem higher, inch by inch, he grabbed both of my hands, pinning them above my head while kissing the nape of my neck. "As much as I would love to claim you right here in front of this beautiful view, I was raised to be a gentleman," he struggled to say through staggered breaths.

I pulled my dress back down and fixed my hair while making an effort to stand. Any other time I would be grateful for a gentleman, but that's not what the fuck I wanted right now. Raine readjusted his shirt and firmly placed both palms down to lean over the desk. "If you need anything at all just snap your fingers twice. I have business to tend to before Solstice, but I'll see you at dinner." He tucked a curl behind my ear and vanished into the hallway, closing the double doors behind him.

"Why the fuck does he have to be a gentleman?" I mumbled to myself and started scanning the shelves for a new book to read.

Chapter Eighteen

I was barely able to read the book I plucked off the shelf after my second encounter with Raine in the library. With high levels of frustration, I found myself exploring the palace and wandering into the garden before dinner. *Why on earth did I let him lay me on that damn desk anyway?* Determined to get answers, I decided that I was going to question him about what was going on between us after dinner. I had less than a week left in Solaris, and I didn't know how I felt about that. I began making a pros and cons list in my head about staying here or going home, which I found even more absurd than me almost letting Raine fuck me on a library desk when I still partially despised him.

Do I go back home to a life of poverty yet, a family that loves me unconditionally? Or do I stay in an unknown world to be waited on hand and foot? Let's not forget the handsome king that irks me despite how much he arouses me.

The sun began to set atop the palace, and my chest ached as I wondered if I'd ever see a place this beautiful again once I returned to Medlar. Another hint of frustration raised within me, and I abruptly stood from my favorite bench overlooking the lotus flowers in the fountain.

Smoothing my dress, I ran through exactly what I was going to say to Raine to get all of the lingering questions off my mind. With the sun setting, I figured that it was almost time for dinner, and my assumption was correct because Millie came to the back steps of the palace to summon me with her sweet smile.

Guiding me to the dining room, Millie opened the door to reveal Raya sitting by herself at the table looking just as confused as me.

"Where is everyone?" I questioned with furrowed brows.

"I'm afraid the High King and Eryx will not be joining you for dinner tonight. They have important business to tend to in preparation for Solstice. The High King asked me to send you his regards," Millie said to me with a tilt of her head.

Raya sneered at Millie's explanation. "If it's in regard to Solstice, why was I not summoned instead of Eryx?" I winced at the tone of her voice.

"Hey! At least we have some alone time together," I pointed out, hoping to erase the thought of Eryx handling Solstice business instead of her. I strode over to where Raya was sitting and plopped in the seat right next to hers. "I'll even have a glass of wine with you," I said with a wink. Raya's shoulders relaxed from her tense demeanor, a minute smile forming on her lips.

The house provided our food along with two glasses of red wine for dinner. I picked up the glass to make a toast. "Cheers to a night without masculinity," I roared probably louder than I should have, which made Raya laugh.

I promised a glass of wine, and by the end of dinner we had drank an entire bottle to ourselves and opened another. To say that I was feeling the effects of my decision was an understatement.

"I probably should've warned you that the wine in Solaris is stronger than the human realm because it takes a lot for us to actually feel anything thanks to being Fae," Raya said with an apologetic look.

"Well, it's too late now. Might as well finish off the bottle," I declared with a hiccup and poured the remaining liquid courage into our glasses.

"So, I know it may be none of my business, but what's going on with you and Raine? Has he eased up a little?" Raya asked before taking another sip of wine. Stunned by her question, I set my glass back down.

"I'm not sure. I'm confused because when I got here, he hated me and now he wants me in his bed." I provided my answer before remembering that she's his sister after all. Raya looked at me with hesitancy and put down her glass.

"Amira, are you saying that you might actually have feelings for my brother?" She began searching my face for any trace of information that I could be withholding from her. Reluctantly, I decided to provide her with the truth.

"I...I think I do have some sort of feelings for him. Whenever he touches me, I feel some sort of... I can't really explain it but—"

Before I could finish, she cut me off.

"You cannot fall for my brother, Amira. I won't allow it," Raya yelled as her eyes started to turn dark.

"I'm not a child Raya, I can make decisions for myself. And last time I checked, Raine let me know that you were the one that talked to him regarding showing his feelings for me."

"I let him know that he was mistreating you because he doesn't know how to treat women that he's attracted to. I didn't know that you would actually return the lust he offers. Please reconsider your— "

"I don't need to reconsider anything, Raya," I spat before I could stop myself. In that moment, all I could see was my sister talking down to me like she always did, throwing me into a rage. "Raine was right. You're controlling and it's annoying to say the least."

I immediately recognized the hurt in Raya's face. The darkness from her eyes faded, returning to big teal eyes that began to fill with hurt and betrayal and what almost looked like a plea.

Taking a deep breath, I brought both hands to my face as I prepared to apologize. Using her brother's words against her was out of line. Parting my lips to speak, a thunderous noise echoed throughout the room.

Raya slammed both of her fists on the table breaking off a piece of the granite. I jumped up from my seat afraid of what she might do next.

"Raya, I'm so sorry. I didn't mean it," I said while reaching out to comfort her. Dodging my touch, she swiftly moved to the doorway. *Damn Fae with their quick movements.*

"Amira, don't believe anything you're—" she said through strained words as if she couldn't speak. Instead of finishing her sentence, she snapped her mouth shut and clenched her eyes closed. Shaking her head, she left me alone in the dining hall.

More than anything, I wanted to go to Raya's room and beg for her forgiveness. How could I have been so cold to the only person that has had my back since the first day I got here? Entering my room, tears began to form in my eyes as I closed the door behind me. Naturally, they didn't make their way down my face, only increasing my irritation with each passing second. Walking to the mirror above the white wooden dresser, I stared at the same girl I evaluated that morning.

Perfect. You possibly lost the only real friend you had here, asshole.

Chapter Nineteen

I tossed and turned in bed throughout the night, providing little sleep to my overly tired mind. On the way to my room after last night's dinner, I stood in front of Raya's door before convincing myself to not bother her with my stupidity. I wouldn't know how to apologize to her while being upset with myself at the same time anyway. After pushing the thoughts about last night's argument to the back of my mind, I threw back the covers and got dressed for the day. I asked Millie and Ellie if I could have the morning to myself. By the look on their faces, I had a strong feeling they already knew about our dinnertime quarrel, saving me the hassle of explaining why I requested solitude. After asking if there was anything I needed, they departed without interrogation.

Leaving my room, I noticed Raya's door was open, but she wasn't inside. I couldn't decide if I was grateful or upset that she wasn't there. Forcing my feet to shuffle forward, I continued down the steps and through the great hall to the library. Placing the book I borrowed back on the shelf, I snagged one that caught my eye and snuggled myself into my favorite chair. Shortly after, I found myself jolting forward to the sound of the library doors opening and Raine heading toward me with a smirk on his face. Startled and disoriented, I realized that I had fallen asleep without even making it through the first chapter.

"Rough night?" Raine asked while placing both hands on either side of my chair and leaning over me.

"Something like that," I said while looking out to the field of sunflowers.

"Want to talk about it?"

"Not really."

"Is that because it's me? Or you truly don't want to talk about it?" He asked while attempting to close the space between us.

"A little bit of both," I said, leaning around his arms to place the forgotten book on an end table. He took a step back and offered me his hand.

"Come. Let's have breakfast in the garden, and you can decide if you'd like to talk about it with a full stomach." After quickly studying his face, I took his hand and let him guide me out to the garden where a full breakfast awaited, accompanied by two gold chairs and servants.

"I can pull out my own chair you know," I expressed while sitting down and being pushed up to the table by Raine.

"Sounds to me like you've never been treated like a lady," he replied, staring into my eyes and sitting in the seat across from me. I didn't have an argument to make because unfortunately for me, his statement held true. Thankfully, the servants started piling food onto our plates to save me the embarrassment of trying to think of a rebuttal.

"Speak, Amira." Raine commanded in a different tone than what he was using previously. Caught off guard, I explained everything that happened between Raya and I last night. When I was done Raine let out a chuckle.

"I wasn't asking about that. I had already expected something like that to happen. Raya can't deal when others don't follow her requests, let alone her demands."

Baffled, I let the irritation seep through my tone. "How could you know something like that would have happened? What made you so sure that I could possibly have feelings for you?"

"Amira, darling. You seem to forget that I'm Fae. I can smell your arousal a mile away, let alone when I had you spread out on a desk willing to give yourself to me freely. And trust me, I wanted to take." His tongue skimmed across his bottom lip as he searched my face for denial, but all he found were cheeks the color of the strawberries in the fruit bowl at the center of the table.

"You also allow others to read your face like a book," he said while popping a breakfast potato into his mouth. "Now tell me what you were thinking when I said you've never been treated like a lady." It wasn't a request. It was an order delivered with the gruff voice that made an appearance every so often.

Studying him in the sunlight did something to my core that had me quickly squeezing my thighs together on instinct. I took a sip from my cup and explained in full detail how my father and I provided for my family without anyone else raising a finger, leaving little time for me to have any type of relationship with someone. *I made sure to leave out the information about random hook-ups here and there.*

Confessions were flowing like a river from my mouth as I unexpectedly shared that I'm not entirely sure if I even miss Medlar while being here.

When I was done babbling, Raine studied my face and provided a simple, "I see." Embarrassment settled within me, and I began to eat the food in front of me without speaking again. Why did I willingly provide so much information to this asshole? Taking my last bite, I noticed Raine rise out of his chair and make his way over to my side of the table. With a wave of his hand the dishes and left-over food vanished while he perched himself on the edge of the table next to me.

"Do you miss them, Amira?"

"My family? Of course I do. Especially my father and brother," I looked away and started to chew on my bottom lip. "But there's also something that makes me want to stay in Solaris."

"And what is that *something,* that has you conflicted?" he asked with his ice blue eyes locked on my lips. As badly as I wanted to say he was the reason that I wanted to stay, I fought every urge to let those words come out of my mouth. I knew deep down that I wanted to stay to see if I could find happiness. To find love in a world that I never knew existed. To be loved the way I'd never been loved before. Instead, I avoided all of those truths.

"I've never seen a place this beautiful before. And I would hate to have to leave so soon."

The half-truth, half-lie left a bitter taste in my mouth as I met his gaze.

Raine studied my face for a few seconds, letting my lie settle through the brisk morning air. "I don't blame you. You'll never find another place like this. Not within the mortal realm I can assure you."

I should have known that he wouldn't show any type of emotion to my bullshit of an answer.

Getting up from where he was perched on the table, he let me know that I would be alone for dinner tonight since Raya, Eryx, and he would be tending to Solstice preparations.

"Can I help?" I asked before I could stop myself.

"There's nothing for you to do, but thank you for the offer," he nodded with a smile on his face. I swear this was the most that I had seen this man smile since my arrival, and it sent butterflies to the pit of my stomach every time.

"When you're ready for dinner, snap twice wherever you are in the palace and you'll be provided with your meal. Millie and Ellie will be available for anything else that you may need tonight."

Planting a kiss atop my head, he made his way out of the garden and past the gate. I wanted to run after him and beg him to lay me on the table we had just eaten our breakfast on. I wanted to stop him and tell him that he was the reason I wanted to stay in Solaris, to ask him what the fuck was going on between us.

But I glued myself to my seat. I refused to give him that satisfaction. I refused to let him know that just his presence alone set my entire body on fire.

Chapter Twenty

After breakfast, I filled my day relaxing in the garden and touring the palace with Millie. When the sun began to set, I ventured back to the library, remembering that I didn't get to start my book that morning due to me falling asleep. Content, I snuggled up in the same chair with a blanket that Millie provided to me. A few chapters in, I grew hungry and snapped my fingers twice to have dinner by myself, but no food appeared in sight. Confused, I snapped my fingers twice again and waited, but only an empty plate appeared.

"Did I do something to make you mad?" I asked the palace out loud. It was then that I realized it was waiting for me to make a request. "Are you waiting for me to request what I want to eat?" I asked.

You're talking to an empty room dumbass.

As if my thoughts were heard, the plate vanished and reappeared in answer.

Okay, maybe I'm not a dumbass.

Taken by surprise, I straightened in my chair and closed my book. It took me a few moments to decide on a proper meal request once my stupor subsided. I'd never had the opportunity to request a meal for myself back in Medlar. I either ate what was provided or went to bed with an empty stomach, but I never chose the latter.

After arguing with myself for several minutes, I made a decision.

"Could I please have roasted chicken with potatoes? And a glass of water?" After a few more seconds I had one more request. "And a piece of cake for dessert?"

Everything I requested appeared on the round end table next to me and I thanked the house—or rather its spirit—with a smile on my face, to which it replied by starting a warm fire across the room. When I finished my meal, a large piece of cake appeared on the table, and I devoured it without a second thought. A full stomach had me talking to the palace out of pure contentment. "I think you and I just became best friends."

"Is that what we are?" Boomed a voice from the doorway.

I jumped from my chair, dropping the plate that once held my cake to the floor. The cream-colored glass shattered in tiny glass shards across the floor.

"Goodness Raine, do you not know how to knock or introduce yourself properly?" I asked while clenching my teeth and attempting to pick up the pieces of the broken plate. Before I could lift a piece, Raine's hands were grabbing my wrists.

"What do you think you're doing? The servants will take care of it." He yelled out a command for a servant to clean the mess and they arrived within seconds. Scanning his now narrowed eyes with apprehension, I apologized multiple times to them and offered to help, but they declined. "That is their job, Amira," Raine expressed through gritted teeth. The intensity in his eyes caused my breathing to increase as he crosses his arms in front of his chest.

"I know that, but it doesn't hurt to offer a helping hand," I countered.

"Are you always like this?" he asked with inquisitive eyes.

"Kind? Considerate? Yes. I'm sorry for being a courteous *mortal*," I hissed in disgust. "You *High Kings* could learn a thing or two from us." As the words left my mouth, the same white flash from days before revealed itself, removing the sky-blue from his eyes.

I blinked once and we were face-to-face with only an inch of air between us. The servants could be heard skittering for the door in an attempt to escape what would surely be an uncomfortable confrontation. His tall stature towered over me as he glowered at my remark.

"Say it again," he commanded with the voice he had used at breakfast.

A slight wince reluctantly revealed itself at his order. Regaining my wits, I adjusted my expression to match his confidence.

"How do you get your voice to change like that?" I asked. On the outside I looked unphased, but on the inside I was screaming at the intensity of his command. His facial expression matched, if it did not exceed, the harshness in his voice.

"It is the voice of a High King, Amira. And you will learn to hear it more often if you don't provide the respect that I deserve. Now, say it again."

I clinched my fists as my eyes narrowed to mere slits, "Say what, Raine?"

Glancing at my fists, he let a small laugh release through his lips, "Do you plan on using those?" Gripping both of my fists in his palms, he yanked me forward. "Mockingly say High King again so that I can discipline you the way that you deserve to be disciplined."

Catching my breath, my palms started to sweat, and heat began to rise in my cheeks. I could feel my heartbeat increase with every passing second of him waiting for me to reply. "I'm not afraid of you," I lied with a sneer on my face.

"Then say it and get it over with," he hissed while baring his teeth.

I don't know where it came from, but everything in my soul begged for me to say those two words to find out the consequences. To find out exactly how he thought I needed to... *deserved* to be disciplined.

"*HIGH. LORD.*" I said with a mocking voice, tilting my head to each side with each word.

My surroundings became a quick blur as Raine threw me over his shoulder and briskly walked us out of the library. *Fuck they move quick.* I began pounding my fists on his broad back.

"Put me the fuck down! I'm not some rag doll you can throw around whenever you fucking feel like it!" I felt a sting on my bottom and stopped yelling.

Did he just spank me?

I continued beating his back, which had no effect on a man of his stature, but it was the only defense I had at the moment. When we got to the top of the stairwell, we passed Eryx who was heading downstairs. He opened his mouth, but Raine cut him off.

"Mind your business and close your mouth for once." A look of shock came across Eryx's face as Raine continued walking. His gaze focused on me with a sinister smile slowly spreading from cheek to cheek. His eyes narrowed before he stumbled backwards with a look of confusion etched on his face. My brow furrowed at his actions, but dismissed his behavior when I realized where we were heading.

We passed Raya's room, my room, and finally arrived at Raine's door. It was only once he had closed the door behind him that he sat me down.

"You have exactly ten seconds to tell me that you want to leave. Otherwise, you're mine to discipline how I see fit," he snarled with his chest rising and falling quickly, hands clenched at his sides. My chest quickly tightened from lack of breathing. How many seconds had passed? Am I stupid if I don't scream at him to open the door? Who the fuck did he think he was carrying me here like a child? But one side of my brain (*the stupid side*) liked it. Liked the smack to my ass. Liked the dominance dripping off of him effortlessly like a waterfall flows from a cliff.

Every inch of my body was on fire as the tips of my fingers turned cold, spreading through my hand and up my wrists. *No no no no no... now is not the time for anxiety to consume me. You asked for this because you couldn't shut your mouth.*

"Last chance, Amira."

I glanced back up at him when I heard his voice. My teeth clamping down on my bottom lip as I decided to let the seconds pass between us. The tang of blood flowed onto my tongue and down my throat.

"As you wish," he declared and locked the door behind him. My heart was beating so fast that I could hear the blood pumping in my ears. Raine slowly walked towards me, and I backed up with every stride causing the back of my legs to hit the bed behind me and fall back onto my bottom. "Lay down and raise your dress," he commanded with that powerful voice. The same one that sent a wave of heat straight to my core each time.

Eyes wide, I laid back slowly and raised my dress to my midsection while staring at the ceiling. I knew what I was getting myself into when I didn't request to leave, but now I was starting to rethink my decision.

Raine walked to the edge of the bed and wedged himself between my legs. "Put both of your feet on the bed and spread your legs apart." My mouth dropped open at his request, causing me to freeze. "Close your mouth before I fill it for you. Do as I say." His stare was calm and collected while he provided his instructions through clenched teeth. "*Now*, Amira."

Mindlessly, I pulled my feet to the bed and opened my legs. I could feel my wetness seeping out of me without a single touch from him. He placed both hands on my knees and spread them even further, causing a gasp to leave my mouth.

The confident male before me effortlessly found his way to my underwear and with one tug ripped them away. *"Raine,"* I exclaimed. "I hope you weren't too attached to those," he said with a devilish grin on his lips. "Tell me Amira, are you always this submissive?" His question caused me to rise on my elbows, *"Fuck. You."*

He tilted his head and reached for the straps of my sundress, sliding them down my arms to expose my breasts. Rubbing his hands down his face after glancing over each and every curve of my body, his eyes slowly dropped to my bare core causing me to close my legs.

"You have no idea how beautiful you are do you?" he asked. I swallowed hard at his words, feeling every ounce of rebellion leaving my body as he ran the tips of his fingers from my hip to the back of my thigh.

"If you're going to fuck me, get on with it." I said and slowly spread my legs apart again. That confident girl I had tucked away since arriving in Solaris emerged from the shadows.

"I won't ruin you so soon, Amira," he smirked, "But since I laid eyes on you, I've been determined to know what you taste like." He searched my face again for any ounce of regret. "Are you sure this is what you want?" He asked with questioning eyes and a furrowed brow.

"I'm positive," I assured him while biting my lip. *"Punish me."*

A flash of white passed over Raine's eyes as he pushed on my knees, spreading my legs further apart again. His hands ran from my knees to my thighs before resting them on my belly. My chest was rising and falling so rapidly that he lifted one hand to place it in the center of my breasts.

"Relax, Amira. I promise you don't want to waste all your breath just yet."

I brought my head up to view him, and clouds of white had overrun the familiar blue hue of those beautiful eyes. Slamming my head back down to the bed, I stared at the ceiling anticipating whatever it was that he had planned. Just then, his face disappeared from above me and I feel his tongue at my core, circling the most sensitive part of my body. Soft moans slipped from my mouth at the newfound sensation.

Now is not the time to say you've never experienced this, Amira.

"Say it," he ordered.

I knew what he wanted me to say, but I couldn't will the words to leave my mouth.

He sucked on that same sensitive bud, and my head lifted off the pillow to find his eyes locking with mine. He dipped his tongue into my center and back to my sensitive spot causing me to let out a moan from my lips that I'd never heard before. His gaze remained on my face, eyes sparking with the same intensity that I felt thrumming through my entire body.

"If you're not going to say it willingly, then I'll force it from your lips," he exclaimed while placing a hand back on my chest, pinning me to the giant bed beneath me. I felt a finger dip inside of me and I snapped my legs shut on instinct. Removing his hand from my chest and placing it between my legs, he pushed them back apart and locked them in place. "Try to close your legs again and I'll replace my hand with something else," he growled while leaning over me. I froze on the bed and put my hand over my mouth to keep a whimper from escaping. After pumping his finger in and out of me a few times, he slid in a second finger, and I felt myself spiraling out of control.

"Since my title bothers you so badly, you'll scream my name until you find yourself gasping for air, Amira," he demanded while slightly hooking his fingers inside my core causing my back to arch. "The perfect form of discipline and pleasure for someone with such a smart mouth."

I felt everything in my body giving itself to Raine as he placed his mouth back on my swollen bud while pulsing his fingers in and out at the perfect rhythm.

"*Please*," I cried out.

"Say it, Amira."

Feeling my core tightening even more I blurted out his command.

"Not good enough. I want you to scream it until every piece of glass in this room shatters," he disapproved and quickly moved his fingers in and out of my drenched core while now sucking on my sensitive bud at the same time. I clenched around his fingers so tightly that I feared they'd snap in half along with my own body. My legs began to shake as I heard a victorious groan leave Raine's mouth while he continued his assault.

"Scream it, Amira, or I swear on my life I will not let you finish," he demanded, and my ecstasy was in his hands. My eyes rolled to the back of my head and every ounce of defiance that I had left dissipated. My entire body went rigid as my back bowed off the bed, screaming his demand so loudly that my voice cracked, and stars formed before me.

"Good girl."

Wiping his mouth, he walked to the bathroom, grabbing a towel to clean the aftermath of his punishment from my core and legs. With surprisingly gentle hands, he pulled my dress back down and laid next to me on his side, running his hand through my hair as I fought to regain a normal breathing pattern. In a daze, I sat up on my elbows to look at him.

"I'm sorry for being so loud," I apologized while blushing.

"Darling, you're not loud enough until my palace is crumbling from your screams," he said while gazing into my eyes, and everything I had ever known started to evaporate from my mind except for the sight of him between my legs.

"Amira..."

"Yes?"

"Stay in Solaris, with me," he requested with a serious look.

"As in…never go back home?" I questioned.

Gently grasping my face with his hand, he leveled his eyesight with mine.

"Yes. I will do everything in my power to give you the life that you deserve. The life that you were born to have. I can care for you in a way that your family can't. You will never have to raise a finger here in Solaris like you would in Medlar," he promised before planting a soft kiss on my lips, my taste still on his mouth.

I stared into his eyes and got lost for an amount of time that I was unsure of.

"Okay. I'll stay. For you."

Chapter Twenty-One

The sounds of birds chirping, and rays of sunlight greeted me as I found myself still in Raine's bed. Rolling onto my back, I glanced up at the ceiling and then to my right. Raine laid there with his back to me still asleep. My mind couldn't decide if I was upset or not that I didn't wake up cuddled underneath him. Taking a deep breath, I peeled the covers back slowly and slipped out without disturbing him. Returning to my room I shut the door and thew myself on the bed face down.

"I'LL STAY FOR YOU?"

What the fuck was I thinking to agree to that? I was almost certain that the events leading up to his question swayed me to answer in his favor. And now that I was thinking about the sequence of events, him asking me to stay after making me see stars was completely unfair. *Probably even planned knowing Raine.* How could I be so stupid to let my guard down like that? And to agree to leave my family behind just because of my euphoric state of mind? The little voice in my head whispered that it wouldn't be so bad to not have to lift a finger again or worry about putting food on the table, but I shooed it away before it cluttered my judgement again.

After curling into the chair in the corner of my room for some time while running through the events of last night, I formulated a reasonable plan. I'd let Raine know that I would only remain in Solaris until the end of Solstice and then return to my family in Medlar before answering his request. I needed time to clear my head before making such a life-altering decision. If Raine really cared for me, he'd understand my decision to go home before making such a huge life change. Even though my family had put me through hell and back, I owed it to my father to give an explanation if I decided to leave.

Taking a quick bath and splashing water on my face, I put on the clothes and accessories left out for me by Millie and Ellie last night while I was away from my room. I cringed thinking about how they must know I stayed the night in Raine's room. Could they hear us if we were only one room over? Could Raya here us? My heart shriveled at the thought of her hearing me with her brother and possibly knowing that I stayed the night in his bed. I released a gasp remembering the sight of Eryx at the top of the stairs. Smacking my palm to my forehead, I muttered a group of vile words and headed out the door to the dining hall.

The double doors to the hall were propped open, revealing platters of food already waiting. I shifted my gaze to everyone that was seated at the table. Raine, Eryx, and Raya stared at me as if I was a unicorn with three horns on my head. "Good morning," I managed to mutter to them underneath their stares.

"Good morning indeed," Eryx couldn't resist saying, causing me to turn the color of a tomato within seconds.

Slamming his hand down on the table, Raine stood from his chair.

"Close your mouth or I'll see to it that it's permanently shut. This is your final warning. I suggest you tread lightly in *all* of our presence." Adjusting his shirt, Raine returned to his chair, gesturing to the open seat to his right while glancing at me with a slight smile. I couldn't contain the small smile that crept upon my face looking at Eryx's mouth pop open at Raine's threat.

The trivial parts of me elevated in delight.

"Well, let me try this again. Good morning," I said with a wide smile on my face as I claimed the seat next to Raine. Eryx muttered a good morning in my direction, but not a single word came from Raya's mouth. A chunk of my cheerful mood broke off and crumbled to the floor. For a split second I forgot we weren't on speaking terms and was waiting for a follow-up jab at her nemesis.

After the servants loaded our plates with food, Raine let everyone know he had an announcement to make. My heart sank into the pits of my stomach because I had a bad feeling that it was regarding my promise that I mistakably made last night. With confidence sketched on his face, Raine proceeded to share the news.

"Amira will remain in Solaris."

Raya snapped her head up from her plate, with Eryx turning his head so quickly in our direction that his food fell out of his mouth.

"And who made this decision?" Raya asked with disgust lining her words.

"Seeing as though she's an adult, Amira decided on her own to stay here. In Solaris. *With me.* Do you have an objection to that, *sister*?" Raine challenged Raya with annoyance heavily lacing his words.

Before the situation could escalate any further, I chimed in, "Raine asked me last night to stay in Solaris and I agreed of my own free will."

Raine smiled at my reply.

"But I do want to say that I had a chance to think things over this morning. And while I do feel that I would like to stay in Solaris, I would like to go home to see my family first. I think it's fair to let them know everything that has happened during my time in Solaris instead of just never returning. I don't want my father to live the rest of his life wondering and worrying." Turning to Raine, I could have sworn I saw a flash of white appear in his eyes again. "If it's okay with everyone here, I would like to stay here until Solstice is over and then return home to explain everything and make my final decision," I explained with optimism.

"I take it that your feelings for my brother have escalated since the last time we spoke?" Raya asked with narrowed eyes that were growing darker with each passing moment. Looking back to Raine with those blue eyes that I'd become infatuated with, I touched my palm to his face.

"They have. And I'm sorry if you don't approve of my decision to consider staying here." Raya glowered at my words.

"And tell me, Amira. Did your feelings become even stronger when you were laying in his bed last night? Or was it not until he was done fucking you senseless?" She spat at me with darkened eyes and clenched fists atop the table.

Raine jumped up from the table, reaching for Raya, and without a thought I stood in between them. Raya never flinched at her brother's outburst. I knew there was a possibility that I could be pummeled to dust between two Fae, but my love for Raya hadn't diminished regardless of her not granting me forgiveness. Shocked by his actions toward his sister, I placed both of my hands to his chest, pushing as hard as I could to get him back to his seat. Though he didn't budge, he slowly backed away granting space between the two of them.

"Leave," Raine hissed at his sister. "You too," casting a glance at Eryx and pointing at the door. His sleeves were rolled up exposing forearms that now contained those same black veins that had revealed themselves days ago. My breath hitched as I surveyed the man before me. Those black veins had now extended from his fingertips to the top of his neck. Noting my gaze, he surveyed his arms before closing his eyes as they began to fade away.

"Gladly," Raya answered with a look of disgust. "I expected more dignity from you, Amira."

They both exited from the table, leaving only Raine and me in the dining hall. Sliding back into my seat, I covered my face with my hands. Raine sat back down next to me, quickly grabbing my hands, and removing them from my face.

"I won't ask..." I said without context. Raine knew what I was referencing as my eyes darted to the black veins that consumed the visible parts of his flesh. Parts of me wanted to ask about the constant change of his eye color but thought better of it given the current issues at stake. Ignoring my statement, he pressed the palm of his hand to my cheek.

"There's no need for you to be upset due to their stupidity, Amira."

"I'm upset because I caused this. Raya has shown me nothing but kindness since I came here, and I didn't show an ounce of appreciation with my vile words to her."

"She'll get over it. Give her some time."

"And what about my request?" I asked while biting my lip.

"What request?"

"To go home to my family after Solstice, before I make my decision." Raine's body went rigid once I reiterated my wish.

"I understand. I would rather you stay here with me to ensure your safety from Lorena, but I can't demand for you to never see your family again."

Squealing like a child, I threw my arms around Raine, giving him a kiss on the cheek.

In the back of my mind, I knew the answer he provided wasn't truly the answer he wanted to give.

Chapter Twenty-Two

Weeks went by in the blink of an eye.

One moment I had just awakened in Solaris and the next I was at Raine's side every waking moment of every day. I hadn't had a single interaction with Raya since our dispute about me staying in Solaris. Clearly, she still didn't approve of my feelings for Raine.

"Morning, Amira." Millie announced from the doorway, setting a cup of coffee and letter on the small round table as I looked out to the field of flowers from my balcony. Noting my eyes widening at the sight of the parchment, she huffed a laugh. "The High King just handed it to me to give to you. Thought you'd like to read it with your morning coffee." She subtly pat my shoulder and left me to soak in the beaming sun and crisp morning air.

I'd written letters to my family twice a week for the past few weeks that I'd remained in Solaris. With the help of Raine, they were delivered back to the mortal realm. I'd sent six letters so far and this was the first one I'd received back. My hands shook as I took a sip of my morning coffee, cozying into the oversized chair the *High King* had sent to the balcony for my alone time while reading. Raine had suggested that I leave out certain information within my letters in case they were intercepted. And not wanting to compromise myself, nor my family, I agreed without an argument for once. I had only let them know that I was safe, unharmed, and content. In the last few letters, I reiterated that I would be home within the next couple of months and not to worry about me.

With a deep breath, I slid my finger under the envelope flap and slowly began ripping it open. *What if they told me not to bother returning? What if they were not surviving without my help?* My hands trembled as I retrieved the letter from the envelope, unfolding it and laying the single piece of parchment out on my lap.

Amira,

We've received your letters and are glad to hear that you're okay. We've been surviving well during the winter and have somehow managed to build a supply of food to last us a few weeks should we come up short at any time. Your brother and sister have finally started to help out with hunting and trading.

I understand from your letters that you're not able to tell us where you are in order to remain safe.

Keep in touch.

•KB

Of course my father would be the one to reply, but in such a short letter? He must have been livid with me. My heartbeat quickened at the thought of him reading my previous letters informing him that I wouldn't return right away. But another part of me fumed at the lack of care and concern within the letter after all this time we'd been apart.

Finishing my coffee and pushing the crumpled letter to the back of my desk drawer, I wandered through the palace to find Raine.

Locating him in the study, I eyed him as he stared intently at a litter of papers spread out on the desk in front of him. I cleared my throat to grab his attention, causing him to smile as he quickly gathered the papers, shoving them into the desk drawer.

"Good morning, darling," he purred as he gestured for me to sit on his lap with a pat to his thigh. This had become one of my favorite rooms within the palace. The room boasted exceptionally high ceilings, creating an open atmosphere. The surrounding walls were adorned with gold and ivory tapestries, accompanied by intricate murals while massive windows provided ample light to seep in, accentuating the glistening marble floors. Of course, the sound barrier Raine implemented via his magic made it a plus when we couldn't get enough of each other. Nevertheless, we were still waiting to take that final step of intimacy which Raine refused to give.

I leaned my head on his shoulder as he placed a kiss atop my curls that I had piled into a bun on top of my head that morning. "What's wrong?" he asks as he leaned back, causing me to raise my head so he can study my face. "I figured you would be in a good mood today since I handed the letter your family returned to Millie this morning."

"I thought I would be too," I said as I avoided the lump in my throat that was forming. "It was very short and precise. They let me know they were okay and understood the reasoning that I couldn't provide a location for where I am. It's just odd that it was so short with it being from my father. Makes me think he resents me for not returning home sooner." I fiddled with the dark stone hanging from my neck, reminding me of my mother's habit.

Raine processes what I'd said before replying. "Maybe he was worried to give away too much information within his reply as well." *He does make a good point.* "Don't overthink one letter, Amira." *Another good point.* In the short time that I'd been here, Raine had come to know me better than my own siblings. I'd let something like this letter consume me if I didn't clamp it down quickly.

"Have you talked to your sister?" I asked, changing the subject before I got more upset about my own family. Raine rubbed his hand across his face before dropping it to the desk before him with a thud. "She attends the required meetings for the preparation of Solstice, but once she provides her input she leaves without additional conversation." And once again, my heart ached with despair.

"She will come around, Amira."

"When? It's been weeks, Raine."

"Give her time."

"*Time?* I don't have time. Solstice is around the corner and then I'll be gone for heavens know how long."

I observed the white flash in his eyes that I hadn't seen in weeks as the words about my departure floated into the air between us.

Before I could continue my argument, his lips were on mine along with his hand buried in my hair that had fallen from my bun. I twisted my body to straddle him, wrapping my arms around his neck. The heat from our kiss consumed me with each passing second. I was used to this happening. A single touch from him would send ripples from the base of my spine to the tips of my fingers. I nipped his bottom lip as he pulled his face away from mine, still cradling the back of my head.

"I don't want to hear another word about you leaving," he growled through clenched teeth. I attempted to speak, but before I could utter a word, he held up a finger to cut me off. "I know that you're leaving after Solstice. I try to process the thought of being away from you every single day." His jaw ticked as he clenched his teeth again. "That doesn't mean that it doesn't kill me inside when I have to think about it. Nor does it get any easier to process."

When he was done talking, I looked into his eyes. I could sense the pain radiating from him. *Pain that I caused.* That's it. I need him. Right here. Right now. I'm over his stupid rule.

Running my thumb across his bottom lip, I let my hand slowly trail down his chin, to his chest, and rest on his stomach. My eyes flick back up to his in time to see them slowly dilating.

"Don't." His single word is clipped as he tightens his grip on my waist.

"And if I do?" My words are breathy as I move my hand lower. My chest rises rapidly with my breath as I rub my hand over the growing bulge in his slacks.

Before I have a chance to process his movements, Raine throws the chair back and stands both of us upright. Retreating a few steps away once he stabilizes me, he runs his hands through his snow-white hair.

I want to bury my hands in that hair while he buries himself in me.

"Amira, I've told you that intimacy is different with mates. There's no going back from it. It seals the bond." A growl slips from his lips as he notes the strap of my sundress that slipped from my shoulder. "I cannot make the promise that I would survive you leaving Solaris if we were to..." His voice trails off as he lets his head fall back with an exasperated breath.

"You have no problem with us doing everything else. I *want* you, Raine. And I know that you want me. There has to be a way around this." My voice was a pitch so high I was convinced it could crack glass.

Closing the distance between us, he clasps both my hands in his. "There are no words to describe how badly I crave the feeling of burying my cock inside you. But I refuse to take the chance of breaking both of us when you have to leave. And I won't use me fucking you as a tactic to make you stay." He places a swift kiss to my lips and runs the back of his fingers along my cheek. Without a word he leaves me to myself in that massive, sun-lit room.

It's been days since my encounter with Raine in his study and now I can't even convince him to sleep in the same room as me. We can barely last two seconds without climbing all over each other, and every time I get ready to take the leap of finding out what it would be like to have Raine thrusting into me as I run my hands through his hair, he stops us. *Can a mating bond really be that strong?* I catch myself in a daydream thinking about the pleasure I feel when he thrusts himself into my mouth, hitting the back of my throat. I shake my head when I realize I'm slack-jawed at the thought.

Would it be so bad to stay a little longer if it meant I'd received the intimacy I craved from Raine? I sprinted through scenarios in my head of me staying in Solaris longer than I agreed to after Solstice, but quickly ran from the thought. I hadn't received another letter from my family despite the additional ones I'd sent back after reading my father's. There's no way I could stay here without going home first. I owed him that much.

Sitting across from the fountain in the garden, I though about how Solstice was around the corner and I still hadn't made amends with Raya. While spending my time with Raine and reading was the most relaxation I'd had in my entire life, I missed having her around. And if I have to spend one more dinner with Eryx without another female presence there, I'd rip my hair out. Though his ignorant remarks had vanished, my hatred for the way he continued to treat Raya had not.

I walked over to the fountain, sat on the cool stone, and dipped my hand in the water to lift a lotus flower. Emotions flood through me at rapid speed.

What the fuck am I doing here? I'm slowly falling in love with a man that will surely outlive me. A man that refuses to sleep with me because he's afraid he can't bear the thought of me leaving. A man that I can't see myself without.

I let that last thought sink in, and it scared me to no avail. No matter how many scenarios I played in my head about being okay when I left Solaris, I knew that deep down it was a lie. A destructive, bold-faced lie.

My head snapped up as one of the glass doors to the back of the palace opened. Raya's gaze locked with mine as she stepped out on to the pavement of the back steps. I opened my mouth to convince her to talk, but she cast her eyes down and turned back inside with slouched shoulders.

Waves of hurt washed over me as I threw my head back in defeat.

Carefully, I placed the ivory-colored lotus back in its home as I tried to decide where mine was.

Chapter Twenty-Three

Time seemed to move faster in Solaris.

Solstice Eve was upon us and anticipation noticeably filled the palace through chatter, song, and laughter. Millie and Ellie were exceedingly chipper that morning. Millie was kind enough to let me choose between a dress or slacks during our usual morning routine, so I opted for slacks and a tunic, though she quietly gave her distaste. I'd been in dresses since I arrived in Solaris, and I needed a break from constantly concentrating on sitting with my legs crossed.

After getting ready for the day, I grabbed the new book I borrowed from the library, along with a blanket to shield me from the morning chill and settled into my chair on the balcony. Eager to read and enjoy the garden's beauty just beyond the rails was an understatement. Opening the pages to where I had left off, a voice startled me from the entry way. "I think I've read that book over twenty times after all these years," Raya said while looking out from the doorway of the double doors that I had left propped open.

"You, nor your brother know how to knock before scaring the

shit out of people," I said lightheartedly, shocked to see her standing there.

"Yea well, knock knock," she said while tapping the glass door with a wry smile on her face.

"I'm sorry I don't have a second chair, but you're more than welcome to join me," I offered with a matching smile. "I don't have an extra book either."

"I think I can manage," Raya teased as she brought both of her palms together and slid them apart slowly, summoning a chair across from me that looked exactly like mine. Making herself comfortable, she summoned her magic once more, conjuring two cups of coffee and a table between us.

"I'm so jealous of that," I exclaimed to her while tilting my head in thanks and grabbing a cup.

"Don't be. It comes with a lifetime of burden, even if it does come in handy often."

"Burdens like what?" I inquired while searching her face wearily. She looked at me with a flash of sadness in her eyes and smiled, "I came to apologize, Amira. I- "

"*You came to apologize? What on Earth for?*" I said a pitch higher than I had intended. "Raya, I was so crude to you when all you've ever tried to do was be there for me, be a friend to me, and I basically smacked you in the face without physically doing it."

"Well, we both know who would win that fight now don't we?" She smiled with a laugh and continued, "But I am sorry, Amira. I shouldn't have let this go on for so long and now it's Solstice Eve. I don't know what your decision will be when the time comes, but if this is the first and only one you experience, I want it to be a good one."

Raya held up a finger while standing and sauntered into my bedroom, returning with a gown in hand. "This is for the final night of Solstice. It's an important night in Solaris, and I want you to have a dress that matches your beauty," she said while holding up the dress for me to see. It was a deep midnight purple with a halter top that cut right above the collar bone and extended just below the chin at the top of the neck. It finished with a snatched waist. My eyes followed the hundreds of jewels that subtly increased, causing the partially full bottom to look like a sea of stars. As she twirled it around, I see the back was open and went down as far as it possibly could without revealing my bottom. The article of clothing looked like a god reached for the stars and threw however many they could fit into their hand onto the dress. *I want to sleep in it. Be buried in it. I never want to wear anything else in my pathetic mortal lifetime.*

"Raya...that is the most beautiful piece of clothing I've ever seen. Possibly the most beautiful *thing* I've ever seen."

"My mother gave it to me before she— "

Her words and movement paused for a moment before she carefully laid the gown across my bed.

"I can't accept that," I blurt out before I could stop myself. "I would be terrified to ruin it. I'd never forgive myself."

"Yes. You *can*. And you *will*." Her piercing teal eyes narrowed at me with one raised brow.

"Oddly enough, it can't be destroyed. It's simply indestructible. My mother made it for me because she said I was the most precious thing in her life and wanted me protected at all times when visiting other realms with her. She even made a suit for Raine out of the same material. Whatever it is... she never actually let us know. Of course, my brother got rid of his when he became High King..." Raya said with an eye roll. She looked at the dress and glanced back up at me with anticipation in her eyes.

"It would be my honor to wear it, Raya," I said while jumping out of the chair and throwing my arms around her. Raya hugged me back slightly tighter than I expected and pulled away to level her gaze with mine. "Solstice is an amazing experience, Amira. But make sure you always make good choices and keep your guard up."

"Raya, is there something you want to tell me?"

Her eyes grew darker, and her mouth opened to speak, but nothing came out except a strained gasp of air. Her eyes returned to that beautiful shade of teal and a sigh left her lips. Shaking her head, she hugged me one more time and laid the dress across my bed. Advancing toward the door, she took one last look back at me and a smile spread across her face. Flicking her hand, the door closed, and she was gone.

I briefly stared at the door where Raya was just standing. My mind began mulling over her peculiar behavior until a glimpse of the dress caught the corner of my eye.

I walked over to my bed to marvel at the gown that was placed upon it. I ran my fingers across the fabric and had to talk myself out of slipping into it.

I wonder if I could convince Raya to come back to Medlar with me.

I chuckled to myself and hung the dress in the cabinet with the rest of my wardrobe that was gifted to me by Raine. Returning to the balcony, I settled back into my seat and continued to read my book while enjoying the morning sun.

Chapter Twenty-Four

Solstice was finally here, and it felt like magic was floating through the air from the moment my eyes fluttered open. My clothes for the day were hanging in the wardrobe cabinet with a note from Millie and Ellie wishing me a happy Solstice and informing me that they were preparing the palace for festivities tonight. I was relieved when I saw their last message promising to still assist in my preparation for the holiday. I'd never participated in an event like this, let alone dressed myself in the wardrobe required for such an important affair. My heart skipped a few beats thinking about how I would be attending a festival full of Fae. My family wasn't one to attend or be invited to such events, so this would be a first for me. And depending on my decision, it could possibly be my last.

Sitting at the dining table, Eryx, Raya, and Raine were in attendance together for the first time in weeks. To my surprise, everyone was chatting and getting along as if bad blood had never existed between the three of them. I assumed such an important holiday brought them together, forcing the foolishness to be left in the past.

Breakfast was summoned by Raine and Raya together and a

spread of food appeared on the table that was large enough to feed a family of ten. The sweet smell of magic made my mouth water thinking about the deliciousness being plated before me.

After finishing breakfast, we remained seated at the table chatting with each other. While Raine was discussing Solstice with Raya and Eryx, his hand found its way to my thigh under the table making me freeze in place for a few seconds before I gathered my composure. I calmed my nerves by convincing myself that he wouldn't dare try something in front of the others.

"So, do either of you have any specific plans for tonight?" Raine asked while inching his hand up my thigh. Eryx looked at Raya, holding her gaze. "I have a few plans that I hope follow through." Raya rolled her eyes playfully and took a sip from her cup. "No plans for me. I just want to enjoy the night and embrace whatever the higher power has in store for me."

Raine nodded his head in acknowledgement, his hand making its way to the lining of my underwear. I found myself catching my breath and trying to mask it over with a fake cough. Raya and Eryx glanced over at me, eliciting a blush to slowly rise from my neck to my cheeks. Plastering a smile on my face, I reached for my glass with hopes of their conversation continuing.

"Well, in regard to my plans for tonight, I would hope you allow me at least one dance under the stars?" Eryx asks Raya with desire in his voice.

Raine's hand found its way under my undergarments and playfully tugged on them with one finger.

"Have your manners in order and I'll see what I can make happen," Raya answered with a smile and light laugh.

"Your laugh is good enough promise for me, but I'll make your request happen as well," Eryx confidently replied to Raya, standing to leave. "I'm going to handle some things and get some rest before the start of Solstice. The first night always hits me the hardest every year." Raya rose from her seat as well.

"He does have a point there. I feel like we all get so excited, go all out, and render the worst headache by morning." We all laughed, with Raine and I standing to leave as well.

"We'll see you at Solstice," Raine said while placing his arm around my waist to keep me from leaving and breathing all at once. Eryx and Raya nodded their goodbye and walked out into the hall. Raya looked back before reaching the massive entrance.

"Brother, I want you to know that I am happy. For both of you that is." Raine smiled and nodded to his sister while placing a kiss upon the top of my head. When the doors closed behind them, I turned to Raine to ask what he was doing under the table and instead found his lips on mine. Fisting my hair in his hands, he pulled me into him until I felt like my body was going to join with his.

"I told myself I'd wait until tonight to taste your lips, but I can't control myself. Forgive me?"

"Raine, you can't stick your hand between my legs with other people in the room. What if— "

"If you'd allow it, I'd have my way with you on this table with everyone in the palace present just so they would know the masterpiece that you are when you're naked and who you belong to."

My mouth popped open at his statement, and he planted his lips to mine again, his tongue exploring the inside of my mouth. He finally loosened his grip on me and took a step back.

"Dance with me tonight?" He asked while searching my face.

"I don't really dance," I answered while looking down at the floor. I didn't want to tell him that I'd never had the chance to dance with someone, let alone a man. And I didn't feel like trip-ping over my own two feet in front of hundreds of Fae that already look at me like I was an idiot because I was simply human. *No.* I would save myself from *that* embarrassment.

Grabbing the bottom of my chin, he tilted my head up to look at him.

"Then I'll teach you. You are too beautiful to not be shown off. Do you trust me?"

"I do."

"Then dance with me, Amira."

"Promise not to let me look stupid?"

"You couldn't look stupid if you tried, darling." Cupping my face between his large hands, he planted a soft kiss on my cheek and walked us to the hallway. "Is there anything you need from me before I finish preparing for tonight?" he asked while picking at a piece of lint on his shoulder. His snow-white hair fell over his handsome face that was almost as pale as his locks.

I was tired of staying within the palace walls and took a deep swallow of nerves before I asked my question. "Do you think I could take a walk through the forest? Where we traveled through to go to the Garden of Sanri? I won't go very far. I just thought the fresh air would—"

"*No.*"

His answer startled me, causing me to jerk backwards at his tone.

"I just figured I could get to see the land instead of staying within the palace. I can handle myself Raine," I said while walking forward to cup his face in my hand. Grabbing my hand, his lips thinned before answering.

"Did you forget where I found you, Amira? Did you forget *how* I found you?" My breath hitched at his words.

"*Raine...*" I whispered, but he stopped me before I could provide my argument.

"The answer is no. If you want to see the land, I will take you myself after Solstice. But you will not roam out there, regardless of how strong our wards are."

I nodded my head in understanding, not wanting to upset him on such an important day. A smile danced on his face at my surrender. Kissing the back of my hand, he asked again if there was anything I needed before he departed.

"I don't think I do. How will I know when everything starts and where I'm supposed to go?"

"All of that will be taken care of. I would suggest getting some rest before nightfall."

"Wait, the festival doesn't start until it's actually *nightfall*?"

"Precisely. Once the sun fully sets, Solstice officially begins," he said with a huge smile on his face. "Based off these past few weeks, I'm sure you'll make your way to the library during your down time. Make sure you find time for a short slumber before the festival. I know humans need more sleep than we do."

I rolled my eyes and agreed to rest before nightfall. Bringing his lips to mine and promising to see me tonight, he walked down the hall to the front of the palace.

Solely wanting to prove that he didn't know me well, I avoided the library and made my way out to my favorite bench in the garden. The sun was instantly kissing my golden-brown skin, and I wanted to lay out in nothing but my undergarments until my skin could no longer handle the heat. Considering who might see me, I declined to do as I wish and soaked up the sun while remaining fully clothed.

Thinking about all the events over the past few weeks, I found myself in pure bliss and started weighing what I wanted to do after Solstice. It didn't help that every time I closed my eyes I saw Raine's fair skin, snow white hair, and eyes as blue as the ocean staring back at me. The vision was so vivid that I reached out to cup his cheek, only to palm the open air instead.

A faint buzzing forced my eyes open to see a hummingbird floating above. After a few moments of us staring at each other it swiftly turned upside down and flew into the sun, pulling a deep laugh from my core. I watched its green hue float into the sky toward the forbidden trees of the forest ahead.

How I wished to know that type of freedom. I thought, glancing back at the beautiful palace that I was beginning to call home.

How can my heart yearn so badly to return home to Medlar, when my mind drifts back to Solaris every time?

Chapter Twenty-Five

Nightfall came sooner than expected.

Before I knew what was happening, Millie and Ellie were pulling me left and right to help me get ready for the night. And to make my nerves even more unsteady, two additional servants that I'd never met before were assisting them.

"Is a corset really necessary for tonight?" I questioned the two servant females I didn't know through constrained breaths as they pulled the strings even tighter. Ignoring my complaint, they managed one last pull to tighten the unnecessary piece of clothing and set it in place. If I didn't know any better, I'd think Millie and Ellie were casting sympathetic glances toward me.

Though it was the most constraining gown I've ever worn (considering it was the only gown I've ever worn), I had the privilege of noticing its beauty once I walked in front of the floor length mirror. The gold corset overlaid an all-white floor length gown trimmed in gold. The sweetheart neckline showed more cleavage than I would opt for, but I knew Millie would cast a playful glare in my direction if I tried to hoist it up further. The two new servants exited my room once I was fully dressed, leaving me with Millie and Ellie before the night started.

"When do you get dressed?" I asked gleefully to the two of them.

"Oh sweetie, we don't go to Solstice." Millie looked uncomfortable and started fumbling with accessories.

"What? I thought it was a festival for all of Solaris?"

"The *wealthy* of Solaris. You must be within a certain tier of nobility to attend, and unfortunately us servants don't fall into that category. Now sit and let us finish you up for the night."

The small amount of nerves I was clinging to evaporated. How am I attending Solstice, but Millie and Ellie weren't after all they did for the palace?

"I'm not going without you," I blurted out and crossed my arms across my chest like a child. Millie looked at me in bewilderment, while Ellie couldn't contain her laughter.

"Don't be silly. We don't have the appropriate attire for the holiday anyway," Millie stated.

"I mean it," I said with furrowed brows and a frown. "I'm not participating unless you come with me".

Millie and Ellie glanced at each other with wide eyes.

"I'll let you complete the finishing touches for the night only if you promise to come with me. I know you don't have a lot of magic, but I'm smart enough to know that you can conjure up two dresses in less than five seconds for yourselves."

Silently, they nodded in agreement. "Uh, uh. I know how sneaky you Fae can be. I've been here too long now," I joked as they both smirked. I held out both arms and crossed them to shake their hands at the same time. The three of us laughed as we exchanged handshakes, signaling a promise to accompany me tonight.

Sitting in my designated chair in front of the large gold framed mirror, they began to work on my accessories and hair. Ellie finished up a French braid that created a crown around the front of my face and ended down the middle of my back, gently placing it over my right shoulder to hang in front. Millie placed three gold bangles on my arm accompanied by a small gold tiara encrusted with tiny diamonds in front of the crown of my braid.

"Heavens Amira, you look like a queen ready to sit on her throne," Ellie said with her hand on her chest.

I smiled and reminded them that we had a deal. Glancing at each other once more, they mustered up their magic and two sky blue dresses appeared, hugging their slender bodies in all the right places. Moving swiftly, they threw their hair in identical high buns atop their heads.

"If I didn't know any better, I would think you guys are twins instead of just sisters," I laughed while looking at them. "We're not sisters," Millie said while sharing a laugh with Ellie. Confused, I asked them to elaborate.

"Ellie and I found each other when we were thirteen. Coincidentally, we were both abused by our families and made a run for a better life. Unfortunately, we both got lost and ended up in the dark forest. Hand in hand we fought the demons that chased us and made it here to Solaris where Raine took us in as servants."

"You fought *demons?*" I questioned them in bewilderment.

"Ones that you wouldn't believe," Millie said while taking Ellie's hand. "But we survived, and here we are. Sisters at heart." Ellie looked at Millie and winked, squeezing her hand tighter.

"How did you beat demons with such a lack of magic?"

They glanced at each other fretfully. "Let's get moving! We don't want you to miss the opening night events," Millie stated while rushing us toward the door.

We made our way down the back steps, out the gates and into the forest. We followed a brick path deeper into the woods toward the sound of music. Reaching the last set of trees, I could see an open field up ahead where hundreds of Fae were already dancing and enjoying the night.

"Where in the world did they come from?"

"They mostly live in town, but some live within cabins in the forest," Ellie informed me as she took my hand and guided me toward the field.

Arriving at the edge of the open field, Millie handed each of us a glass of wine from a nearby table while subtly reminding me of its effects on humans. Taking a very small sip of my wine, I peered over the top of my cup just in time to see Raine make his way to the main stage in white slacks and a gold tunic that was unbuttoned at the top, showing just a hint of his bare chest. Reaching the center of the stage, he raised both arms to silence the crowd and caught my gaze. It felt like we stared at each other for eternity until finally, with a wink and a smile from Raine, he faced the crowd and began his speech with raised arms.

"Ladies and gentlemen of Solaris, welcome to the first night of Solstice," his voice boomed over the hundreds of guests.

The crowd cheered so loud and for so long that my ears began to ring.

"It is with great pride that we have been fortunate enough to celebrate Solstice once again within our homeland. It gives me great pleasure to say that we have had another fulfilling year within our court, and I look forward to fulfilling many more. Tonight is about celebrating life, prosperity, and power. As your High King, I want you to know that I am here for you. If there is anything that you should need, please do not hesitate to knock on my door." The crowd erupted into another boisterous cheer. *"With that being said, please enjoy the next three days of festivities. Eat, drink, and soak in the starlight. Happy Solstice!"*

The music resumed, and people returned to dancing with drinks in hand. Leaving the stage, Raine made a beeline to where I was standing with Millie and Ellie on both sides of me.

"Hello, darling." Raine smiled and kissed me on the cheek before taking my hand.

"Millie and Ellie, thank you for assisting Amira in getting ready for her first Solstice. You will be greatly compensated. Have a wonderful night at the palace." He went to turn away from them, but I stood my ground while holding his hand causing him to jerk back and look at me with confusion plastered on his handsome face.

After a small stare down I cleared my throat, "I asked them to attend Solstice tonight. I know that I'm only a guest here, but it would mean a great deal to me if they could stay."

Raine opened and closed his mouth, clearly taken aback by my request.

"My High King, please understand that we did not want to upset your guest by declining her request. We have no problem leaving. Thank you for hosting another wonderful solstice," Millie explained and turned to leave with Ellie. Letting go of Raine's hand I reached out and grabbed Ellie's.

"No." I said firmly, pleading silently to her with my unmoving stare. "If you leave, I leave," I mouthed to them without Raine seeing. His eyes flashed white as I looked back, but returned to their perfect hue of blue before I could fully register him trying to mask his anger.

"You two may stay for the night. Enjoy Solstice." Raine nodded at them and took my hand in his once more, leading me to a table where Eryx and Raya were seated. I waved bye to Millie and Ellie who had a look of unease, causing my stomach to turn in knots.

"Hungry?" Raine asked while pulling out a chair for me.

"Why is it so bad if Ellie and Millie join us? They do a lot for me. And for the palace as well," I asked Raine in front of the others. I watched his face twist with agitation as I moved to sit in the offered chair. He ran a hand through his hair before looking up at the night sky. The blue of his eyes disappeared again in that flash of white. I squinted my eyes at his reaction. Why would a simple question upset him so badly?

"Dance with me, Amira!" Raya jumped out of her seat before my bottom touched mine, grabbing my hand and dragging me out to the sea of people before Raine could provide an answer.

"Raya, I can't dance, and you know that," I exclaimed with a wave of panic taking over me. My usual rush of heat threatened to engulf my body in flames from the anxiety forming within.

"Amira, there are hundreds of Fae here. No one is paying attention to us. Enjoy tonight. Enjoy life. You only get one. And yours is shorter than ours," she quips while laughing, causing me to laugh along with her. Her humor was so close to mine that my heart squeezed in appreciation at having my friend back.

Raya and I danced together until the music finally turned into a slow rhythm, snapping us out of the alternate world we had so easily drifted away to. Finally refocusing on my surroundings, I noticed Eryx and Raine walking in our direction.

"I believe you both promised us a dance," Eryx reminded us with a smile.

"I don't recall that promise," I teased Eryx in return and grabbed his hand for a dance while Raya grabbed her brother's. Bewilderment crossed their faces so harshly that the two men could only laugh.

We danced endlessly with each other, and it wasn't until the end of the night while sitting on his lap that I noticed I had never got a chance to dance with Raine.

Fae began to disperse in opposite directions to head home for the night. A small snicker slipped from my lips, followed by a hiccup as I watched multiple Fae stumble their way into the distance. I made a valiant effort to stand from Raine's lap and quickly fell back down, pressing my back into his chest with my head falling back onto his shoulder. And while I watched everyone leave in their night of bliss, I realized I drank a bit too much trying to keep up with my new Fae friends who drank their liquor like it was water. One last peak through slitted eyes showed me the night sky looming above, the moon a blaring light that caused me to snap my eyes shut again.

"Let's get you to bed, darling," Raine said while cradling me in his arms.

I fell asleep on the way to my room and awoke in the middle of the night alone in my bed. Cursing the heavens above for granting me with such a low tolerance, I rolled over to find a note on the pillow next to mine.

As hard as it was to not lay next to you tonight, I didn't want to disrespect you without permission. Beautiful doesn't explain how you looked under the night sky. I hope you enjoyed your first night of Solstice, and I expect my dance that was promised to me tomorrow. Otherwise, there may be consequences that we would both enjoy.

•R

Those familiar butterflies swarmed my stomach, filling it so much that they made their way up my throat and reminded me that I was still drunk. Clutching the note to my chest with a smile on my face, I drifted back into slumber dreaming about what the second night of Solstice might have in store for me.

And naturally, I repeated the same question in my head that I had since I came here.

How am I ever going to leave this place?

Chapter Twenty-Six

Millie and Ellie must have known I would be feeling the effects from last night because breakfast and coffee were provided on the balcony for me when I reluctantly rolled out of my warm bed.

Though I felt like my head wanted to fall off my shoulders and roll down into the field of flowers, I had the inkling to reach out to my family again. Grabbing paper and a pen from my room I frantically started writing between sips of coffee, leaving out some specific details along the way. They didn't need to know that I was slowly falling for a man that just so happened to be *immortal*. And they *definitely* didn't need to know that I was considering *not* returning to Medlar. I just wanted to let them know that I was still safe and would be coming back home shortly. The intentions of a short letter turned into two pages of scribble. Hopefully my family knew me well enough to be able to read my handwriting.

When I finally finished, I folded the letter neatly and cursed under my breath. In the time it took for me to write the letter, I never once thought about how I would get it to them. It had been weeks since I had sent a letter. How had it slipped my mind to check in with them? Regardless, I had no way of sending it on my own, and I wasn't up for being interrogated by Raine regarding what potentially harmful information I might have slipped about while writing.

"I can send that to them if you'd like."

Whipping my head around and knocking over my coffee, I saw Raya standing in the doorway.

"Damnit, Raya. I'm starting to think you do that on purpose just to see my reactions."

"You could be on to something there," she replied with her hands on her knees while laughing.

With the flick of her wrist, she cleaned up the mess and gave an apologetic smile, which I countered with a playful glare.

"How do you even know who I was writing to?"

"Wild guess," Raya answered while looking into the sky. "I noticed you haven't sent one in a while. Truthfully, you've stopped talking about them as well."

Her words sent unease coursing through my stomach, threatening to send the coffee I was drinking back to the surface. *Had I stopped talking about them? When was the last time I had mentioned their names?*

"I'll send it through the skiff. Another perk of being Fae," Raya said while observing my confused expression at the word *skiff*. She rubbed her temples with both hands. "Magic, Amira. I'll send it through the skiff which is a channel the Fae use to..."

Her explanation faded into the background as I tried to process my own thoughts. *Why didn't Raine think of doing that to avoid interception?* My brows furrowed at my own question as I gave the papers an extra crease and handed them over to her.

"Raya, I—"

"If you tell me that you're sorry or appreciate me one more time I'll throw you off this balcony. And no. I will not jump off to save you right after." She gave me a wink and tapped the folded letter to my forehead while I tried to swat it away. "It's adorable how you try to be faster than me. Maybe one day *human*."

She turned to leave, and words began to tumble out of my mouth. "Am I free to roam the forest?"

Raya stilled in the doorway.

"Is there a reason for wanting to roam?"

"I... No, not really. It just looked so beautiful when Mille and Ellie walked me out to the clearing last night. I thought I'd take some time to clear my head and go for a walk." I tried to seem calm while answering her, but unease settled over me after I asked the question. *Should I tell her that Raine had forbidden me from going alone?*

"I see," she answered while looking past me out into the field. "You're not a prisoner here, and can go wherever you please. Unless someone has told you differently?" She questioned with a raised brow before releasing a breath and continuing. "Do not stray far, Amira. There's a brick path that starts at the entrance from the back of the palace. Stay on it and follow it back. I've told you that nothing is what it seems here and..." Raya's stare went blank as she blinked a few times.

"And what?"

"Call for me if you need me. I'll come."

"But, you just said—"

"I know what I said, Amira. Just call for me."

Raya levitated the folded letter between her two slender hands and within seconds a burst of gold dust replaced the two pieces of parchment.

"Message delivered," she stated with a smile and left the balcony through the double glass doors.

Chapter Twenty-Seven

Mille and Ellie came to check on me once I finished breakfast after Raya left. When I asked them for a small bag of essentials to explore the forest, they looked like they had seen a ghost, paling even further when I let them know I didn't plan on telling Raine where I was going because I wanted time alone. Wearily, they provided me with an outfit for exploring and a small over-the-shoulder satchel to take with me with essentials inside.

Shortly after, I was already going down the back stairs, stopping at the fountain to admire the lotuses, and then heading through the gates into the forest on the brick path Raya had instructed me to follow.

The trees were in full bloom with full, thick green leaves looming overhead, accompanied by dozens of white rose bushes filling the morning air with their aroma. I had lost count how many times I stopped to inhale and appreciate their scent, along with their beauty. Continuing along the provided path, I couldn't figure out for the life of me why the others acted like I was walking to my death when I requested to venture out here.

Bending down to admire another full bush of flowers, I

looked up to see a part of the forest that looked out of place. In the distance, there were no leaves on the trees and the rose bushes were so dark that they looked dead.

Every fiber of my being told me not to venture off the path, but gravity pulled me in that direction.

Nothing is what it seems.

I heard Raya so clearly in my mind that I threw my hands over my ears as if she were with me. Bringing my hands back to my sides, I walked to the edge of the path and teetered at the thought of venturing to the grim area. Heart racing, I set one foot off the path and took an exaggerated breath. "*Well, that was dramatic,*" I mumbled to myself and brought my other foot off the path to the ground before me covered with soil instead of brick.

Once both feet touched the soil it felt like all oxygen had been sucked out of my lungs. Panic crept its way into my mind as I turned to go back to the paved trail, but an invisible wall blocked my effort causing me to bounce back. I convinced myself that I was hallucinating and stretched my arm out, hitting the invisible barrier again.

A silent cry made its way up my throat as I began to pound on the barrier with closed fists.

Raya, I can call for Raya.

Yelling her name, I felt the vibrations from my voice bounce back off the barrier into my face. Above, what seemed like hundreds of crows flapped their wings, leaving their tree branches at the sound of my voice. The familiar cold feeling laced the tips of my fingers as unease steadily crept in.

The urge to scream sat heavily in my chest as I turned back around to face the darkness that awaited me. In the distance was a small cabin at the end of a gravel walkway that was just as dark as the dead roses surrounding me.

"Heavens above... please don't let me die alone," I said, sending a prayer up to whoever was willing to listen. When no one answered, I grudgingly walked toward the cabin in sight.

Twenty feet away I took a hard look at the dead rose bushes only to find that they weren't dead. Each rose was bloomed to perfection but... black. Every single flower was as dark as night, yet fully alive and healthy. Reaching out to touch something so surreal had the tips of my fingers tingling from excitement. Inches away from making contact, the cabin door flew open with a loud thud causing me to drop my bag.

"Welcome to the dark forest, Amira."

I stood slack-jawed looking at the gorgeous woman in the doorway. She was dressed in a black tunic and slacks, her hair in long jet-black waves. Her olive-toned skin and bright green eyes contrasted heavily with her dark attire.

"You are more than welcome to stay out there and admire the roses, or you can come in and have some tea," she offered while walking away, leaving the door ajar as an additional invitation.

Hands trembling, I looked around to see if I was imagining all of this. *And how did she know my name?* I raised my fingertips to my forehead to find small beads of sweat forming. I utilized the back of my sleeve and wiped the building moisture away.

With few alternatives, I picked up my bag and walked toward the open door. When I reached the doorway, I stopped a few feet inside to look around.

"You can come all the way in, sweetie. I don't bite." She was right next to me and spoke directly into my ear causing me to jump so high that I thought the top of my head would hit the ceiling.

"Fuck. I think I need to sit down," I exclaimed, feeling dizzy from the panic I felt moments before.

"Was going to offer it anyway," she said with the wave of her hand and a smile toward the tall, dark wooden table in the center of the room. "Feel free to hold that dagger in your bag in your hand if it makes you feel safer."

Confused, I searched in my bag, and sure enough, a dagger was in the side pocket.

"How did you—"

"Oh sweetie, I know all. It's what I do," she said through a genuine smile. "Tea?"

I hesitated to answer.

"If I wanted to harm you, I could do that in many other forms. No need to waste good tea for that. Relax."

"Tea would be nice," I answered still confused on what was happening.

She walked over to the fire and grabbed the pot, poured the liquid into two black mugs, and strode back over to the table to join me.

She really loves black, doesn't she?

Sliding my cup over to me, she picked hers up and took a sip while cocking one eyebrow, her stare cool and collected. Picking up my cup and looking into it, I peered back up at the sound of her loudly sipping the same liquid from her mug. *Same tea, from the same pot.* A subtle hint of *it's not poison, dumbass.*

I took a sip as the most delicious tea I'd ever tasted swished over my taste buds, bringing them to life. Snapping my sight back to her with a look of surprise, I quickly downed the entire cup. "Thank you," I said shyly while wiping my mouth, "That was the most delicious tea I've ever had."

"My pleasure. I'm sure you have questions, but I've been quite rude. I know your name and didn't provide my own. My name is Anya, and welcome to my home." She smiled while holding both of her hands palm up to the air. "A lot to take in I know," she said with a wry smile. "Now... fire away with your questions."

I found myself staring at her with my mouth parted, head cocked to the side, and eyes wide. Figuring that I probably looked rude, I fixed my face and smoothed out my shirt. Where do I start with the questions? *Hi, thanks for the tea. How the fuck do you know who I am?* Clearing my throat, I slid the mug to the center of the table and fired away with my questions.

"How do you know my name?"

"I only let those in that are worthy. And you, Amira, are worthy. I've been waiting."

"Waiting? On me?" I asked with bewilderment. "I'm not even from here."

"I'm aware. Next question," she politely commanded.

"Why can't I get back onto the trail? You have a very nice place, but I'd like to get back to the palace and—"

"You are not held captive, Amira. I can read the worry on your face. You are free to leave whenever you like. The forest waits for me to grant entrance and exit. You have been provided both as of this moment. Press firmly with both palms against the barrier and it will provide you with an opening."

My body wanted to bolt up from my seat and run as fast as I could back to the trail without asking any more questions, but the inquisitive mind that I was born with forced me to remain seated and continue my interrogation. Anya, stepped away from the table with my mug in hand and poured more of that delectable liquid, sliding it back over to me once she claimed her seat again.

"Why are you here? All alone in this cabin. Why aren't you in the heart of Solaris with everyone else?"

Anya produced a laugh that didn't seem like it came from the heart, but rather vexation. She took a glance out her small, lone window and back to me. "I live alone because the Death Dealer killed my entire coven. There were only three of us left after the attack. But the other two were caught on the other side of the barrier and despite my power, I couldn't grant them entrance to be with me. Thankfully, the dark forest cannot be seen by those that it doesn't welcome. They come back every so often, but we can only speak through the barrier. And a piece of my heart breaks off each time they leave me."

"Coven? So you're a –," my words left me as I swallowed.

"It's okay to say it," she pressed on with her eyes full of life, "A witch. Yes. Yes, I am. And you seem to get along great with our kind." She had a smug look on her face that irritated my soul.

"What are you talking about? If you're talking about the old hag that caused me to be here in the first place, I wouldn't quite call that getting along."

"I know exactly who you are speaking about. And Lorena is not of my origin. The darkness has consumed her with no hope of return." She gritted her teeth at the sound of Lorena's name. "I'm speaking of Millie and Ellie."

Choking on my tea I wiped my mouth with my sleeve. "You're lying. They barely have any magic. I've never heard of a witch that doesn't have distinctive powers," I bit back at her.

"Oh, but they are more powerful than you know, Amira."

My eyes searched hers for any hint of a lie, but all I could find was hurt and despair.

"I found Millie and Ellie running for their lives in the dark forest at the age of thirteen. I took them in and taught them the ways of my coven. It's amazing what one can do when they realize the magic that flows through their veins." Anya's eyes skimmed over my face with endearment. "Allows for one to fight their own demons without relying on others. To care for themselves and find their purpose within this cruel world."

"Why aren't the three of you like the tales that I've heard? Why aren't you evil like Lorena?" I questioned her frantically while trying to ignore how she was surveying every inch of me.

Anya once again stood from her chair and walked over to a shelf next to the fire. "You believe in too many myths, Amira. We're not all evil," the corner of her lips lifted. "Just like the dark forest isn't bad. It's just skeptical on who it lets in." She returned with a small black box and placed it on the table. Her slender hand lay atop the box as she slowly slid it over to me. "In my *many* years of life, I have never met a human worthy of our secrets. But I trust you, Amira. And Erebus himself guided you to the dark forest to find me."

Surely she can't be referencing to the God of Darkness. Was my name and the God of Darkness just used in the same sentence? My mother would fall to her grave if she heard those words. I've never in my life called upon him, nor do I wish to do so.

Opening the box, I gasped at the lotus flower inside. Like the rest of the dark forest, it was black. The edges had a silver hue to them that lit up the inside of the container. I spread my fingers to touch the gorgeous flower in front of me and a shock rippled through my arm, causing me to snap the box shut. Internal flames were threatening to claw their way out as I studied Anya for answers. Steadily, she stood from her seat and glided to the door.

"Our time is up, Amira. When the time is right, consume the petals and find clarity for your questions while in Solaris."

"I'm sorry, consume the petals as in *eat*?" My voice carried within the small cabin from shock. A hearty laugh came from Anya.

"Yes, Amira. That would be the meaning of *consume*." My face contorted from confusion as I put the box in my satchel.

"Are you sure that the barrier will allow me to leave?"

"Make sure to keep your visit and the information you've gathered here to yourself. Do not speak of this interaction within the palace walls." She winked and formed a ball of green dust in her hand.

"Wait!" I exclaimed with my hand out. "You said the Death Dealer killed your coven. What is a Death Dealer? Where are they?"

Anya let the same look of hurt and despair from before come over her face and whirled the ball of dust in the air. "All of your questions will be answered and you will be set free, Amira. But I am not the one to provide clarity. Be protective of your mind and understand that free-will is your right, as that is not something that is easy to come by in Solaris."

My heart began to pound so hard that I was convinced my ribs were about to crack. She blew the green dust into the air between us, the particles gliding over to me as they painlessly traveled up my nose and through my mouth.

"Be wary of the one that brings death to those that are not at their end," she warned as her eyes darkened. "That time is for Erebus to decide."

Those were Anya's last words before the dust encapsulated me and I found myself in a free fall back onto my bed at the palace.

When my mind and heart stopped racing each other, I urgently rummaged through my bag to ensure that the little black box wasn't there and confirm my suspicions that it was all a dream, that the dark forest wasn't real, that it all been a construction of my mind. But the moment that the tips of my fingers felt the smooth surface and round edges of the box, all oxygen escaped from my lungs.

"You ventured off, didn't you?"

A small scream escaped from me before I could stop it as I slapped my hand over my mouth. Raya was standing in my doorway with her arms crossed and eyes dark. I wanted to lie to her, but I couldn't. Her face twisted in anger as I let her know I drifted off the path, leaving out all the details Anya forbade me from sharing including the onyx lotus that now rested comfortably in my bag. Raya glided over to me and gripped both of my hands in hers. "Do not tell Raine where you were."

I searched her face for answers, but nothing was there to read, and I didn't want to press my luck any further.

"Why were you in my doorway?"

"I came to let you know that I already received a response back from your family," she stated while walking over to the desk and putting the letter in the drawer. "Before you ask, I didn't read it."

A knock at the door startled both of us.

"Come in," my voice squeaked.

Raine stepped into the doorway and apologized for being away all morning. "I thought you might like to take a walk into town before the festivities pick back up tonight?" he asked with a smile on his face. "I've had all wards rechecked and re-enforced to ensure zero chance of anyone entering without clearance." I didn't need to ask to know that he was speaking about Lorena specifically.

"I would love that," I answered with a genuine smile.

Raya provided a small smile of her own while stating that she would see me tonight, offering a nod to Raine on the way out. I tucked the bag into my wardrobe cabinet and followed Raine out the door, looking back at the desk in my room wondering what my family replied.

A few steps down the hall and a shiver made its way up my spine.

Why did they reply so quickly?

Chapter Twenty-Eight

Raine had the palace horse and carriage waiting for us when we reached the front steps. Two white horses with grey manes were tied to the gold and white carriage, with a guard holding one of the doors open.

"This is a bit fancy for just a ride into town, isn't it?"

Raine chuckled and kissed the top of my head. "I figured you wouldn't want to walk the distance. And besides, I've been on my feet all day taking care of the final plans for the last few nights of Solstice."

Holding out his hand to assist me, he tilted his head toward the open door of the carriage. I placed my hand in his and hoisted myself into the golden carrier. Raine informed me that we'd be taking the scenic route into town so that I would get a chance to view the forest and all its beauty.

My stomach lurched forward at the mention of the forest. I wasn't stupid enough to admit where I was earlier, nor was I going to mention anything about my venturing off into the *dark forest* and my time with Anya.

As the horses tread their hooves onto the brick path, my mind wandered back to this morning's unexpected adventure. I couldn't stop myself from silently pressing my nails into the palms of my hands out of anxiousness to travel down the same path I was on only moments before Raine knocked on my door.

Making our way into town, I noticed the curve of the pathway that had led me to the discovery of the dark forest up ahead. Would Raine be able to see it? Could he cross the barrier?

"The dark forest cannot be seen by those that it does not welcome."

Anya's words played in my head as Raine talked to me about the events that would take place tonight during Solstice. I had a feeling that I would regret not knowing the details later, but my mind was incessantly wondering if I could afford to sneak a peak in the direction of Anya's cabin. *Would I even be able to see it? Was it real? Was Raine welcomed there?* I knew the box was still in my satchel, but technically I never opened it to see what was inside. Everything very well could have been a hallucination.

Raine placed his hand on top of mine, startling me and bringing me out of my deep thought.

"Everything okay? You look like something is troubling you. Did something happen while I was away today?" He questioned, removing his hand from atop mine and placing it on my cheek.

"I'm fine. Just worried that I won't fit in at the remainder of Solstice, that's all. Any other details that I should know about before tonight?" I plastered a smile on my face and firmly placed his hand back on my knee. I returned to my thoughts about the dark forest while Raine kissed the back of my hand and continued talking.

Though Raine was continuing to feed me additional information about day two of Solstice, all I could hear was the clacking of the horse's hooves bringing me closer to the curve of the path. A mere thirty feet away I decided I would sneak a peek to ease my mind. I needed some sort of confirmation that I wasn't going crazy while away from home for this amount of time.

I couldn't tell which sound was louder, the sound of the

horse's hooves connecting with the pavement, or my own heart-beat drumming in my ears as we made it to where I spotted the black roses and lone dark cabin from earlier in the day.

My eyes had been averted down since I made the decision to look in the direction of Anya's house. The sound of my thumping heart increased in my ears as I slowly craned my neck to the right and brought my eyes up for a deeper look into the forest.

In unison, my heart skipped several beats as my breathing ceased.

Anya was standing in the doorway of her cabin. She clutched the same mug in her hand that she sipped her tea out of with me earlier. Her opposite hand was waving at me with a smile beaming across her face, as if she was waiting for me. As if she *knew* I would be coming at this very moment.

"Amira."

How did she know?

"Amira."

Heavens, could Raine see her?

"Amira."

He would surely know that I left the palace earlier. He would know that I spoke with her. Otherwise, why would she be waving at me? That lying bitch...She set me up...

"Stop the carriage!" Raine yelled ahead.

"What's wrong? Are we in danger?" I asked him through my cracked voice and a tight hold on his hand.

"You tell me. You're sweating profusely and mumbling to yourself."

I looked down to find my knuckles had gone white on the hand that was holding Raine's from gripping it so hard. My other hand was bleeding from digging my fingernails into my palm. Unclenching my fist, I reached my hand up to my hairline where beads of sweat had collectively formed for the second time in one day. "I'm sorry," I mumbled. "I had a horrible nightmare last night, and my mind drifted off to the memory of it." Sneaking a glimpse of his immaculate face told me how concerned he was, but I was determined to visit the town of Solaris. I needed to pull myself together if I was going to convince him to not turn the carriage around. More importantly, I needed to know if I was going crazy.

Glancing back over to Anya's cabin with her still planted in the doorway, I decided to take the risk. "Aren't those the most beautiful rose bushes you've ever seen?" I asked while making sure to point in the exact direction where Anya was standing with her head tilted and wide smile still pressed onto her narrow face.

"Um... well, yes. They're beautiful. But they look the same as all the other roses," he answered with concern. "Actually, you're right," he said as my breathing hitched. This was it; he had seen the difference and would question me. I tucked my hands under my thighs as the tips of my fingers became chilled. "The way they're all bundled together is quite peculiar in a way," he pointed out while reaching for my hand and kissing the back of it once more. "Your hand is freezing...would you like to go back to the palace, Amira? I don't want to take you into town if you're not feeling well. The best healer in Solaris is closer to the Palace. If you're coming down with something—"

My heart kick started and began wildly thumping again, as if it were as upbeat as the music playing in the field at Solstice the night before. How did he not see her?

Heavens, I'm going mad.

"I'm fine. I promise. Please, let's continue into town?" I begged while cutting him off.

Raine nodded with his lips pursed before telling the guard to continue on.

Taking one last glance back at the cabin, I could see Anya still standing there, but she was no longer alone. The black cat that belonged to Lorena was standing next to her in the doorway. My mouth popped open and my eyes bulged at the site of him.

"You're not going mad, if it makes you feel any better," Anya yelled while waving as we turned down the brick path.

I'm definitely losing my fucking mind.

<h1 style="text-align:center">Chapter Twenty-Nine</h1>

Sometime after the pounding in my ears dwindled away, I noticed the number of trees were thinning the further we went. Shortly after, the town of Solaris was in clear view before me. The horses trotted their way over a golden bridge connecting the forest to the smooth cream-colored cement pavement of the town. Once they stopped, I jumped out before Raine could greet me on my side to help me out of the carriage.

The crisp cool breeze blew its way through my loose curls, carrying the smell of freshly baked loaves of bread and wild lily's mixed together. The laughter of kids filled my ears, causing my heart to grow bigger by the second. *I'm not sure how many more emotions it can take today.*

"You're making me look bad. I could have at least helped you out of the carriage," Raine whispered teasingly in my ear with a smile on his face. He wrapped his arm around my waist. Turning to look at him, I placed my hands on his chest.

"This place...it's...". I couldn't find the words to describe it.

"Astounding? Stunning?" Raine answered for me.

"Yes." Was all I could bring myself to reply.

I turned back to look at the town before me. We must be in

the marketplace. Nearly fifty tents were set up displaying fresh flowers, freshly baked bread, trinkets, and foods I'd never seen before but smelled delightful. My overstimulated senses guided me over to a tent that had multiple baskets of peaches. The lingering tropical smell encased me the closer I got to the merchant's tent.

"Not handpicked from The Garden of Sanri, but a close second in taste," Raine whispered with his hand pressed to the small of my back. "Go ahead."

Picking up a perfectly plump peach, I bit into it and let the juices flow into my mouth. He was right. It was almost as delicious as the fruit from the garden, but without the unsettling electric shock. I devoured what was left of it in the most lady-like manner that I could allow and properly disposed of the remains afterwards.

"Heavens, I'm so sorry. How rude of me. I don't even have any money to pay for what I've taken. I can give you this bracelet to offset the cost if you'll accept it." I apologized to the merchant and reached to take my bracelet off that Raine had gifted me before he gently grabbed my wrist, stopping me in my tracks.

"Charge it to the palace would you, Annetta?" Raine asked the lady with a wink of his eye. She agreed and let him know that it was a pleasure to see him. Nodding at me with a smile as well, she placed another peach in my hand and kindly waved us off.

As much as I wanted to stop and admire every trinket and bit of food the market had to offer, I now realized I had no money to buy anything, and I was born too stubborn to borrow money from Raine. I stopped my gawking and continued walking through the market until the tents were no longer in view.

Though the pavement was the same shade under my feet, my surroundings were not. An abundance of homes and shops came into view with hundreds of Fae wandering about. The homes were distinct from the shops—cream-colored houses with deep golden colored roofs and white fences. The shops lined the streets with windows big enough to view the entire store without having to walk inside. Lilies bloomed along the streets where children played with each other, and their mothers chased them to come back home.

Medlar didn't hold a candle to the town that stood before me in this moment. Tears welled at the thought of never being able to have a life like this. Never being able to raise my children in a town so beautiful. Never having to worry about when my family will eat next. *Did I just mention myself and children in the same sentence?*

Raine turned to speak and noticed my tear-filled eyes gazing ahead. *Why won't the damn things just fall for once?*

"Did I do something to upset you?"

"No. Nothing at all. Quite the opposite actually," grabbing his hand before continuing, "Seeing this place just made me realize that I'd never be able to have any of this in Medlar."

Raine searched my face with eyes so blue they could easily blend into the sky above. Placing both hands on my shoulders, he turned me around and firmly pressed my back into his chest.

"You see that building up ahead?" He pointed his finger in the direction of a breathtaking structure. It was no less than five stories tall with long golden stairs leading up to the front double doors that were trimmed in gold.

"Yes."

"That's my home away from the palace. What's mine is yours. You're free to visit whenever you'd like. When you go back home..." he stiffened at his words, "I can send someone to bring you back here as often as you'd like."

Every emotion that I could muster up came to the forefront of my mind, causing me to turn and throw my arms around Raine's neck.

"You would do that for me?"

"There's not much I wouldn't do for you, Amira."

I pulled back from my grasp and peered into those beautiful eyes I longed for each day.

"I'd much rather you stay here. With me in Solaris. But, as I said before, you are of your own free will. And if that time comes for your decision to be to leave after Solstice, I'll be broken but I will abide by your wish to leave."

"You don't mean that..." I trailed off in shock and many other feelings that I couldn't place in the moment.

"Amira I- "

The guard that brought us here came running up behind us, causing Raine to tighten his grip on me. "Apologies, High King. But Eryx has sent word via the channel that you're needed at once back at the palace. He sent the message with urgency."

Irritation flashed on Raine's face before he peered back down at me.

Channel? Did he mean the skiff that Raya had mentioned earlier?

"I'm sorry to cut our visit short. But if you'd like, I promise to bring you back here after Solstice." I nodded in agreement. "What were you going to tell me?" I asked, hanging onto his words like a child hanging onto their last piece of candy.

"Later, darling."

A wave of sadness washed over me while he took my hand in his and lead us back to the carriage. What was it that he was going to tell me? When would *later* be? He seemed so genuine and sincere that not knowing was gnawing at my insides. I had to fight the urge to ask him again on the way back to the palace. Thankfully the ride back was silent unlike on our way to town. Raine still clasped his hand in mine, but his brow was furrowed as he looked out the window.

Lost in thought due to the silence of the ride back, I found us at the front doors of the palace sooner rather than later.

"I'm sorry about our time in town being cut short, but I promise to make up for it tonight." Raine embraced my hands in his and kissed both knuckles, "If you need anything, you know to snap twice, and it will be taken care of. I'll see you tonight." He ventured to the front of the palace without looking back.

Two guards opened the double doors to the backside of the palace for me to enter. Arriving at my room, I closed the door behind me as I gently knocked the back of my head to the frame. Impatience, frustration, and curiosity were brewing in the pit of my stomach all at once. Wandering over to the desk that held the letter from my family, I ripped the top of the envelope open when a knock at the door startled me.

Zero fuckin' privacy in this place.

Shoving the envelope back into the drawer of my desk, I turned to see Ellie peaking her head around the door. "Safe to enter?" she asked with a smile.

"Considering you've both seen me naked multiple times now, is there even a reason to ask anymore?" I joked while standing.

"Good point," Millie said while walking around Ellie to enter my bedroom. "I'll start your bath. Time to get ready for day two of Solstice," she said while clapping both of her hands together.

Chapter Thirty

R ed.

That was the color of the dress Millie arranged for me to wear for the second night of Solstice.

"Are you sure there's no dark color options for tonight?" I subtly begged her from the golden chair sitting in front of the mirror. Millie let out her usual frustrated puff of air before playfully narrowing her eyes at me.

"You can't live your entire life in the dark, Amira."

"Says who?" I quipped back and raised a brow. Ellie threw her head back and let out a high-pitched laugh with a hand resting on her chest. Once her laughing fit was over, she wiped the tears from her eyes and began her assault on my curls.

My hair was fixed on top of my head in a giant bun with four tendrils of curls falling around my oval-shaped face. Ellie was putting the finishing touches to my red lipstick that she insisted I wear, when a dull ache found its way into my head.

"Everything okay?" Ellie stepped back, examining me intently.

"Yes, sorry. I just feel a small headache coming on," I answered while squinting my eyes. Smacking her lips together, she summoned a large glass of water to the end table next to me.

Tilting her head toward the glass, I grabbed it while rolling my eyes, consuming half of its contents in one gulp. Reluctantly, I had to admit that I felt better moments later.

Ellie made a joke about me ruining her masterpiece before continuing the crimson red assault on my full lips. Millie jostled both of my feet into a pair of shiny gold heels and started to rush me out the door like the night before. When we reached the back steps of the palace I stopped in my tracks at the bottom. "Why aren't you two dressed?" I asked, eyeing them up and down while crossing my arms.

"Amira, we're staying here tonight. We can't impose on the High King twice," Millie snuck a quick glance at Ellie, "We already risked a lot to accompany you last night."

I opened my mouth to speak, but Ellie cut me off as she raised a hand. "We simply cannot go," she said in a stern voice that I hadn't heard from her before. I glared at both women before shrugging my shoulders and dropping down to sit on the bottom step.

"Then neither can I." I raised my chin along with my eyebrows and looked at both of them haughtily.

The stunned look on both of their faces almost made me break my solemnity to burst into laughter. We had an additional twenty-second stare down until they realized that I wasn't budging from my seat. Throwing their hands into the air at the same time, they conjured their magic and appeared in front of me with matching forest green gowns.

"What the hell?" I yelled while throwing my own hands in the air. "Why do you get that *gorgeous* dark color and I get *this*?" I went to pinch a piece of the fabric from my dress, but it was so tight I found myself pinching my own skin instead. They laughed as I winced at the pain I inflicted on myself. Both Fae came to my sides to link arms with me before heading to the clearing.

We laughed the entire way to the festival, but as soon as we got there, they fell silent. Before I could question why their mood changed so drastically, Raine was only a few strides away from us. My heart leaped to my throat when I spotted his narrowed eyes at the servants beside me. I assumed they were equally as nervous as me when they both unlinked their arms from mine, dropping them to their sides while looking straight ahead at their High King.

"Ladies," he acknowledged us with a tilt of his chin. "I assume you came here to ensure Amira's safety through the forest. I appreciate your dedication to my special guest." Raine reached for my hand, and while taking it I gestured back at Millie and Ellie.

"Actually," I said while clearing my throat, "I asked them to attend tonight because I feel somewhat sick. I have a small throbbing in my head that just won't go away. I was hoping they could assist me throughout the night if I don't feel any better." I cast a smile in his direction. It was the quickest white lie I could come up with to get them to stay. Although, the headache truly was slowly making its return.

Raine eyed me with concern. "I could have the healer provide something to you to take care of that." He turned his gaze back to the two servants, "Could you two retrieve an elixir from Merlin to relieve Amira of her headache?"

Millie and Ellie agreed and quickly turned to leave. "No!" I blurted out, louder than I wished. Three sets of eyes were now staring at me, along with whoever heard my accidental outburst in the clearing. I forced a small laugh out of embarrassment. "I'm not very fond of taking medicine for something so minor. I would much rather just have them here to help if needed." I placed the palm of my hand to Raine's chest and placed a quick kiss on his lips before looking into his eyes with hope instilled in mine.

"As you wish."

His answer was stern, with no sense of cheer. But it was the answer I wanted, so I smiled at Millie and Ellie, subtly nodding for them to head into the clearing before letting them know I'd find them if my headache got any worse.

When we were separated, I asked Raine why he always seemed so upset when I asked for Millie and Ellie to attend a night of Solstice with me. He took in an exasperated breath and looked out to the crowd of Fae dancing in the moonlight. "Since Solstice began hundreds of years ago, the servants were not allowed to attend because we didn't want them distracted from their duties. If we don't have them working quickly and efficiently throughout Solstice, then it won't run as smoothly as it does each year which allows for everyone to have a relaxing and peaceful holiday." He let out another breath of air before tucking a loose curl behind my ear.

"But don't you think that they deserve a break as well? They do so much for the palace year-round. Certainly, they could use a night or two of relaxing." My brows furrowed in annoyance that this wasn't a consideration for him already. He ran his hand through those snow-white locks of his and placed it on my cheek before studying my face.

"Amira, I don't want to argue. They're here now. That's all that matters." He placed a kiss on my temple and cupped my face once more. "Now you owe me a dance." My eyes grew as wide as saucers when I realized he was leading me out to dance in the center of the clearing. Every set of eyes was already fixed on us.

"Everyone is staring," I said with panic overpowering my voice.

"So let them stare."

This was different than dancing with Raya the night before. Now I was in the hands of their *High King*. And a human at that.

"I can't dance, Raine. You know that."

"I do know that." He laughed while holding my waist. "Do I have permission to use my magic on you?"

"What? No! Not a chance in hell am I allowing that."

"Okay, then we can just stand here while everyone stares. I don't mind."

His lips spread into such a wide grin I could see every single one of his immaculately white teeth. Glancing at the crowd surrounding us, my panic was starting to show on every inch of my skin that wasn't covered. The heat seared me from the inside out. "Fine," I answered Raine while glancing at the surrounding Fae. *I'm so sick of him getting his way.* With a laugh leaving his lips, he placed one hand on the small of my back and the other in the palm of my hand. A slight chill raced through me as my body subtly started moving to the sound of the music surrounding us. I was making no effort to move, yet I was moving at the same speed and rhythm as Raine. Truthfully, I was dancing so elegantly that I was convinced I'd done this my entire life.

"How the hell am I doing this?" I asked with my mouth agape.

"Language," he hissed at me. "You asked me to not let you look stupid, and that's exactly what I'm doing. Would you like for me to stop?" he asked with a wry grin.

"No," I said as quickly as possible. He let out another laugh and pulled me closer to his chest.

"I didn't get a chance to tell you this, but you look absolutely exquisite in red," he said with his gaze trailing down my body between us. I wanted to say thank you, but the throbbing in my head revealed itself again causing me to clutch one side of my head. Raine cupped my face and asked if I needed to take a seat. Shaking my head and resting it against his chest, we continued dancing.

After what seemed like an eternity of chatting and gliding throughout the clearing, I no longer cared about the stares from others nearby. Leaning on the small amount of confidence I gained from dancing, I asked him the question that had been weighing heavily on me since this morning. "What was the urgent matter that caused us to leave town earlier?" My face was calm and collected, while my insides were screaming. Raine tilted his head to look down at me.

"You're not going to stop inquiring until I answer, are you?" he asked with an exasperated breath.

"Nope," I beamed back at him. Looking around to make sure that no one was eavesdropping, he pressed his lips to my ear.

"We're on the brink of war with another realm. And it seems that they no longer want to take the peaceful route if they don't concede to our demands."

My head snapped back to look into his eyes at the information that I had just processed. *War?* That was a thing in these realms? Why would they have a need for war amongst each other when they could have whatever they want, whenever they want through magic?

"What realm?" I inquired, letting my curiosity get the best of me. Raine cleared his throat and looked around us once more.

"Another time, darling." He pulled me back to him and continued dancing. I placed my forehead on Raine's chest while letting the music guide us and reminisced on my time here in Solaris. I knew deep in my heart that I'd miss this place. But what I didn't know was if I would come back. And if I did, when? How long would I be away from this world? A world that I didn't know existed until mere weeks ago. My heart sank even deeper at the thought of Raine going to war without me here. Not that I could assist an army of Fae in any type of way, but the sole thought of him getting hurt made me sick to my stomach. My train of thought was snapped in half when Raine grabbed the tip of my chin and tilted my head upwards until our eyes met. My eyes fixated on the point of his ears. *Why doesn't Raya possess the same feature?* Minutes passed before he uttered a single word to me while staring into my eyes.

"Marry me, Amira."

A wave of shock so strong passed through me that I stumbled backward into someone dancing. *Magic be damned.* Raine caught me by the waist, pulling me back into him.

"Marry me." His eyes were frantically searching mine as a dull pain was traveling its way into my head once again. I clutched my necklace, rubbing the onyx stone for comfort. For *anything* to calm my nerves.

"Raine I—"

"You can still go home to your family, Amira. I just can't bear the thought of you leaving Solaris without knowing if you'll ever come back to me."

My head was so cloudy from surprise that my knees threatened to buckle beneath me. Raine had me pressed to his chest with a hand tucked behind my head. "I'll wait for you. However long it takes. But I must know if you'll be my queen. Rule Solaris with me. There is no one in any Realm that I'd rather have sitting next to me on the throne, lying in my bed, or in my arms other than you, Amira," he begged. "Hell, I'll even go with you to Medlar if that's what it takes."

I shifted my gaze to the sky above. Hundreds of stars were shining brightly providing us the most gorgeous night sky I've ever laid eyes on. Was anything or anyone in Medlar worth this feeling? Could I have the life I wished for back home? I knew one thing that wasn't back home, and that was Raine. Weeks. I'd known him only weeks. But I've never felt this strongly for someone.

Heavens above, please don't let me look foolish.

"Heavens, Amira. Say something...please," he pleaded with parted lips. I studied his face once more. This is the face of a God. Those piercing eyes and high cheek bones would be the death of me.

"What was the question again?" I asked jokingly. Raine rolled his eyes with a smirk tugging at his lips as he moved to cup my face with both hands. Time stopped in that moment as he leaned in closer, slightly bending at the waist. "Will you marry me, Amira?" he asked once more as his lips brushed mine.

"Of course, I will."

Chapter Thirty-One

At the end of the night, I found myself in Raine's bed. We were both so exhausted from dancing and socializing that we curled into each other and drifted off without so much as a goodnight to each other. Waking up before him, I replayed his question from last night over and over in my head. *I agreed to marry him.* That's not something that I could take back. I'm not even sure that I'd want to take my answer back if I could.

I turned my head slightly to look at him as he slept. He looked like an angel created by the God's themselves. How could I compare to someone this beautiful? The thought of mortality and immortality slid its way to my thoughts, paralyzing me where I laid. Tears pricked my eyes when I realized that there would come a time when I'd be gone, and he'd still be here.

"Good morning, beautiful."

Startled, I focused back on Raine's face to see his eyes were intensely blue in the morning.

"Hi," I purred with a broad smile.

Raine took his hand and ran it up the center of my stomach under my nightgown. My breath hitched once he reached my breasts.

"I'm not happy," he said while finding the peak of a nipple.

"Why is that?"

"We went to sleep before I could please my future wife."

Raine's eyes darkened at his own statement. Before I could provide a reply, he maneuvered himself between my legs while I remained on my back. Bending down to kiss my forehead he scanned my face, and I could feel the heat rising within me.

This was it. I had agreed to marry him, and he was now willing to complete our bond as mates.

"I want you, Amira. I want all of you. But I'll wait until you're ready," he said while caressing my cheek. I considered his statement and couldn't stop myself before I said what I truly wanted.

"Take what you want."

Raine's body stiffened at my offer. My thighs clenched at the sight of him at a loss for words. Studying his face reminded me of his previous words. *"I've told you that intimacy is different with mates. There's no going back from it. It seals the bond."* I shuddered at the thought of being his, solely his and no one else's until my last breath.

"Do not tease me, Amira."

"It's not a tease, Raine," I countered while lifting my nightgown over my head and laying back down.

He gazed over my entire body before kissing me with a force I'd never experienced, sending shivers down my body. Slowly, his kisses trailed from my lips to my collarbone, and to the peaks of both nipples. The sensation caused my body to shudder, bringing a smile to Raine's face that I could feel on my bare skin.

"Please," I begged. "Please don't tease me like this."

"Darling, this isn't a tease," he said while raising his face to show his determination. "I'm just preparing you before I bury myself inside of you."

He plunged a finger into my entrance without warning, causing a moan to escape from me. "That is the most beautiful sound I've ever heard in the morning," Raine admitted while taking another nip at my breast. "I think I'd like to hear it again." My eyes grew wide as he sat up on his knees and placed his thumb on my clit, repeatedly making full circles. Before I could muster another sound, he slipped an additional finger inside me and smirked. My lips had popped open at the surprise but snapped shut once he started to pump them in and out of me without mercy.

"Raine, please."

"I like it when you beg," he countered in his morning rasp.

"I'm going to— "

"Then do it, Amira. Just make sure the entire palace can hear you."

My eyes were so wide, I feared they'd fall out of their sockets. The release was right there, and he knew I was doing everything I could to keep myself from bubbling over. The last thing I wanted to do was to have anyone outside of this room hear what we were doing. I was still a guest here.

Bringing his body to a hover, his eyes bore into mine. "Don't you dare think about suppressing that pretty little voice." He placed his lips on mine, parting them with his tongue while moving those two fingers in and out of me. The arousal was too much for my body to handle as I bowed off the bed and the moan that Raine was searching for escaped my throat. Riding out my release, he dropped himself back between my legs and sucked on my pulsing bud until I came again. Every ounce of energy that I awoke with was depleted from me as I found myself panting from the release with him still between my legs.

"Your moans are the most beautiful melody I've ever heard," his eyes roamed the length of my body. "Now, I believe you said I could take what I want. And I assure you, there's something very specific that I want."

I lifted myself up on my elbows to make a smartass remark to him when I was reminded of the length of him. My mouth was agape, and I didn't care how stupid I looked. How was any woman supposed to handle a man of his size? Licking my bottom lip, I slowed at the sight of him stroking himself while staring at the entrance of my sex. Instinctively, I wanted to snap my legs shut thinking about the pain that would cause.

Raine opened his mouth to speak while leaning over me, the tip of his erection at my core, when a knock appeared at the door. I shrieked, pushing Raine off me and pulling the covers to the top of my chest. Raine let out a deep laugh before calling out to the guest on the other side of the door.

"What is it?"

"Sorry to interrupt, High King. But we have an urgent matter that requires your presence," Eryx answered from behind the door.

"Heavens above, can't it wait until after breakfast?" Irritation painted Raine's face as he sneered at the sound of his best friend's voice.

"I'm afraid not. I'll be in the foyer awaiting your presence."

Raine cursed under his breath as he threw on his clothes and stalked to my side of the bed. Planting a kiss to my forehead, he apologized and let me know that he'd find me as soon as the issue was handled.

"There seems to be a lot of issues arising out of nowhere," I stated with a pout on my face, making it exceedingly noticeable that I didn't want him to leave.

"I'm so sorry darling, it's not always like this. I promise to pick up where we left off as soon as I handle whatever situation has arisen." He kissed my forehead once more, "Forgive me?"

"Forgiven." I rolled my eyes while suppressing a smile.

Chapter Thirty-Two

When Raine left, I forced myself out of bed, slipping my nightgown and robe back on before I returned to my room. A fresh set of clothes was laid out for me on the bed thanks to Millie and Ellie.

After a warm bath I sat at the desk where I hid the letter from my family. *They don't know what I've agreed to.* I covered my face with the palms of my hands.

What if I was making decisions with lust instead of with my heart? Everything was moving so fast that I couldn't decipher what was up from down anymore. We had yet to say we loved each other, but with every touch, every breath I knew how strong our feelings were for each other. Well... my feelings at least. He wouldn't ask me to marry him if he didn't love me. *Three words didn't define how I felt for him, nor him for me.*

Though I had already opened the drawer to retrieve the letter, I was not in the right state of mind to comprehend anything. The executive decision to consume food before upsetting myself with reading another lackluster letter overrode any other options.

Throwing my curls into a plait, I headed to the dining hall for breakfast. When my foot hit the last step, I was startled by the sound of Raine reprimanding Eryx.

"You made me get out of bed for this?"

"Raine, they're fighting back. We've already lost five soldiers. Do you know what this looks like for us to lose five soldiers to—
"

"No. *You* lost five soldiers. If I had been smart enough to realize that my best friend couldn't handle such a weak realm, we wouldn't be in this predicament in the first place."

"If you had stuck to the plan from the beginning, we wouldn't have even needed to go this far."

I heard a scuffle and strained breaths coming from Eryx before Raine spoke again.

"We needed to go this far because you couldn't handle the goddamn army on your own. This war has been brewing for *centuries*. Don't you dare act like this came about when—" Another scuffle ensued before Raine continued speaking. "I sent my men there to search for confirmation. Not to start an all-out war. That was *not* my intentions."

I heard a thud and what I imagined to be Raine dropping Eryx to the ground. They continued their quarrel, but no matter how hard I strained my ears I couldn't make out the substance of their conversation.

"With all due respect Ra— "

"High King. I am your High King, Eryx. And you will address me as such from here on out."

Eryx cleared his throat before continuing his statement.

"We have known for many years the plans for an uprising within that realm. The land is far too valuable to leave it in the hands of— "

"I don't need you to explain to me what I have already known for hundreds of years," Raine spat at Eryx.

"One last thing my High King," Eryx said in between ragged breaths.

"More good news I suppose?" Raine inquired threw gritted teeth. "What is it?"

"Suspicions of the Death Dealer of Solaris are beginning to rise again throughout the realms," Eryx relayed the information slowly. "Word of mouth I suppose. People love to talk about the— "

"Enough," Raine roared so loudly that the palace shook. "Get out of my sight until I can clean up your mess."

I turned to run back to my room before either party emerged from the foyer, but I slammed into someone on the stair above me. Raya caught my shoulders before I tumbled backwards and raised a finger to her lips. We quietly and swiftly snuck back to her room, quickly shutting the door behind us.

"How much of their conversation did you hear?" I asked her with my heart threatening to escape its cage.

"Enough." She replied with her arms crossed over her chest. "And exactly why were you eavesdropping in the first place?" she asked while looking me over. I began to wring my fingers together.

"I need you to take me back to The Garden of Sanri," I requested without answering her question. Raya dropped her arms as her body stiffened.

"Why?" she questioned with a furrowed brow.

Taking a few steps toward her I pleaded, "I promise to tell you everything if you take me there. I need answers. Answers that I know the garden can provide to me when no one else will."

Raya stared at me for a few moments before crossing her arms over her chest again and letting out a long uneven breath. "We would have to go now." She swiftly eyed my wardrobe. "And for the love of God change out of that dress and into something you can travel in." Before I could thank her, she summoned slacks, boots, and a matching tunic for me to wear. I changed into my new set of clothes and reached for the doorknob when Raya grabbed my arm.

"What are you doing?"

"You said you'd take me to the Garden…"

"There's not a chance in hell we would be able to sneak past Raine right now. Nor would I want to catch him in the middle of the rage he's experiencing with Eryx at the moment. I'll beam us there."

Before I could question what she meant by *beam*, a cloud of purple dust immersed us. A familiar pressure, like a bear squeezing my chest, seized me. *The same sensation I experienced when Anya sent me back from the dark forest.* I clenched my eyes shut at the pressure and within seconds the two of us were in The Garden of Sanri. We both smoothed our clothes out and surveyed each other before Raya threw her arms out to the side.

"Well, here we are. Now what?"

"I have to drink from the pond," I stated, turning to where it was with determination, but Raya stepped in front of me.

"Are you crazy? Drinking from that pond has been known to knock out some of the strongest Fae I know for *days*. Gods knows what it'll do to a human," she lectured me without knowing this wasn't my first time.

"I'll be fine, Raya. I did it once before with Raine. I passed out for a moment, but I came back without any issues." She eyed me suspiciously.

"I can't risk you harming yourself, Amira." Raya prepared to beam our return to the palace, but I stepped out of the purple dust cloud she summoned. Her eyes grew wide as she reeled her magic back in.

"You're serious?" She inquired with her hands on her hips.

"I don't have a choice. I made a promise to Raine last night and I need answers."

Before she could interrogate my statement, I swiveled around her and sprinted to the pond, scooping a handful of water into my mouth. Unlike last time, there was no jolt of pain. Nor was there a vision presenting itself to me. Confused, I took another handful of water and waited for the jolt of electricity to flow through my veins, but it never came.

"I don't understand," I said as I turned to Raya confused, but was terrified when I saw her. Her eyes were dark instead of the teal blue I've grown accustomed to. She stood where she was with a blank expression, as her throat worked to speak.

"Raya? Are you okay?" I asked while inching toward her, touching the tips of her fingers at her side. I jolted back at the electricity I felt through our touch, but she had gripped my hand too quickly.

"Amira, Solaris is..." She paused, closing her eyes, and breathing deeply before looking to me once again.

"Solaris is what?" I searched her face for answers, but her expression never altered.

"You can't—"

"For the love of Gods, Raya. I can't what? Why are you speaking in riddles?"

Raya loosened her grip on my hand and fell backwards at the same time I did, resulting in us both falling to the ground. Crawling over to her, her eyes were back to the beautiful teal color I was accustomed to. She grasped my face between both of her hands, "We have to go back. *Now*."

Chapter Thirty-Three

Raya beamed us back to my room within seconds of a knock landing at my door. We both jumped at the sound and made our best efforts to look casual before I projected my voice for a greeting. "Come in," I offered to whomever was on the opposite side of the door.

"Is it proper for us to enter?" Ellie and Millie sang in unison from a crack in the door. Raya and I let out the breaths we were holding in fear of receiving a male's voice instead.

"Goodness, of course! Come in." I shuffled across the floor to open the door wider.

"Everything okay, Amira? You look disheveled," Ellie said with a glance over to Raya. "You as well. Should we be worried? Did something happen?"

"Not at all," Raya offered encouragement as she stood from her chair. "We were just discussing the last night of Solstice and all that it has to offer." A tension filled the air between the three of them before three sets of eyes found mine.

"Actually we—" I was going to say we didn't discuss any of that, but Raya cut me off before I could continue.

"We didn't get to go into specifics, so would you ladies mind filling Amira in on the festivities for tonight? I have business to attend to before I head to the celebration myself."

They both stared at Raya as she patted my shoulder and left the room without another word. When she was gone, they quickly began to make small talk about what I should wear. "Actually, I have a gown to wear already," I chimed in while they both looked at me in bewilderment. "Raya, provided me with a gown a few days ago that she thought would be perfect for tonight." I grabbed the dress from the giant armoire and held it up for them to see as they both gasped.

"What? What's wrong with it?"

"Absolutely nothing," they replied in unison.

"Then why are you both about to fall over in shock?"

"Because that belonged to— " Ellie started, but Millie elbowed her to shut up.

"Raya said it was given to her by her mother. If you deem it inappropriate, I'll—"

"*No,*" they both answered once again in unison.

I laughed at how awkward they were being and laid the dress on the bed. I sat in my usual chair as they primped and preened me with everything needed to make a meager mortal presentable among the angelic Fae that would be surrounding me. My eyes lit up in delight when I saw that Ellie was opening a tube of dark purple lipstick. "You and these dark colors are going to be the death of me," she said through a lighthearted laugh. Once my makeup and hair were set, they helped me shimmy into the skintight dress that was gifted to me. Millie zipped the dress upward to where it ended at the lowest part of my back just before revealing too much of my ass. "I know you've heard me say it before...but you are gorgeous, Amira," Millie whispered with her hand over her mouth.

As she guided me over to the floor length mirror in the corner of the room, I gasped when I saw myself in the midnight purple dress. My lips parted as I noticed that they were such a deep purple they could easily blend into the night sky. My hands traveled to my hair that fell past my shoulders, brushing my back in deep full waves. *How on earth they finessed my curls into waves is something I'll never understand.*

The bronze-colored eyeshadow with hints of violet and green that Ellie provided brought out every spec of green that was hidden in my brown eyes. "Fae nor mortal could ignore your beauty if they tried. They'll fall to their knees when they see you, Amira," Millie announced while gripping my shoulders from behind, as we stared into the mirror in unison. A pang of guilt struck. I wanted to share my knowledge of who they really were. To tell them their secret was safe with me.

Ellie jokingly pushed Millie out of the way to set a crown upon my head. "The High King requested that you wear this tonight since you'll be at his side," she said with hesitancy while placing it atop my head. I'm not sure if it was the sight of the crown or the thought of it representing a queen that caused panic to rise within me.

I surveyed the onyx jewel hanging from the necklace around my throat as I whipped my head toward the two women. *Now or never.*

"Can I ask a favor?"

"We're not going to Solstice tonight, Amira," Ellie replied. Even though that made me sad, I continued with my request. "Fine. I won't twist your arm to accompany me again. But I..." I couldn't figure out how to explain about the flower Anya had given me without mentioning her name or where I went. "I need you to prepare something that was given to me." They looked at each other confused before Millie answered, "Okay? Well, what is it?"

I walked over to my chest where I hid my satchel from the day I wandered into the dark forest. Locating the black box that Anya slid over to me, I placed it in Millie's hands with a small smile painted on my face as she opened it. "*WHERE? HOW?*"

She yelled, as Ellie peaked into the box and slammed her mouth shut.

"Can you help me or not?"

"Amira we—"

"Don't. Don't say you can't help me. Everyone has hidden secrets from me since I set foot in this place. Now either you tell me what the third night of Solstice entails, help me figure out how I'm supposed to eat a fucking flower without vomiting on myself, or I find my way home. *RIGHT NOW.* The choice is yours." They both looked at each other with wide eyes before Ellie finally spoke to me.

"For the third night of Solstice, all we can tell you is to make wise decisions and let the stars guide you."

"What does that even mean?"

"It means think with your soul, heart, and mind. Not lust."

Mille smacked the back of Ellie's head with her hand and snapped the box shut. Pointing her long, thin finger at me she continued, "We can help you. But so help me stars and moon above, we're going to have a long talk in the morning." I nodded my head as they told me to remain here and wait for their return.

It was almost time to leave when they returned with a bowl of broth. "I thought we usually ate at Solstice?" I questioned them confused. "The broth contains the flower girl. So, either you eat it now and fake being hungry later, or you don't eat it at all," Millie scolded me while holding out the bowl with a spoon. *Fake being hungry? This isn't even a snack.* Sticking my tongue out at her I grabbed the bowl from her hands and thanked them. Putting the spoon to the side, I drank the broth directly from the bowl as quickly as possible in fear that I couldn't handle the taste.

I sprang up waiting for some magical episode to happen and explain everything I needed to figure out what the fuck had happened to my life within these past weeks.

Nothing.

Not a swirl of magic.

Not a mythical creature in sight.

Nothing.

I turned with wide eyes to Millie and Ellie, waiting for them to provide an answer, but all I received were two sets of shoulder shrugs and sympathetic smiles.

Ellie beamed with her arms outstretched wide, "On the brightside, your dress has pockets."

Chapter Thirty-Four

Displeased with the outcome of eating the lotus from the dark forest, I confidently told Millie and Ellie that I could find my own way to the festival. They sighed with displeasure but allowed me to venture to the clearing on my own. Proceeding toward the giant double doors in the back of the palace, I stopped to admire the bright lotus flowers drifting in the fountain. *How can something so beautiful derive only from mud?* Picking one up to admire its' beauty, I placed it back into the fountain and followed in the direction of the music filling the slightly humid night air, thankful for the peach to snack on that I plucked from the bowl Raine left for me in my room.

I swiftly found Raya who looked concerned as she gestured to the seat next to her.

"Everything okay?" I asked, searching her face for answers while trying to ease my own nerves.

"Yes, yes. I'm fine. It's just..."

"Just what?"

"The third night always makes me uneasy."

"Can someone please explain to me what the fuck happens to—"

As I was about to finish my sentence, Eryx took up a position at the center of the stage, commanding everyone's attention. Hundreds of Fae were shoulder-to-shoulder, making every effort to get as close to the platform as possible. The crowd became so silent that one could hear a pin drop all the way from Medlar. Raine confidently strode to the center of the stage with grace as he thanked Eryx for his assistance at quieting the crowd, offering a large smile to the sea of Fae before him.

"Citizens of Solaris, it is with great pleasure to have everyone gathered here once again for the most important night of Solstice." The crowd cheered among the clapping that erupted in praise at their High King's words. "Tonight is about devotion. Solaris would not be what it is today without the ongoing reverence and passion you all provide. It is with great pride for me to provide my blessing to each one of you that have had, *and will have,* the privilege of experiencing the mating bond."

Raine briefly stopped his speech to glance over at me, tipping the corners of his mouth up into a smile. I provided a small smile back as Raya glanced at me with an odd expression. Before I could continue quizzing her about tonight, Raine continued his speech. "I myself believe that I have found my mate in this lifetime as well." The crowd got so loud with cheers that my ears began to ring. I immediately realized that he was speaking about me as all eyes shifted in my direction. My heart raced as Raya placed her hand on my knee underneath the table. I focused back on Raine's speech as I worked to calm my nerves. The familiar icy feeling poured into my palms.

"It's not my desire to have you listen to me speak all night. Enjoy the final night of Solstice. And may the heavens above lead you to a lifetime of happiness within your devotions tonight." Raine exited off the stage and strode over to our table. Before he could claim his seat next to mine, Raya stood from her chair to speak in a hushed tone with Raine as I did my best to eavesdrop on the conversation.

"How dare you," She spat in his face in the quietest voice she could muster.

Raine slowly turned his head toward Raya's outburst. Clenching his jaw, he found his seat and calmly claimed it. I braced myself, ready to feel their wrath explode before my eyes.

"Stay within your line of succession sister," Raine gritted through clenched teeth while offering a venomous glare.

"Piss off with your obsession of rank. How could you place that much responsibility on her without discussing it with her first?"

My heart raced at her words. And my mind decided to jump in the race as well as I tried to decipher her question. *What responsibility?* If she's talking about the possibility of being the queen of Solaris, it would take some time to learn everything I need to know about this realm, but I could handle it.

A menacing grin spread across his handsome face, causing my stomach to drop. I was fearful of what his next words would be, but nothing could prepare me for the blow that he delivered.

"As a matter of fact, Amira has agreed to take my hand in marriage."

Before I could say anything, Raya shifted her attention to me with a look of hurt and concern etched across her face.

Not again. I can't take losing her trust again. I should've told her. I should have-

"He's lying. Surely, he's lying to get a rise out of me," Raya insisted while maintaining her focus on me. I opened and closed my mouth to answer her but couldn't form the words needed to explain. "Tell me that he's lying, Amira. You certainly can't be that foolish to agree to this so soon. You've only been here a few months," Raya reprimanded me while her hands shook at her sides.

"I can explain," I offered but she held her hand up to silence me.

"I've done what I can to help you see the darkness. But all

your eyes wish to see is the light," she said as she excused herself and vanished into the crowd.

I stood from my seat to go after her, but Raine softly grabbed my arm and suggested that I let her go. Making a mental note to find her later to explain everything that happened last night, I nodded in agreement and sat back down to join him at the table. With it being just the two of us I figured now was the best time for me to inquire about the argument I had heard between him and Eryx.

"I left my room earlier to find you and overheard you having a disagreement with Eryx in the foyer," I revealed while popping a grape into my mouth. Raine stilled with his chalice to his lips. Setting it down he continued the conversation.

"Oh? And what did you hear?"

"Well, I heard mention about a dealer of death? Or death healer? I'm not exactly sure."

"I see. Dance with me while we continue this conversation?" He requested as he glanced around. "I'd rather show you off than sit at a table all night." Raine held his hand out for me as he stood from the table. Placing my hand in his, he guided us out into the sea of Fae that were dancing and enjoying the festivities.

"May I?" Raine asked, implying that he would once again be using his magic to guide me while dancing. "You may," I approved with a smile. As we began to glide across the clearing to the sound of musical instruments in the background, Raine picked up where we left off on our conversation at the table.

"The Death Dealer is a myth that has been passed down through generations. The elders here refuse to let it die because it gets a rise out of everyone from time to time. Eryx came to let me know that another rumor was spreading within town that the so-called *Death Dealer* has returned. As you can imagine, that caused a bit of chaos within Solaris."

"So...he's not here?"

"*He* isn't real. Therefore, *no*. He is not."

Raine's response was filled with irritation, causing me to move on to my next question. "Well, that makes me relax a bit," I said to ease the tension. "I also heard a mention of an army?" Raine's grip tightened on my waist before he provided a reply.

"I received word of a possible rebellion from another mortal realm some ways south of Solaris. I dispatched a few of my men to ensure our treaty was still in place."

"Treaty?" I asked confused. In my twenty-four years of life, I had never known of the immortal realm. How could there be a treaty? A subtle laugh left his lips.

"Yes. You may not have been aware of the immortal world, but I assure you that many elders from your mortal realms do. A treaty was set in place thousands of years ago to allow for all realms to live in peace after an unnecessary war ended over our land."

"I'm sorry... did you say *realms*? As in...more than one? And why can't you just say you have an alliance?"

"Surely you didn't think that your human realm was the only mortal one in existence? Medlar is not the only realm to host mortals, darling," Raine explained in amusement. "And mortal does *not* always mean human." The thoughts flowing through my mind held every type of emotion except amusement as I looked at the smile slowly spreading across his face.

"Okay. Explain the alliance you keep talking about."

"The treaty that we have across all realms is not the same as an alliance."

I was done dancing around words.

"Then what is it, Raine?" I asked as annoyance swirled through me.

He studied me hastily before releasing a forceful breath. "It's an agreement that as long as they don't interfere with our realm, we don't interfere with theirs." Chills traveled up my spine at his words.

"And how does that agreement play into marriage between a mortal and immortal?"

Raine released a breath before answering. "The treaty would most likely need to be amended within the human realm, but they have no say over a mating bond."

"Exactly *what is* the mating bond anyway?" I began to shake my head in confusion, "This is a lot to take in and I'm not sure if—"

"Amira, the only thing that matters is our love for each other. Surely you know I care for you more than anything my world or yours has to offer." He searched my face for agreement. "There's nothing I wouldn't do for you. And there's no one in this universe that could keep us apart."

Raine's grip was getting tighter and tighter as he spoke. Before I could say anything regarding his statements, he halted our dancing while still gripping my waist.

"Marry me, Amira."

"I already agreed to that, Raine."

"I mean marry me tonight. Under the brightest stars that Solaris has to offer."

I could feel the numbness spreading from the top of my head down to my feet as my mouth went dry. I swallowed multiple times before words could be formed to leave my mouth. "Raine, that's quite soon. My love for you is real, but I would prefer that my family be present for such a big part of my life. I haven't even had the chance to inform them of our plans."

I placed my palms on his chest as I often did but cowered back as white clouds replaced the blue eyes I had fallen in love with. Gripping my wrists in his hands, he snatched me toward him so quickly that I collided with his chest. "You will *not* embarrass your High King after I've professed my love for you in front of my entire realm," Raine hissed under his breath baring his teeth, as his clouded white eyes bore into mine.

"This is not my home. Therefore, I don't have a *High King,*" I hissed back at him through gritted teeth. "You're hurting me," I added while attempting to free my wrists from his grasp, but he held tight. Letting out a cryptic laugh, he brought his lips as close to mine as possible without touching.

"Darling, you haven't experienced pain yet." Fear and panic took over as I started aggressively tugging at my wrists to get out of his grasp. Internal flames licked at my flesh as I began to overheat. *Now is not the time to panic, Amira.*

Suddenly, a hand was on my shoulder as a voice spoke from behind me. "Let her go, Raine. Don't embarrass yourself in front of everyone."

"Ah. Glad to see you, sister. Just who I was looking for," he exclaimed in Raya's direction as Eryx appeared next to him. Releasing my wrists, I scrambled next to Raya. With a snap of Raine's fingers, we were back at the palace in front of the fountain.

"What the fuck was that?" I questioned as I looked around to confirm where we were. "Welcome to dark magic, *Pixie*," Eryx mocked. A strange metallic aroma floated in the air as I scrunched my nose. "And before you ask again what it means, it references someone who is worthless. Just like all humans." I was seething. Nothing would feel as good as sinking my nails into his deep brown eyes right now. Before I could act on my intrusive thought, Raine began speaking again.

"I've decided that you'll be married off to Eryx tonight, *sister*."

Raya took confident strides to meet Raine face to face before she let out a condescending laugh. "Over my dead body," she challenged with her head held high. Raine let out a laugh to match hers, "As much as I revel in the idea of that, there's no need for such drastic measures. I've already given word to the council of the plans *we* have both agreed on. Along with documentation accompanied by your signature and seal upon the family crest."

Raya stumbled backwards before bumping into me.

"You bastard."

Raya reached under the slit in her dress brandishing a dagger, but before she could lift it, she writhed in pain and dropped to her knees. I attempted to drop down beside her, but halfway down Eryx gripped both my arms standing me upright. "Don't fuckin' touch me," I hissed while trying to remove myself from his grip, but he ignored me as if I wasn't there.

Raine knelt in front of Raya, forcefully grabbing her chin so that her eyes met his. "You've done nothing but disappoint me our entire lives. Your compassion and sincerity for those below us makes me sick. One of the worst things our parents could've done was bring you into this world. Many nights I've begged the heavens above to rid me of your presence, and every morning you were still there. But I'll make sure tonight is the last night you threaten to have any type of power."

Raya spit in Raine's face while trying to lunge at him but was frozen in place. Wiping the saliva dripping down his face, he let out a grueling laugh. Forcefully gripping her chin again, a smile spread across his face. "I hope you enjoy being Eryx's bitch for the rest of your pathetic life." Tears spilled from Raya's eyes as Raine stood above her. A burst of light came from her palms throwing Raine back.

Snapping her head in my direction, she eagerly attempted to get her words out through force. "Amira, it's all a lie. Look around you for fucks sake. Everyone and everything has been touched by death itself. The ones he couldn't break were— "

Before she could finish her sentence, Raine flicked his wrist and where Raya's lips once were on her face was now a vacant stretch of skin. With Eryx's grip loosened I leaned forward and threw my head back into his face, dropping to clutch Raya as he released me. The sound of Eryx's bones crunching echoed in my ears as he clutched his nose. I dropped to my hands and knees at his release, quickly noticing Raine halting his friend's effort of landing a blow to my back with his boot.

Raine rolled his eyes before landing a blow of his own to his sister's ribs, sending her hunched over on her side.

"Very touching indeed. My guards will transport you somewhere safe while Raya is escorted to her sleeping chambers." I gawked at his actions while pulling Raya into my arms. "I'm not leaving her like this," I exclaimed while latching on to Raya.

Walking to where I was on the ground, Raine grabbed the back of my neck, pulling me from his sister and to my feet. Before I could focus on him standing before me, my head snapped back as what felt like hundreds of lightning bolts were set free throughout my body. My eyes rolled back as visions of a different time and place consumed my mind.

A male stood with his back to me in the beautiful town of Solaris. One by one he struck male and female Fae down that were running at him. Another group of Fae stood paralyzed behind him. A golden mist fell overhead as the ones charging him dropped like flies. Hundreds of Fae crawled to him attempting to kiss his feet and apologize. Many begged for his forgiveness as the dark-haired male next to him laughed.

A single Fae, immune to the mist, spat at the feet of the unknown man before speaking, "I'll sacrifice my life before I worship the Death Dealer that has brought disparity into my home." The dark-haired male stalked forward, placing his foot on the neck of the defiant male. "Then sacrifice, you shall," he declared as he unsheathed his sword, plunging it through the male's back as blood spurted from his mouth.

That voice. I know that voice.

The vile man turned around to flash a smile I'd seen one too many times.

Eryx.

Tapping the shoulder of the man next to him, he too turned around to greet me as he removed his ivory-colored hood.

"Hello, darling."

My mouth dropped open as Raine stood before me, eyes

white as snow with clouds swirling within. Black veins encased his entire body accompanied by huge white wings beginning to protrude from his back as he stalked toward me. My head snapped forward from the vision and my body went limp. Refocusing, I found myself in Raine's grasp.

"Y-you're the—"

Moving his hand to my throat and tightening his grip, he looked irritated and irrational.

"Spit it out, Amira."

"You're the Death Dealer," I sputtered through small gasps of air. "*You lied.*"

Tilting his head, he smiled while brushing my hair from my face. "Surprise my love," he cooed as the gold mist from my vision was blown into my face from his palm. Gasping for air and clutching at my throat, I heard laughter from Raine and Eryx ringing in my ears before he picked me up in his arms. The corners of my vision blurred to black as I saw Raya being carried over a guard's shoulder in front of me. Reaching out to her, I lost all sense of reality and let myself succumb to the darkness encapsulating me.

Chapter Thirty-Five

I jolted awake to find myself submerged in darkness save for a small, barred window. The cool metal against my wrists let me know that I was chained to either the floor or the wall but it was too dark to decipher. The air was thick with a musty scent that let me know I was no longer within the confines of the palace.

Tugging at the chains, I cursed the heavens for not granting me an ounce of magic to produce some type of light. Making the effort to stand, I felt a tug at the base of my throat. Bringing my hands up to meet the pulling sensation, I noted a chain fixated around my neck. The visions from Lorena's cottage flooded my mind as a scream left my lips that was so loud and filled with rage my own ears began to ring.

The same chains from my previous vision were now reality. The blank walls that haunted me in that very same vision were now surrounding me, save for a lone barred window.

Wandering over to the small window, I could see the stars above Solaris. How could a place so beautiful be ruled by someone so evil.

How could I fall for someone so evil?

Gripping the window bars above me and lowering my head between my shoulders, I heard rustling from outside the door before it swung open. The man I agreed to marry stood in the doorway holding a ball of light in his hand, similar to the ones on the wall behind him. He flicked two balls of light into holsters in the wall, illuminating the room. As he took two steps closer to me, I took two steps back, causing him to tilt his head with a sinister smile.

"You're *afraid* of me now?" He asked with an arched brow as he closed the door behind him, placing a bowl of fruit on an end table that he conjured with one flick of his wrist.

"Don't."

"Don't what, Amira?"

"Don't play the role of the savior. You're the reason I'm in here. I did nothing but love you and this is your response?"

Raine laughed as he walked over to me under the moonlight that now flooded through the small window. Grabbing my face, he examined it before running his thumb across my bottom lip. "I told you before, there is no one in this realm or universe that can take you from me. Love me or not, you're mine to keep...and keep I shall," he informed me before leaning in to kiss me. Before his lips could touch mine, I slammed my head into his nose causing drops of blood to fall onto his white shirt. He stumbled back from shock. *I'd rather die alone in here than feel this fucker's lips on mine again.*

Gripping the chain connected to my throat he yanked it in his direction causing me to stumble forward. I saw rage-filled blue eyes, and then before I realized what had happened, I stumbled back toward the stone wall behind me. Raine had slapped me, and my face stung from the impact, but seeing the blood run into his mouth from his broken nose was worth it. A devious smile painted my face before he quickly strode back to me, gripping the same chain a mere inch from my face.

"You worthless bitch," he seethed while those milky white clouds took over his eyes again. "You're lucky I have a small bit of respect left for you and don't take what's rightfully mine right here."

I felt his other hand slip under my dress to my inner thigh. Panic rose in my throat while I tried to swallow it down. "Scream. No one can hear you within these walls except me." His cloud-filled eyes searched mine. "And I've waited so long to bring such a noise from that pretty mouth of yours with my cock."

My body began to overheat from rage, or panic, or both. I knew so much about him yet, he knew nothing about me. Not once had he made the effort to find out about my life, my family, or anything for that matter. As if my mind and heart were screaming at me to wake the fuck up, realization slammed into me that he never asked what my name was. The sensation was so overwhelming I was convinced I would burst into flames just from looking at him. "How did you know my name?" I asked him with wide eyes.

"What?" he asked, his grip on my thigh loosening.

"When you found me in the forest. How did you know my name when we spoke for the first time within the palace walls?" My lips trembled, my knees weakening as I stared at the man I thought was my knight in shining armor. The knight I swore I never needed to survive. A venomous smile formed on his lips.

"It seems like my damsel is finally piecing together the puzzle that was hidden from her after all this time," he replied as he gripped my face in his hand while running his tongue up the side of my face. "Let's just say, I've been waiting for you longer than you know," he taunted me while tightening his grip on my jaw. Eyeing the blood smeared across his face and the deep red stains on his shirt that I put there ignited a flame within.

Just as I was about to attempt to draw blood again, the door flew open once more and Raine took a step back, releasing the chain around my throat. Eryx was gripping Raya by her arm. Her gaze connected with mine as my mouth fell open at the sight of blood and sweat covering her clothes. Her weakened body was barely able to remain standing as he threw her unceremoniously into the cell in front of me. Raine laughed as he flicked his hand, bringing a replica of my chains to Raya's wrists and throat as well.

"Think of all the things we could do right now," Eryx observed while ogling both of us.

"Let's take care of business first, then we'll have our fun, brother," Raine approved as I knelt beside Raya. Both men exited the cell without a second glance in our direction.

"Where have you been? I've been worried sick about—," Before I could finish my sentence, I noticed the marks on Raya's face and body. "No, no, no, no, no... No!," I yell in anger as I grabbed her face. "What did he do?"

Tears spilled onto Raya's face as she sobbed uncontrollably. "He did whatever he pleased to me before he brought me here," she confessed as her sunken teal eyes met mine. "He took what he knew he could never have."

Squeezing Raya as hard as I could, I dragged us both back to the stone wall so my back could rest against it as Raya laid in my lap. Caressing her hair, I watched as she drifted into a deep sleep. A different type of rage flowed through my veins at her words. An equal swirl of fire and ice rippled through me.

Leaning my head back against the wall, I almost woke her as I jumped at the figure staring back at me. The black cat from the cottage was standing right outside the barred window. Without a single noise, he dropped a small object from his mouth and pushed it through the metal bars with the tip of his wet nose where it dropped into my hand. Mesmerized by what I was holding, I gaped upwards to the window as he scurried off into the night.

Afraid that Raine or Eryx would enter unannounced, I shoved the object into the pocket of my dress and leaned my head back against the stone. I had so many questions and needed so many answers, but I let Raya sleep. I took one last look at the blanket of stars above us.

Stars above...don't let us die in here.

Chapter Thirty-Six

The water dripping onto my face from the cracks in the ceiling startled me awake before Raya who was now laying on the stone floor next to me. Leaning my head against the stone wall I could see the sun starting to rise through the barred window above. I shouldn't have slept. I should have organized a plan to get us out of here. *Or at least get Raya out of here.*

With the sun illuminating the entire cell I could finally take a good look around. Not that there was much to see.

The walls of hewn stone held the base of our chains, while the ceiling was so low it felt like it would collapse at any moment. The concrete floor was cracked and crumbled in so many places it was apparent this area was left in purposeful disrepair.

Raya barely fluttered her eyes open as I bit into an apple from the bowl of fruit Raine had left the night before. The subtle electricity traveling through me let me know it was from the Garden of Sanri. *How thoughtful.* I thought to myself with a scowl.

Without warning, Raya slapped the apple from my hand. Before I could question her actions, she propped herself up to her knees. "Tell me you weren't stupid enough to eat from the

Garden of Sanri." Dread ran its course within. "Fucking hell, Amira," Raya spat as she furiously tipped over the bowl of remaining fruit. I gaped at her with wide eyes, confusion etched across my face. "That fruit hampers all ability of logical thinking. It can even go as far to break down shields that Fae use to protect their thoughts and mind." Splotches of red had bloomed across her neck and face from her anger.

I ate multiple pieces of that fruit the night Raine asked me to marry him.

"How did you know it was from the garden?" I questioned her, searching for proof of her accusations.

"You can't smell the tang of magic? There's no sweet smell, Amira. What you smell is dark magic."

I focused on the aroma in the room as that same metal fragrance from last night arose. I detected the same smell when Raine brought us back from the clearing. I inclined my head to survey Raya who was now getting a deeper shade of red by the minute.

"Fuck," I muttered. "A fresh bowl was left for me in my room every morning." I winced at my words and Raya's reaction as she clenched her jaw so tightly, I feared I would hear her teeth crack at any moment.

I finally gathered myself to speak when two guards forcefully pushed the door open without so much as a knock. "Stand up," the tallest one commanded from the doorway with his hand on the hilt of his sword. Raya and I both did as we were instructed but stayed in close proximity to each other.

The guards unlocked the chains from the wall but left both wrists chained together with a connection to the one around our necks. "I'd rather not walk you through the halls like rabid animals on a chain. Long as you don't start any funny business, we'll allow you to walk on your own," the muscular one declared before leading the way. Raya and I followed behind as the tall guard trailed behind us.

The same hewn stone from the cell lined the passageways that we followed. Progressing deeper, multiple branches of pathways offered different route choices. Even if I were to make a run for it, I'd surely be caught before making any real progress. The halls were so eerily quiet that I'd have done anything just to hear a pin drop as we walked through the deserted hallways. Though the halls were lit with balls of Fae light, the darkness sent shivers down my spine.

The further we walked, the more uneasy I felt as regret gnawed at my insides. Regret of not creating a plan to get Raya and me out of this situation. I glanced back at Raya who looked just as uneasy as I felt. The guards never said we couldn't speak, so I took a chance at conversing with her.

"Where are we?" I asked hesitantly, glancing at the guard in front of us. Raya swallowed before answering.

"This is where prisoners are sent to bide their time before trial or death." I winced at her answer.

"Well, that's...pleasant," I murmured before I stumbled into the back of the guard in front of me.

"Unless you want what's behind these walls to have a feast, I suggest you shut up with your questions," he instructed me before he started walking again. Rolling my eyes, I followed along several more feet before we turned left down a dimly lit pathway. The guard opened a large wooden door to reveal Eryx and Raine sitting on a dais in two large throne chairs. Seeing them sitting in such an elegant room with smiles on their faces had my stomach turning in knots. "Keep it moving," the muscular guard ushered us from behind with a not-so-subtle nudge in my back.

Walking closer to the dais, I could tell that we were somehow back within the palace walls. *I should've paid attention to the path we took.*

Before me, the towering ceilings were supported by large golden pillars adorned with intricate designs of the heavens above. The floors were complete with the same white and gold marble from my room that I had come to adore. My eyes finally raised back up to meet Raine's. Despite showing his true self, he was still nothing short of godlike. The extravagant golden throne bedazzled with jewels only accentuated his looks and portrayed him as the rightful ruler of Solaris. I took one more look at the man I had come to love before I forced myself to look away as the hurt began to chew away at the remainder of my heart. I could feel the bile rising in my throat as I thought about the intimate moments we'd shared.

"I don't suppose that you're still willing to move along with our marriage arrangement?" Raine asked as he studied me from head to toe, arrogance dripping from his muscular form.

Realizing that I was in the same skintight dress from the night before, I curled my lips inward and bit down so hard that I was afraid my teeth would pierce through as I glared back at him.

"Figured as much," he continued with the same annoying smile plastered on his face. "Since you've declined to continue with our previous engagement, my second-in-command and I have a new proposition for the both of you," he stated while making a gesture toward Eryx at his side on the additional throne.

"Second-in-command," Raya seethes, "What a fucking joke."

Raine tilted his head as he turned his palm upright, then closed his fingers to make a fist. Raya screamed in pain, dropping to one knee.

"Enough!" I yelled at him. "Stop it. Say what you need to say but leave her be."

Raine released his hand as Raya collapsed to the floor on her hands and knees. Her shoulders trembled as she coughed while working to regain her composure. With deep labored breaths, she slowly returned to her feet. I subtly shook my head at her as the look in her eyes read retaliation. The look on her brother's face showed he was hopeful that she would ignore my warning and follow through with her intrusive thoughts. After several seconds passed, Eryx spoke from Raine's side.

"Your High King has decided that you both will be married off. Amira to Raine, and Raya to me," he held up his hand as we both began to protest. "If either of you would like to decline, that is an option." Raya and I looked at each other, surprised that there was an option to decline the proposal.

"And if we decline?" Raya asked.

"If one of you declines, the other shall be punished by death," Raine answered while crossing one leg over the other and leaning back into his throne. "For the sake of Solaris, I pray to the heavens above that Amira declines my offer," he commented while staring at his sister. The two men laughed from the dais as Raya and I looked at each other knowing we couldn't allow for the other to be put to death due to the decisions we *truly* wanted to make.

"The heavens wouldn't accept shit from you," Raya spat from my side as I huffed a laugh at Raine's infuriated facial expression.

"You're wasting valuable time here. What are your decisions?" Eryx demanded from his throne. Raya and I looked back at the men before us as we answered in unison. "*We accept.*"

Raine clapped his hands together as he stood. "Excellent. The ceremonies will take place tonight in the garden. The council has already provided a letter giving their blessing," he announced before he dismissed us back to our cell. As we turned to follow the guards back, he called for our attention again. "One last thing," he announced as he stepped down from the platform. "If either of you speak out of turn during the ceremony. If you even *think* about defying us in front of the citizens of Solaris or the council, I'll see to it that the other is killed." He walked over and placed a kiss to the side of my head. It took every ounce of restraint not to pull away from his touch as heat simmered within. "See you tonight, darling," he said as the guards ushered us back out to the dark passageway.

Neither guard showed the same kindness that they did before on the way back, gripping each of us by the arm and forcefully chaining us back to the walls once we arrived. "Funny how powerful this one was destined to be. Now look at her, not a single ounce of fight in her," the muscular guard said while advancing on Raya. Stepping in front of her, I was aware that I was no match for Fae strength, but I would take my chances. Both guards laughed at my gesture before leaving the cell. We heard the locks click into place on the other side of the door.

"How the fuck are we going to get out of this?" I asked while placing my forehead against the cool stone wall. "All I have is mortality and a smart mouth," I said as I pulled the crystal Thackery dropped to me last night from the pocket of my dress. I began playing with it in my hand to alleviate the amount of stress I'd experienced in the last twenty-four hours. Raya's face paled as she looked at the onyx crystal in my hand from Lorena's cottage.

"Where did- How did-... do you know what that is?" She stammered while staring at my hand.

"When you fell asleep last night, the black cat that followed me around that old hag's cottage was outside the window and dropped it in."

"I'm sorry, did you say a *cat* brought that to you?

"Yes. A black cat. Thackery. He's actually quite sweet once—"

Raya's right hand shook as she stretched it outward toward the crystal, placing her palm flat on top of it. Her teal eyes darkened as she shook uncontrollably and muttered incoherent words out loud. My mouth dropped open at the sight of her. Every inch of her was glowing as if the sun was filling her from the inside out. Her head snapped to meet my eyes, "Heavens above, it worked. I don't have my powers back, but it worked. I have free will to speak."

"You have what?" I questioned her with a look of bewilderment.

"I don't know how much time I have to explain, but I'm not as weak as I've appeared. Raine has my powers suppressed," she professed with her hand still on the stone. "I'm half witch, half Fae, Amira. The gift of enchantress was given to me by my mother's sister before she died. The only one that knows this is Raine, because unlike the man he's become, there was a time that I confided in him."

I opened my mouth and closed it like a fish out of water as I searched for the right questions to ask.

"Why would he suppress your magic?"

Raya closed her eyes, rolling both lips between her teeth before loosing a breath and connected her gaze with mine again.

"Before you came here, Raine placed a hex over Solaris. Prior to that, we ruled this realm equally as we awaited the council's decision on who would take over due to the untimely death of our parents. It was unknown at the time of their death which of us was the most powerful, therefore the rightful heir was up in the air. As we got older, Raine knew his chances were slim because my magic is stronger than his."

"You let him put a *hex* on Solaris?"

Raya winced before narrowing her eyes, a deathly glare consuming her now darkened eyes. Though I knew she would never hurt me, I swallowed in fear for those that evoked her wrath.

"I didn't *let* him do anything," she hissed. "One night while we were having dinner, he slipped an elixir into my wine and since then my magic has been heavily hampered, along with my freedom of speech. I've been trying to tell you this whole time that nothing is what it seems, but due to the hold he has on me, I couldn't get the words to come out."

I gawked in realization at her last statement. I moved towards her, the tug of the chain around my throat serving as a sharp reminder of our captivity. I reached for her free hand, taking it in mine as I squeezed tightly.

"That's why you would stop mid-sentence during some of our conversations..."

Raya nodded her head exaggeratively with wide eyes as I pieced everything together.

"Precisely. Raine knows how to get into the minds of those

that don't know how to shield. And the goddamn fruit threw all of your logical thinking out the window. For heaven's sake, Amira... had he even told you that he loved you before you agreed to marry him?" My breath hitched as her words slammed into my core with the force of ten gods.

"Amira, listen to me. If for some reason I don't make it out of here, we have an older brother named Ezra. You *must* find him, as he is the rightful heir to Solaris. He disappeared the same night as my parents. Had he not disappeared, the council wouldn't have a say in who rules Solaris due to the bloodline. With Raine and I being twins, there was no distinction for who was next in line. We cannot let Raine reign over Solaris. He will rip apart everything that my parents built."

Before I could ask Raya questions about the information she'd thrown at me, the air around us turned frigid as the lights in our cell flickered. Raya grabbed my face with her free hand, "Whatever happens, promise me you will fight for Solaris as if it's your home. As if you're my blood sister," she searched my face, "*Promise me, Amira.*" I tried to form words, tried to beg the heavens for time in my mind as I heard shuffling outside the door.

"You have my word."

Raya snatched her hand back as her teal eyes came back to life and I shoved the crystal back in my pocket. The door flew open once again and Raine appeared with milky white eyes and trails of black veins covering his body.

"You *bitch*," he spat at Raya from the doorway as he quickly marched up to her. I couldn't react quick enough as the back of his hand connected with her face so hard that her head snapped to the side.

I gasped as her limp body fell into my arms.

Glaring at Raine, I held her lifeless body as tight as I could as the same two guards entered and wrestled me for her. I kicked my legs as forcefully as my weakened body allowed while tightening my grip around Raya.

A few vulgar words and forceful kicks later, a guard was able to get close enough to grab me by my hair. Successfully pulling me away from Raya with a fist full of my curls, I was once again forced to watch as they unchained and carried her away from me. My hair fell into my face as I looked up at Raine from my hands and knees. He towered over me.

"What did she tell you?"

"Nothing."

"Lie to me and I will make sure that you receive her head on a platter as my wedding gift to you."

The rage that had been building up inside me boiled over as I lunged at Raine. My palms were as cold as ice, but my body seared from the flames within.

He was so quick that he was nearly at the door before I leapt from the floor. Blood dripped down my wrists as I pulled with everything I had at the chains binding me to the wall. White-hot rage flowed through me when I heard him laugh, turning his back to me with his hand on the edge of the door.

"Save your energy for when we consummate our bond tonight darling," he remarked as he closes the door behind him still laughing. I yanked on my chains once more in desperation, eager for a chance to rip his throat out. When the room was sealed shut, I screamed so loudly that I heard birds flapping their wings at the sound echoing within the confined space of my asylum.

Chapter Thirty-Seven

Daylight was fading away as I stared at the wall in front of me, wondering how my world came crumbling down within weeks. I dug the nail of my index finger into a crack in the floor to settle the anxiety gnawing its way into my mind as I wondered where they took Raya. Scenarios kept playing in my head as to what I could've done differently to get us both out of there. Just as my mind began to drift, eyelids becoming an unbearable weight, a light knock presented itself at the door. Confused, as no one had knocked since I had arrived in this putrid cell, I answered, "Come in."

Millie and Ellie rushed in, throwing their belongings to the ground, and wrapping their arms around me. I couldn't hug them back because of my chains, but I nestled my head into their shoulders as we stood there in silence. Millie twirled her hands together for a few moments before speaking.

"We were instructed to assist you with getting ready for your um..." She drifted off with her sentence before getting her mouth to form the word. "For your... *ceremony* with the High King." She bit her bottom lip after she spoke, her eyes wide and filled with sympathy. *At least she was kind enough to not call it a wedding.* A wedding consisted of two people in love, and this was *not* that.

"Are you sure he's your mate, Amira? I can't see—" Ellie questioned, but was elbowed in the ribs my Millie, followed by a tilt of her head toward the guards right outside the door. "Sorry," she whispered with an embarrassed smile, "Let's get you ready." My chest caved in at the realization that I wouldn't have a chance to explain everything to them due to the guards standing right outside the door.

After completing my hair and makeup, they pushed and pulled me every which way to get me into the hideous white dress that Raine had provided. Graciously, the guards removed my chains so that I could change clothes. They declined when Millie and Ellie asked if I could bathe, but I thanked them for trying at least.

"For the record, this dress was chosen by the High King. Not us," Ellie stated while scrunching her nose and surveying the dress after it finally formed to my body. Millie fluffed out the giant shoulders of chiffon fabric that were so big they brushed the bottom of my jaw. The sleeves stopped right above my elbow, which made absolutely no sense at all. And the corseted waist led into a ballroom skirt with a five-foot-long trail. I looked like a fairytale princess' wet dream when Millie held up the mirror that she bullied the guard into fetching for her.

"I brought something for you," Ellie's youthful smile appeared as she rummaged through her bag and opened the same box that I handed her the black lotus in. She plucked the gorgeous ivory lotus flower from the box and instructed me to turn around. My hair was in a low, loose bun with a few tendrils flowing around my face. "I picked the smallest one that I could find," she said as she secured it next to the bun. She squeezed my shoulders as she whispered in my ear, *"Growing from the mud allows us to birth our most beautiful selves."*

Stunned, I surveyed her face as she took a step back to stand next to Millie. The latter put her arm around Ellie's shoulders as she smiled, "Amira, I want you to know that we will always— ". Her sentence was cut short as both guards threw the door open and walked in.

"Times up for chit-chat," the tall one spat as he held the door open.

Ellie opened her arms to say goodbye, but the other guard caught her by the forearm, "Save it for later. The High King has requested his bride." I seethed seeing his hand wrapped so tightly around her arm.

"Take your hand off of her...now."

The guard slowly turned his head toward me as a smile crept across his face. "Pixie, just because you think you can tell me what to do, wait until you hear what my hands do to her after your ceremony." I clenched my jaw as I threw myself at him, scratching the side of his face as deep as my nails were willing to go. He shoved me off him, bringing his hand to his face to witness the blood I'd drawn. A grin of satisfaction danced across my face. His eyes blew wide with anger as he drew his dagger from his belt and stood over me, "You stupid fucking—". The other guard grabbed his shoulder.

"Relax, Felix. Wouldn't want to dirty her up before her big day. They're just a few scratches. Take it out on this one instead," he said as he threw his thumb in the direction of Ellie.

Both guards backed away from me after reapplying the chains to my hands and neck. "Rylan, will be in shortly to escort you to the ceremony. I suggest you don't try any of this shit with him. Rumor has it he strikes first and asks questions later," Felix said as they moved to escort Millie and Ellie out of my cell, leaving their belongings behind. Before she was out of the door, Millie made sure my eyes connected with hers. She gave a nod to my dress from last night on the floor before vanishing from my line of vision.

"Hells angels," I muttered to myself while banging my fists into the stone wall. Glancing down, I saw my gown from the night before. *Fuck his demands.* I ripped the horrid white dress from my body as quickly as possible and pulled the midnight purple gown over my curves. Rummaging through the pocket, I found the onyx-colored stone gifted to me. The door creaked and I shoved it into my bodice without a second thought, assuming a guard had returned. Thank the gods it was only my paranoia. In the same pocket, I found my necklace and quickly clasped it around my neck, running my thumb over the smooth surface.

The second pocket of the dress crinkled as I ran my hand over it, causing my brows to pinch together. I hadn't placed a single thing in there last night. Shoving my hand inside, I gasped as I felt the smooth surface of paper. *It can't be.* My mouth went dry as I pulled the folded envelope from the pocket. How could Millie have known about the letter? *"It's now or never,"* I muttered to myself as I slid the contents from the envelope that was already ripped open, unfolding the parchment with slightly shaking hands. The page was half-full of handwriting, and it was a handwriting I knew very well, causing the blood to drain from my face as my mouth dropped open.

Amira,

I don't know if you will get this in time, but the uprising has come to Medlar. Our home is no longer safe. I know that we have had our differences, but as your mother I need you to listen to me. Protect your heart and mind while you are in Solaris. Whoever helped you send your letter to us, keep them close. I don't have enough time to write everything that I want as the Saurians have reached Medlar and will be coming any time now. I will find you. Despite what you may think of me, I love you more than you will ever understand. You are strong. You are smart. And you know your way better than anyone else in this family. It is too late to tell you what I should have told you after all these years, but fate will lead you. If anyone can get you to Aravis, you are safe with him, and he will tell you everything that I've kept from you for far too long.

Find your inner strength and set it free.

Before I could re-read the letter, it floated into the air and burst into tiny golden particles in front of me. "*No!* No No No No," I repeated to myself trying to catch the pieces as if I could put them back together. But the letter was gone without a trace. How would I remember everything that she said? Tears pricked my eyes as I replayed the words from the letter in my mind. *How did she know about Solaris? Who is Aravis? What are Saurians? And what the fuck is this talk about an uprising?*

As soon as I asked myself that last question, I staggered backwards into the stone wall from realization. My palms were already sweating from panic and the room began to spin while my vision blurred.

The war that Solaris was preparing for was against Medlar.

Ceremony be damned. I'll burn this entire fucking place to the ground before I bind myself to this fucker.

Chapter Thirty-Eight

The new guard, Rylan, walked in just as scary as he was described moments earlier. His broad shoulders were held high as two Sai blades were strapped to his back. Our eyes locked on each other before either of us said a word. "I don't like to be rough with females. If I unchain you from that wall, do you think you could contain your wrath until we get to the ceremony?" He leaned against the wall with his arms crossed while looking annoyed at the request. I nodded my head in agreement as he walked over and unchained me. With a raise of his hand, he gestured for me to walk out of the cell while guiding me with his voice through the passageways. Though he was scary to look at with his jet-black hair and overly dark eyes, he didn't seem as vicious as the other guards. I glanced a look back at him to see his eyes were burning a hole into the back of my head.

"Something you need?" He questioned, which caused me to startle and trip over my own feet. His hands gripped both my shoulders, standing me upright. "How about you keep walking? I don't need to deliver a bloody bride," he stated while making another gesture for me to continue. The other guards would've let me fall flat on my face. I took one last glance into those obsidian pupils before I continued my stride. Something was off, and I couldn't decide if I was scared or intrigued.

Taking the same route that I did with Raya earlier in the day, we finally made it to our destination which was the throne room instead of the garden. A sinking feeling strangled me as I viewed Raine and Eryx in their previous attire, residing in the same giant golden chairs. Confused, I looked around and confronted Raine.

"You said our ceremony was to be in the garden. Why are we here?" Raine laughed a menacing laugh as he stood from the dais and made his way over to me.

"Fuck you. If you so much as touch my family I'll kill you. I know *exactly* which mortal realm you sent your soldiers to. Get them the fuck out of Medlar."

Raine gripped my face *hard*. "Rylan, thank you for bringing my bride to me. You'll make a great addition to the Saurians of Solaris. Your services are no longer needed," he instructed the new guard as he roughly released my face, whipping my head to the side. Nodding his head in thanks, he proceeded to clap Rylan on the shoulder, barely moving him. Rylan bowed his head as he clenched his jaw and headed out the wooden door to stand guard.

Saurians.

I rustled through bits and pieces of the letter from my mother that still floated through my exhausted mind. That must be the title of Raine's army that he sent to Medlar. *What could he possibly need from a mortal realm that isn't already available in Solaris?*

"Where is Raya?" I asked, snapping my focus back to the asshole in front of me, and casting a burning glare at Eryx. "Funny you ask," Raine said as a menacing smile spread far too wide across his face. I knew by the look in his eyes that he had something sinister planned for the evening. My mouth went dry at the possibilities that were playing in my head. Raine clapped twice and the door to the entrance opened. Raya was being dragged by the chain around her neck to the dais. On the far wall in the hall, I could see Rylan. His facial expression grim at the sight of Raya. I went to move toward her and Raine grabbed me around my waist, pulling my back to his front. "Not so fast," he hummed in my ear, causing me to clench my jaw.

Raya's clothes were ripped and tattered, along with a small trail of blood coming from her lip. "Before we get to that pathetic excuse of a being... I have a special surprise for you," he sang to the room filled with guards before redirecting his words toward me. "I figured our ceremony could wait until morning. Give the council time to arrive and get situated. This is just a little something special I threw together for you before sending you back to think about your recent actions." My heartbeat was flooding my ears as a door on the far side of the room opened, presenting Millie and Ellie who were dragged to the center of the room by their hair. I turned my head to look up at Raine, "No. Please no. They did nothing wrong. Please, Raine." I begged so hard my body began to tremble.

"Now Amira, as my wife, one thing that won't be tolerated is being a lying bitch," Raine instructed as Eryx's laugh boomed from the dais. He was stroking Raya's head like she was a fucking animal. Each time she tried to pull away he would yank her back by her clothing that barely remained. She was an arms-length away and I couldn't even comfort her.

"I believe these two *servants* went out of their way to assist you quite a few times. Not only did they break the rules of attending Solstice and attempt to make me look like a bad leader letting trash into the celebration. But residue of a black lotus was located in their chambers. Now, if I'm not mistaken, that particular flower has been banned from Solaris for how long now, Eryx?" He tagged in his second-in-command. "Centuries I believe," Eryx answered with his ominous smile still plastered on his face.

"And what is the punishment for something like that?" He

once again quizzed his right-hand-man. Eryx leaned forward, gripping Raya by the nape of her neck. "Death."

I thrashed and kicked as Raine lifted me in the air, holding my arms to my sides, as multiple guards chained Millie and Ellie to the center of the floor. Neither of them shed a tear, nor fought back as their lives inched closer to death's door. Raya and I screamed for mercy as two guards stood behind them with daggers drawn. I screamed as Raine held me in place.

"I am so sorry. I am so, so sorry for everything. Please forgive me. Please forgive me for putting you here. Take me instead," I cried to Millie and Ellie while begging Raine as the guards moved closer to them. They were shoulder to shoulder as they smiled.

"It was an honor to serve our *High Lady*." They both were staring at me when they let the phrase *High Lady* leave their lips and then interlocked their hands. As our eyes met, the two women I had come to know changed before my eyes. The long grey hair I was accustomed to slowly transformed into thick jet-black manes. Their brown eyes swiftly shifted to bright green ones. Their previously monotonous pale faces were now splattered with freckles and full of life. Their unfamiliar full lips spread into a set of wide smiles as they raised their heads high. Their beauty radiated from the inside out as their youthful faces stared straight ahead, ignoring the surrounding guards gawking at their newfound features.

"How kind of you to remove your glamour," Raine drawled toward Millie and Ellie. "Please do tell how you snuck them past the palace wards." The two women glanced at each other before Millie answered, "Anya sends her regards." The blood from Raine's face drained as he studied the female prisoners.

"Kill them."

The guards grabbed each under their jaw and brought their daggers to their necks. I was so lightheaded that I dropped to my knees, yet Raine held my arms tight to my sides. "Wouldn't want you to miss the show, darling," he whispered in my ear as he wrapped my body with one arm and used the other hand to grip my jaw, holding my line of vision to where the two women who had become my friends knelt. The icy sensation of panic and dread in my palms threatened to break through.

The daggers were slowly dragged across their throats. Bright red liquid ran down their dresses. Neither made a sound except for the gurgling when the daggers completed their assault. Both of their bodies fell as their hands remained interlocked.

My heart fluttered as I threw up whatever remained in my stomach. Raine yanked me to my feet as the corners of my vision went dark and a trail of sweat ran down my back. As much as I tried to hold on, I collapsed into him.

Chapter Thirty-Nine

I regained my vision with Raya curled at my feet begging for me to wake up. I was seated on the dais, in the very throne that Eryx had resided in earlier. Only I wasn't freely seated, I was *chained* to the golden chair, an exact replica of the vision I had at the Garden of Sanri.

"Now that you're awake, you'll be happy to know you didn't miss the main event, darling," Raine announced as he paraded up to the dais. My vision was still slightly blurred as I saw Rylan enter the room, casting a glance at my fallen friends and averting his eyes to the floor.

Raine grabbed Raya by her hair, pulling her from the dais to stand in front of me. "Funny thing about Fae, if they're not alert it's quite easy to read their mind. Isn't that right, Eryx?" Raine questioned as his right-hand man provided a nod. "You see, Eryx here was able to see everything that Raya told you in that tiny cell of yours. The only thing he can't see is how she was able to break the hex that bounded her free will. You wouldn't happen to have an answer to that would you, Amira?"

Shaking my head in denial, a smile crept its way onto Raine's face. "Another peculiar thing we came across pertains to you, *darling*." I swallowed hard at the tone of his voice. "In Eryx's decades of life, there's never been a human who's thoughts he can't read. And now he tells me that ever since that day at dinner, he hasn't been able to hear a single thought in that pretty little head of yours. Want to explain that for me?"

Surely he noted the confused expression I genuinely gave as my mouth popped open to speak, but Raine continued speaking.

"During your stay here, I was unable to read your thoughts as well," he searched my face for a reaction that I refused to give. "I couldn't even do what I do best and control your mind. Thankfully, you enjoyed the fruit from the garden well enough to grant me some leeway there. Care to explain?"

"I... I don't know. I don't have an answer as to—"

"Thought so." Raine had cut me off before I could attempt to reason with him. "She's all yours," he stated as he thrust Raya into Eryx's arms. In true character, she slammed her head into Eryx's face, causing blood to spurt from his nose. He placed both hands around her neck, tightening his grip.

"Easy brother, you wouldn't want to end the show early," Raine commanded as Eryx removed his hands from her throat and dragged her to the center of the room. My breathing subsided as I saw Millie and Ellie's bodies lying on the floor in pools of blood. Eryx kicking Ellie's arm out of the way sent me over the edge.

"This wasn't the fucking plan, Raine," I seethed.

"Language, darling," he said as he settled into the throne next to mine. "You inquired so heavily about the Death Dealer, allow me to show you how I *earned* my name."

Raine extended thick black ropes to Raya as they wrapped around her neck and torso. Her eyes began to bulge as I dropped to my knees in front of Raine, placing my hands on his knees. "Please don't do this. Whatever you want. I'll give you whatever you want. Spare her, *please*," I plead at his feet. Raine retracted the leathery ropes as Raya gasped for air, those white clouds taking over those blue eyes I now loathed.

"You look *pathetic* begging for a life such as hers to be spared. Stand up. No wife of mine will look this *weak* at my side." The milky white hue in his eyes swirled as he grabbed the hair at the back of my head and tilted my eyes to look even further into his.

"An heir," he hissed. My blood ran cold at the thought of not only having a child, but *his* child.

"Over my dead body," I spat back at him. A menacing laugh left his lips.

"Well, we already have two among us, let's make it three, shall we?" His gaze drifted to his sister.

The guards shoved me back into the throne next to Raine and held me down as I fought to move toward Raya, as if I wasn't attached to chains. Every thought I had of how I treated her terribly ran through my mind. Her kindness. Her loyalty. Tears were building as I screamed her name repeatedly, still fighting to break my chains.

"You see, her betrayal caused a small change in plans. Due to a little manipulation, the counsel believes that Raya and Eryx's ceremony took place weeks ago. Therefore, once she's gone, I don't have to worry about her trying to take my place as ruler of Solaris. And Eryx doesn't have to bother with having a worthless bitch as a wife for the rest of immortality. Life is good," he explained while reaching for my hand. I jerked away from him as my spit connected with his face.

Grabbing me by the jaw, he squeezed tightly as my saliva ran down the side of his face. "I'll make you regret that. Know that her blood is now on *your* hands." He turned to face Eryx, "Do what I should've done years ago."

Eryx forced Raya to her knees as he grabbed the sides of her head. Her arms were stretched out wide by two additional guards as she thrashed, tears streaming down her face.

For the first time in a long time, warm wet streams were trailing down my own.

"The heir! I will give you an heir! Do not do this. *That is your fucking sister, Raine*," I begged as he squeezed my jaw tighter. "Blood does *not* mean a damn thing to me," he seethed.

"Finish it," he spat at Eryx before refocusing his gaze to me. "I'll get my heir regardless."

My wrists stung from my skin peeling back as I pulled with every ounce of human strength to be freed. To gauge those pellucid white eyes from his head. To save another friend from a death caused by *me.*

A guard stood before Raya and unsheathed the sword from his side, aiming it at her heart. My own heart fluttered rapidly at the tragedy unfolding in front of me. The skin around my wrists chilled as the chains were now encrusted with ice.

From the corner of my eye, I noticed Rylan had now inched his way to my side of the dais. With Raine distracted and facing the center of the room, Rylan leaned close enough to where only I could hear him.

"The crystal. Break it."

I averted my gaze to look at him bewildered through tear-filled eyes.

"You want your friend to live or not? Shatter it," he insisted again with raised brows. "*NOW.*"

Swiftly, I tugged the crystal from my bodice, tossing it to the ground and smashing it under my foot. Raine's gaze turned toward me in shock as a strong aroma of lavender filled the dais and the area surrounding it.

"You idiotic mortal," he roared as he swiftly rose from his seat.

"*Show time,*" Rylan said as he drew the two blades from his back while running his tongue between his lips in a maniacal form.

The ceiling began to crack as I stood from my seat.

"Sit the fuck down," Raine lashed out as he placed a hand on my shoulder, shoving me back down.

I whipped my head back to Rylan who winked at me, accompanied by a wiggle of his brows. My mouth dropped open at his gesture, as if someone wasn't about to be *murdered* right in front of us. Frustrated, I opened my mouth to profess my anger toward him when fragments of the ceiling crumbled around the room. Dust engulfed us and subsided as two men with large jet-black wings dropped to the floor, sending cracks in the foundation spidering in different directions.

The male with slightly smaller wings possessed two large daggers, one strapped to each of his thighs. His short black hair contrasted his bright green eyes which complimented his insanely handsome face. Ripping my gaze from him, time froze as my heartbeat slowed looking at the male with the largest wings, shoulder length black hair, and hazel eyes so deep they were almost gold. He reached behind him to brandish a long black sword that gleamed as if it were made from pure crystal.

The same crystal I shattered moments ago.

His eyes locked mine before sliding down to survey my chains and back up to my face. His eyes went dark as he moved at the speed of light and gripped Raine by the throat, handing his sword to Rylan who severed the chains attaching me to the dais and swooped me into his arms. I gaped as he winked at me again.

"That's enough, Silas," the golden-eyed male barked in our direction. Confused, I looked at Rylan who slightly shivered while holding me, unveiling completely different features than before. A broad smile consumed his handsome face. "The name's, Silas. Nice to meet you...again." I paled at his words entwined with the magic that had just unfolded before me.

The male gripping Raine by the throat slammed him into the dais, sending a large crack up the middle of the marble platform. The High King of Solaris' white wings extended to reveal themselves.

My eyes drift to the other green-eyed male that was now looking at Raya like he'd known her his entire life. He seemed to swiftly observe every bruise and mark on her body before he rapidly moved to the guard holding the sword in front of her, ripping his arms from his body in one swift motion. Before the guard could voice his pain, two hands were secured on each side of his head which was then twisted and plucked from his body. The winged man looked back up to the ceiling after nonchalantly discarding the guard's head to the floor. "How's it holding, Nova?"

A petite woman with black wings had her arms outstretched to the ceiling holding open a portal as she floated midair. "I can't hold it much longer, Xavier," she replied while surveying the ground below her and shook her head at the male hovering over Raine. "Don't start a war that our realm doesn't need, Thane. Get what we came for and let's get the fuck out of here."

"*Fuck no.* I'm leaving here with something for my troubles," Xavier said as he eyes Eryx who was now steadily backing away from Raya.

"I say we add to the collection," Silas bellows with a laugh that I could feel reverberate from his chest.

The male bent over Raine had his mouth pressed into a thin line as he looks at Silas and then back at Raine. Moving closer, he stepped on a shimmering white wing, purposefully moving his foot from side to side. Raine writhed in pain as black ropes extended to the male hovering above him. But despite Raine's attempt, the ropes failed to grip his tormentor.

"I'll be seeing you," Thane said as he pulled away from the High King. "But he won't," he hissed as he nodded at Eryx. Before I could fully focus, Xavier was in front of Eryx, grabbing the back of his head and plucking out his right eye. Eryx howled as he dropped to his knees, grabbing at the socket that was now empty.

Xavier studied Eryx's eye that was now in his hand. "Nothing special, but it'll do," he said before dropping it into the satchel that was strapped across his chest. The sight had my stomach in knots, threatening for its contents to escape again.

"Guys!" Nova bellows from above as beads of sweat dripped from her face. "Wrap up your bullshit before dinner. *Please.*"

Silas brandished black wings that had my eyes about to pop out of my sockets. He looked toward the portal and was about to flap his wings when I finally opened my mouth. "I'm not going anywhere without her." I reached my hand out to Raya who was as pale as clouds and drenched in sweat. What remained of her tattered clothes barely clung to her body.

Xavier who was already kneeling in front of her nodded. "Never planned on it."

Silas threw the large sword to him that he used to sever my chains, and I watched in hysteria as Raya collapsed into Xavier's arms before her face hit the floor.

My attention retreated to Raine who was casting me a glare so fierce that my skin felt like it's on fire. Before I could process his movement, he reached at his side, brandishing a dagger. The blade flipped twice through the air before it collided with my torso, the tip of the blade bouncing off the bodice of my dress and clashing to the ground. My heart slowly continued its rhythm as I remembered Raya's words while running my hand over the dress where the tip of the blade had connected.

Oddly enough, it can't be destroyed. It's simply indestructible.

Thane gripped the front of Raine's tunic, ensuring his focus was on him. "If you so much as *think* about either one of them, I'll come back without my warriors. And I'll make sure you can't eat, breathe, or walk right for the rest of your immortal life." Raine's lips curled back as those white clouds swirled in his eyes. "You've crossed a line, Thanasis," Raine seethed.

The dark-haired male stood while sheathing the sword that was tossed back to him. Bringing his leg up, he swiftly dropped his foot to Raine's face. A crunch rang so loudly it sounded like a thousand bones shattered at once. Raine spit blood out the side of his mouth as he attempted to find his balance to stand while Thane forced him backwards with a boot planted on his chest.

"We'll see how many more lines I cross before the council sees who you really are," he retorted while studying the damage to Raine's face and plunging the same dagger he threw at me into his thigh. Thane's eyes darkened again as he pierced two additional daggers through Raine's flesh, pinning him to his throne. Raine's roar of pain and fury caused stone to crumble from the surrounding walls.

"Let's go," Thane called out to his group as he stilled to focus on the male before him once more. "Do us all a favor and have someone rip off those fake ass wings you conjured up for yourself."

If looks could kill, the glare Raine cast in the male's direction would have incinerated him where he stood.

Guards could be heard rushing down the halls toward the room as each male flapped their wings, moving us toward the portal being held open by the female above. Before Xavier ascended, he threw a purple dust over Millie and Ellie's remains. My chest tightened as their bodies disintegrate below me. I made an oath to them that Raine would pay for their lives before my view filled with the night sky.

Waves of shock crashed into me as a bright blanket of starlight surrounded us.

Epilogue

The cool night air taunted my face as I soared through the sky in the arms of a muscular male with black wings, his companions surrounding us as we all made our way somewhere unknown. I tried not to think about how I could fall hundreds of feet to my death if he lost his grip. *My life is once again in the hands of a man that I don't know.*

I glanced to the left of us to see that Raya was out cold in Xavier's arms. He surveyed her with warmth in his eyes. The hysteria and realization of the events that just took place hit me before I could control it. My eyes grew wide as each breath I took became shallower than the last.

"Thane, say something. The girl looks like she's going to pass out before we even get there," the female warrior said with a grimace on her face, offering me a small, sincere smile. He cleared his throat from above, gazing down at me while searching for the right words to say. His eyes still portrayed a golden hue in the midnight sky as our eyes connected.

"I know you don't know us. But you're safe," he said in a steely, calm voice.

Silas offered a sympathetic smile and shrugged his shoulders as we drifted further into the night sky.

"I thought I was safe once already," I murmured as I glanced to the male above me, focusing on his wings effortlessly drifting through the darkness. He closed his eyes before releasing a subtle growl.

"*Do not* compare me to him," he said through a clenched jaw. A pang of guilt hit me in the chest. Afterall, he did just save me.

"Where are we going?" I asked the four of them.

Nova offered a broad smile in my direction before answering with the name of our destination.

"*Obsidian.*"

Acknowledgments

I truly and honestly don't know how to put everyone together in one paragraph, so here goes nothing.

Andrew/Sir Hubbington/My Everything: I have no words to express my appreciation of you. You've supported me through the highs and lows throughout this entire process–including when ten chapters somehow got deleted and I cried at Starbucks telling you that I was done writing. The drive you gave me to keep pushing regardless of the hiccups I encountered was exactly what I needed. I thank God for you every single day. I love you to the moon and back.

Mom and Dad: Thank you for the MANY hours of babysitting to allow me to work on this book. I have no idea if I would have been able to complete this without you. I love you boomers more than you know!

My In-laws: Thank you for watching Phoenix so many days while I wrapped up this project! You're the best in-laws a girl could ask for! Love you guys!

Janna: Girl...girl! I don't have the words. This book would not be what it is without you! Having you be the sole editor for this project was the best choice ever! Thank you for everything. Thank you for your expertise. And thank you for being such a great friend. I love you!

Meg: Goodness. Is there really a way to say how much I appreciate you and everything you have done for me? Everything you STILL do as well. The way you handled my anxiety and panic throughout this process makes you a solidified angel. I'm so happy that we connected. You're the best assistant a girl could ask for! Thank you for everything!

Lexie: This cover art and map is perfection. The way we work so well together makes my heart full. Thank you for being so flexible and easy to work with! (Follow her at @lexiesmebooks on Instagram)

Phoenix/My baby boy: Thank you for asking me "what dernin?" every five minutes while writing and the thousands of kisses on my breaks. Each one of those kisses caused me to keep pushing. I love you more than anything.

Khloe: Thank you for the best puppy cuddles a girl could ask for.

To everyone that donated to help me publish this project, I appreciate you beyond words!

To my friends and additional family that made this possible, thank you and I love you! (Brittany, Rhea, and Jenna... you already know what you mean to me.)

Anyone that I may have forgotten, please don't yell at me! I thank you and appreciate you too!

Rest In Peace Grandpa.

Rest In Peace Paw Paw.

You two will never know the impact you had, and still have on me.

About the Author

O'Junea Brown is an emerging author of Romantasy. This is her first published novel with many more to come. She was born and raised in the suburbs of Chicago, Illinois.

She loves her books, comics, video games, sports (go Cubs!), and anything fitness related. O'Junea has a bit too much dark humor and somewhat of a sailor's mouth, but her husband loves her the way that she is and that's all that matters.

Her baby boy Phoenix and dog Khloe are her only babies.

Follow her on Instagram and Tik Tok at @fit.and.fiction